The 7 Puzzles Of Life

God's Plan To Save The World

by
Allen C. Liles

The 7 Puzzles Of Life
God's Plan To Save The World

by
Allen C. Liles

Published By
Positive Imaging, LLC
9016 Palace Parkway
Austin, TX 78748
bill@positive-imaging.com

ISBN: 9781951776206

THE 7 PUZZLES OF LIFE

1. FREE WILL

2. FAMILY

3. LOVE

4. WORK

5. SPIRITUAL SERVICE

6. DEATH

7. GOD

DEDICATION

For Jan

ACKNOWLEDGEMENT

I would like to thank my publisher A. William "Bill" Benitez (Positive Imaging, LLC) for his outstanding expertise and professionalism. His contribution in bringing THE 7 PUZZLES OF LIFE to reality were numerous and indispensable. I am forever grateful, my friend.

Contents

God's Warnings To The World

"The LORD regretted that He had made human beings and His heart was deeply troubled. So the LORD said "I will wipe them from the face of the earth and with them the animals, the birds and the creatures that move along the ground—for I regret that I have made them."

GENESIS 6-7

"But My people have exchanged their glorious God for worthless idols. Be appalled at this, you heavens and shudder with great horror," declares the LORD"

JEREMIAH 2: 12

"The end! The end has come upon the four corners of the land! The end is now upon you, and I will unleash my anger against you. I will judge you according to your conduct and repay you for all your despicable practices. I will not look upon you with pity."

EZEKIEL 7: 1-4

"Woe to the wicked! Disaster is upon them. They will be paid back for what their hands have done."

ISAIAH 3:11

"Suddenly the fingers of a human hand appeared and wrote on the plaster of the wall. The king watched the hand as it wrote. His face turned pale and he was so frightened that his legs became weak and his knees were knocking."

DANIEL 5:-5-6

Author's Note

Dear Reader,

I've been asked to tell you a story.

The request comes from the same Source that I hear during my daily meditations. This Higher Power, whom I choose to call God, is worried about the state of our planet. This is not about the Coronavirus Pandemic or the climate change that could someday imperil us. My Source is warning of a more imminent danger. From what I'm hearing in the silence, time is running out. God is angry. As the Holy Bible in the Old Testament tells us, the earth's people are always subject to spiritual judgement. In the past, many nations and even entire civilizations have felt God's wrath. Why would it be any different today?

There is no question that God Itself is under attack. We openly embrace and worship various idols. Science and technology rule our thoughts and lives. Our culture insults and disdains spirituality. We act as though a Higher perspective is no longer needed. Our scientists have now slammed God with the ultimate rebuke. They have assumed, through Artificial Intelligence, the task of creating human life. It is no matter that these robotic beings lack "soul". They are programmed for the benefit and use by human beings alone. God's input is nowhere present in this new creative process.

I hear in my meditations that this usurping of God's role will not stand. The end could be near for every living thing and the earth itself. That's why you need to hear Lorena Mae Johnson's story. It also concerns 7 Puzzle boxes, the battle between Good and Evil, and how we might survive the dangerous days ahead. This might be our generation's "handwriting on the wall". We all need to pay close attention. Our lives may depend on it.

Blessings,

Allen C. Liles

1

The Old Man On The Bench

The disheveled old man disgusted Lorena Mae Johnson. He was becoming a pest just by being in her line of sight.

As she had pulled into her designated parking space on each of the last three mornings, the ancient bum was already there. He sat on the public bench with his arms folded, as if waiting for her arrival. His appearance was creating eye pollution for the entire area, in her opinion. The tattered fool was not just a "dirty old man". He was an "old dirty man." She had never spoken to him, or even looked in his direction. As far as the 35-year old real estate agent was concerned, he didn't exist.

If that old creep is still there tomorrow, I'm calling the cops, Lorena told herself.

The elderly man was positioned a couple of doors down from Lorena's real estate office. She assumed that he was entitled to his perch. But the rancid character was detracting from the exclusive near-beachfront area where Lorena now worked.

The dirtbag is easily past 80 and looks it, she thought. He's 20 years older than my own parents.

At least he had never spoken to her. That is, until today.

"Good morning, Lorena," the old man called out in her direction.

His unexpected greeting confused her.

How did this creep know my name?

"Pardon me?" she called out in his direction, "What did you say?

"I just greeted you with a 'good morning', my dear," the old man replied with a near toothless grin.

This fool might be drunk, delusional or even dangerous, Lorena warned herself. I need to exercise some caution.

"Look, man," she said with a firm voice, "I don't know how you knew my name. But I've got my cell right here."

She reached for her purse on a shoulder strap.

"If you don't stop harassing me right now, I'm calling the cops."

To accentuate her point, Lorena reached into the purse and fetched her phone. In a quick move, she punched in 9-1-1.

I didn't really mean to do that, she reflected, but it's OK. I need to exercise some caution.

"No need to worry," the bum called out with a smile and friendly voice, "I'm harmless."

A sudden thought crossed Lorena's mind, just the dispatch operator answered, "9-1-1, what's your emergency?"

I'm just a newbie at work, she thought. What if I'm I overreacting? Having a scene outside of work might not be the best optics.

"9-1-1 Operator, state your emergency please."

"I'm sorry operator," Lorena answered. "I hit the wrong speed dial. My bad."

"O. K., fool," she called out to the man, "I'll let you off the hook for now. But you better leave me alone. Park your ass somewhere else. I don't want to see you on that bench tomorrow. If you do, I will call the cops. Do I make myself clear?"

Lorena turned and began to walk toward her office.

"But you won't be in your office tomorrow," the old man said, "You're taking the day off. You'll either in yoga class, shopping at the beach or maybe having lunch with your friend Carole. Maybe you'll be doing all three. That's why I'm here today. I didn't want to miss you."

His all-correct statement about her plans halted Lorena.

How did this ancient dude know any of these things?

But it was his next comment that really drew Lorena's attention.

"Now," he said, "Can you confirm for me how much you still owe on the Camry? I believe the current payoff is $8,634.50. Am I right?"

"What did you say?" Lorena asked. "How do you even know what kind of car I drive?"

"For one thing," the bum answered, "I watched you drive up and park this morning. Now, am I correct on what you still owe the dealer's finance company?"

I think he might be close, she thought. I do know that I have a $400 payment due tomorrow. I wonder how he got the payoff information.

"That's probably about right," she said, "Where did you get that number?"

"I have my sources," the old man replied, while digging into his pocket and producing a folded piece of paper.

"Here's a cashier's check for $8,700," he told her, "I put in an extra fifty bucks or so, in case they charge you a fee for an early payoff of the loan."

He handed the check to a surprised Lorena. She hesitated, but then accepted the piece of paper.

"Take a look," the man smiled, "I think you'll see that it's the real deal."

Lorena inspected the check, drawn on her own bank. It was indeed authentic.

"Who are you?", she asked the tattered man.

"I'm a messenger," he said with a grin.

"What does that mean?" she asked, "What kind of a messenger?"

"I'm the kind you read about in Sunday School many years ago. You know, the kind that brought people messages from Heaven."

"You mean like an angel messenger?"

"Yep, that's the kind. I came here today with a message for you."

I wonder if it's time for another 9-1-1 call, Lorena thought to herself.

Sensing her uncertainty, the man quickly followed up.

"I have a proposition for you, my dear. If you will sit with me for 15 minutes, I can explain why I'm here. After that, you are free to take the cashier's check and leave. You never need to speak with me again. That will be your decision. There won't be any coercion or funny business. What do you say?"

The cashier's check does seem real, Lorena pondered.

Without a word, she zipped open her purse and deposited the check inside her bag.

"There's your answer," Lorena told the messenger, "You're on the clock."

2

The Puzzles Of Life

As Lorena settled in on the bench, she noticed a battered carboard briefcase by the old man's side. He fetched the case and snapped it open. He reached inside and pulled out a disorganized sheaf of loose papers.

"What's all that?" she asked.

"It's the reason why I'm here," he answered, "By the way, my name is Seth."

The old man extended his hand for a shake, but Lorena just stared at it. The idea of shaking hands with this filthy fool repelled her.

"Oh-kay, I guess," Seth said as he withdrew his hand.

He waved the papers and repeated, "Again, this is the reason why I'm here. Remember that I am only a messenger. I did bring everything in writing. My memory isn't what it was 1,000 years ago. Let me assure you that this information comes from the highest levels."

"Like who?"

And don't tell me God, she thought.

"God HERSELF," he responded with a mostly toothless grin.

"Now I'm sure you're crazy," Lorena said with a wave of her hand.

"You might want to hold off on the judgments for a bit," Seth cautioned. "These papers contain crucial information that could impact the earth itself. They explain God's anger and His threat to pull the plug on everyone and everything. But I'm also here for another important reason. God needs your help. Spirit has selected you for a critical assignment in the days ahead. Only you can handle it."

"Pardon me," Lorena bristled, "I think I just heard some BS."

"Don't worry," the messenger angel said, "You can always say no to any request from God. That's what "Free Will Choice" is all about. The LORD allows human beings to choose their own spiritual path. Of course, there are consequences for every choice. Let me tell you the way that God operates. When you agree to do what Spirit asks of you, It picks up the complete tab. When you choose to do what you want, you get stuck with the bill. When you say "yes" to GOD, everything needed to complete the task is provided. You are never left holding an empty bag."

Without warning, the clear blue sky above them was filled with a burst of pure light. It was though the sun had received a sudden jolt of energy.

"Wow!" Lorena exclaimed, "Did you see that?"

"God is with us," Seth proclaimed.

"No kidding!" she agreed, "Something just happened."

"Let's proceed," he said, "I only have 11 minutes and 45 seconds remaining of my time with you."

"I'm listening," Lorena said, checking her watch.

"God creates every soul in His image and likeness. However, every soul comes into human life with its own unique characteristics. Just like fingerprints, no two souls are precisely the same. Each human journey is pre-planned to some extent. You are sent here to continue your soul's evolvement. Past incarnations determine the specific lessons planned for you in this parenthesis. Hopefully, you will choose to accept these learning opportunities. Of course, many souls choose not to evolve. God has a definite plan for your life but allows you to make the final choices."

"That sounds a bit deep," Lorena opined.

"Yes, it is," Seth continued, "God helps the process along by providing some hints. In fact, there are 7 different "Puzzle" boxes assigned in your name. Each separate puzzle contains 500 pieces. Figuring out how to make those pieces all fit together is the key to a happy life. Of course, God always remains available to help you with any of the puzzles. However, most people never ask for assistance. They want total control of their lives. Free Will allows you to do that. As a result, virtually no Puzzle ever gets completed without a few major speed bumps along the way. People spend most of the time trying to force the puzzle pieces to fit. That's why so many human lives end up bent and out of shape."

"Hmm," Lorena mused, "That kind of makes sense. What are the 7 Puzzles of Life?"

"Good question," the angel answered, "They are labeled like this: (1) Free Will; (2) Family; (3) Love; (4) Work; (5) Spiritual Service (6) Aging and Death and (7) God. Believe it or not, there are a few enlightened individuals who breeze through the Puzzles. Of course, no one does them all to perfection. But the people that excel are the human beings who seek conscious union with God. They have somehow discovered the secret to a happy and fulfilled life: "Oneness" with Spirit. They allow God to live Its divine life through them."

"How is that possible?" Lorena asked, "I guess I don't understand."

"One of the key decisions in life involves seeking unity with the sacred force that resides within you," Seth explained.

"When you and God link up, every hardship and difficulty can be handled from a spiritual perspective. If you separate yourself from Spirit, everything becomes harder. The material life can be a killer without God's help. When you embrace "Oneness", the answers come."

"What Puzzles give people the most trouble?" Lorena inquired.

"Every Puzzle has some degree of difficulty," Seth replied. "Personally, I think "Free Will" offers the biggest challenge. In that one, you must confront the human ego. Everyone is born with an ego. Sometimes it overwhelms the soul. With other people, it can be more balanced. However, even when the ego seems dormant or subdued, don't be fooled by its quietness. Every ego can be activated at a moment's notice. A raging ego can erupt when you least expect it. Then the human ego goes straight to self-promotion, tossing God aside. Surrendering to God's Will involves humility. To the ego, that makes no sense at all. It seeks total control over its human host. It never gives in without a fight. That's the basis for the "spiritual warfare" that you hear about. "Satan" and the ego can often be interchangeable. The bottom line: You can trust God with your life. You can never depend on the ego to have your best interest at heart. Big egos often mean big crashes. With God, you are always guided to the best outcomes."

This is all sort of interesting, Lorena thought, But I need to get into work.

"Your 15 minutes are about up," she told the angel. "Is there anything else? And, again I must ask you: how does this all affect me?"

"I'll try to wrap up," Seth said, "The bottom line is that I want to meet with you again tomorrow about the same time. Then, I promise to give you the specifics of what God needs from you. I think you'll want to hear about that."

"I don't know," Lorena replied, "I did what you asked for the 15 minutes. I'm sorry, but this all seems a bit crazy."

"The cashier's check for your car is still good. In fact, I suggest that you go by the dealership and pay it off today. Then you'll know that I mean business. Let me quickly take a minute and summarize what I've shared so far. There are 7 major puzzles in every human life — Free Will, Family, Love, Work, Spiritual Service, Aging and Death and God. Right now, Spirit is unhappy about the world's worship of false idols. Technology and "self" are probably the top two offending idols, but there are others. God hopes that spending time trying to spiritually solve the 7 Puzzles might awaken a dormant interest in one's own spirituality."

"I still don't understand where I fit into that equation," Lorena said, "I've got a lot going on at my job."

"I think you just proved Spirit's point," Seth smiled. "You're automatically putting work ahead of a request from God. Don't worry. That's typical. But maybe you can now understand how the One who created you feels. Most people put God dead last in their priorities. There is also one more quick thing I need to share. It might affect whether you and I have a second meeting."

"Do make it quick," Lorena insisted.

"You may want to consider how God responds to being shunned, disrespected and ignored. In case you're interested, you can read about it in the Old Testament. The people dissing Yahweh always received a punishment of some kind. You know about Noah and the Great Flood. But there were many nations hit by famines, pestilence and economic calamity for their disobedience. I will tell you confidentially that God is seriously considering a physical end to the world."

"What?" Lorena exclaimed.

"It's called a Solaster," Seth said. "If you show tomorrow, I'll tell you about it."

3

Lorena

Lorena sleepwalked through the rest of her day at the real estate office. She excused herself shortly after lunch, claiming a migraine. There was one errand to run: to the Toyota dealership to pay off the Camry. Seth's cashier's check was accepted without incident. The clerk said the car title would be mailed within the next seven days. Lorena left the finance office with a positive feeling

Not having a car loan is a good thing, she thought. That's one benefit from this morning's meeting with the "angel", no matter where it goes from here.

Lorena's small condo was less than two blocks from the beach and only 10 minutes from work. She quickly changed into walking shorts and plopped down in her favorite chair in front of a bay window. There was a slightly obstructed view of the endless ocean nearby, but she treasured it.

Life is good right now, she mused. I've got a promising job and I'm happily single. No more marriages for me. I've been there and done that — twice.

The real estate agent sat and reviewed her life. Her most recent marriage had lasted 5 ½ years. Ted was a decent guy. He was a high school physical ed teacher and assistant soccer coach at a large high school, also located near the beach. Since Ted had been a surfer dude at the same school growing up, he was happy to be back as a teacher and coach. However, his passion for surfing evolved into a consuming addiction for sports on TV. He was into world soccer and had a cable subscription that allowed him to watch matches from any venue in the world. There was always a game happening somewhere. Lorena fought Ted's addiction for a while, but it was a losing battle. She first detached emotionally and then legally. When Lorena informed Ted that she had filed for divorce, he just shrugged and changed the channel.

Her first marriage provided far more passion, but it was briefer. Tom was her high school sweetheart. He was a typical jock, but with some talent and potential. He was the #2 quarterback on an excellent team that went to the regional championship before losing on a last second field goal. The team's first string QB had a spectacular college career and a few good years in the NFL. Tom skipped college, even though he was recruited by several small colleges. "I guess I'm just tired of football", he had told Lorena before taking a job in his father's auto parts store. "Besides", he had added, "I want us to get married and start having babies." They were married within a few months, but no babies arrived. In fact, the couple's hot sex from high school soon vanished entirely. The marriage lasted almost two years before Tom quit coming home after work. Lorena heard that he was a nightly patron at a local strip club. He offered no objection when she suggested an amicable divorce. Like Ted, he shrugged and changed the channel.

Twice-bitten, Lorena promised herself to be extra cautious about any future marriage. She decided to focus her energy on getting an education and advancing a career in business. She enrolled at a nearby community college and received her Associates degree in 21 months. Then, she attended a state university and got her BBA while working in retail at a famous department store. Her teacher parents were so pleased with her educational interest that they financed most of her studies. Lorena graduated with less than $10,000 in student loan debt. Many of her college friends had racked up so much debt they simply quit paying back the loans. Lorena was happy to avoid the extra stress in her life.

At the urging of a friend in real estate, she took a two-week prep course for the state licensing exam. She aced the test and soon found a newbie job in residential sales. An office headed by a successful husband-wife team was looking for someone to help stage open houses. Lorena got the job, had a good attitude and worked hard at making every showing important. When one of the firm's regular agents resigned unexpectedly, she was offered a full-time job. Lorena became a full-fledged rookie agent and even notched one closing during her first three months on the job. A second closing was set for the end of next month. Both of her bosses seemed pleased with her.

Real estate isn't easy, she often thought. It takes time, hard work and some luck.

Lately, Lorena had started thinking about the lack of romance in her life. She still was not interested in marriage, but neither did she enjoy the lack of companionship. Miranda, a married girlfriend, had recently badgered Lorena into accepting a blind date with one of her male cohorts. A dinner date had been arranged for tonight at a local restaurant. The girlfriend and her husband would be bringing Lorena's date.

Now this strange old bum named Seth, claiming to be a full-fledged angel, has plopped himself into my life. Two new men in one day seems kind of unusual for me. I do wonder how the so-called angel knew so much about me, especially the exact payoff on my car. And, what about that scary stuff about God being so upset with the world? Anyway, I did get the car paid off today. That's a big plus. And I do have a date tonight. What's his name? Franklin, I think Miranda said. Oh well, it should be uneventful.

On the sidewalk in front of Lorena's condominium, a lanky red-haired man in his mid-30s stood unnoticed. Franklin had decided to take a quick walk near the beach before his date with a certain real estate woman.

Uneventful? Franklin smiled to himself. That's what she thinks.

4

Franklin

Lorena arrived at the restaurant first. Miranda and her husband William were bringing "Franklin", her blind date. She decided to wait at the bar, ordering a Vodka Gimlet. She was sipping her drink when the threesome showed up. Accompanying the couple was a tall and breathtakingly handsome man.

Lorena's heart raced at the sight of him.

OMG, she thought, this guy's a 10-plus!

Being seated at the bar as the others stood next to her, Lorena found herself eye level to the huge bulge in Franklin's khakis. She swallowed hard and tried not to stare.

"I'm sorry we're running a little late," her friend Miranda said.

Lorena attempted to speak but her voice had temporarily vanished. She was only able to nod in response.

"Lorena, I want you to meet our friend Franklin," Miranda offered.

Lorena's voice broke as she replied, "Nice to meet you."

What's the matter with me? I feel lightheaded.

She later recalled extending her right hand toward Franklin as a greeting. But before he could react by shaking it, Lorena pitched forward off the bar stool in a dead faint. She vaguely remembered the jolt of hitting the floor.

Her sudden fainting created an immediate scene in the restaurant. Several patrons and a waiter rushed over to help. One woman quickly identified herself as a physician's assistant. She reached down to check Lorena's vitals. Franklin went to his knees and placed a comforting arm under her shoulder. As he squatted down next to her, Lorena opened her eyes. She found herself gazing directly at Franklin's enormous package. With a sudden moan, she passed out again.

When Lorena's awareness returned for a second time, she found herself being supported and escorted by Franklin in the parking lot adjacent to the restaurant. Mindy and her husband were both walking close behind them to help as needed.

"Where am I?" Lorena managed to ask in a weak voice.

"We're taking you home," Mindy replied. "We'll stay until you're OK."

In the back seat of the car, Lorena felt the strength of Franklin's protective arm around her shoulder. His cheek gently brushed her hair. His manly presence felt natural and comforting.

The car made a sudden left turn to enter a nearby expressway. To brace herself, Lorena's hand inadvertently brushed over Franklin's crotch.

Oh my God, she realized, he is HUGE!

There was a brief pause before Lorena moaned "Oh! Oh! Oh!" Then she climaxed. The unexpected orgasm started in the lower half of her body and then cascaded throughout her entire being.

The suddenness of the physical event stunned everyone in the car.

"What just happened?" Miranda's husband asked.

There was a long silence and then Franklin began to laugh.

"Well, this is one blind date I'll always remember," he said with a good-natured humor.

His nonchalance seemed to ease the tension and soon everyone, including Lorena, were cracking jokes about her sexual awakening.

I may as well laugh about it, she told herself.

Franklin reached into his pocket and retrieved a small bottle. He unscrewed the cap and produced two rust-colored pills.

"That PA said to give you a couple of these babies after you woke up," he said, offering Lorena the medications. "It's sort of a super acetaminophen. It's supposed to relieve any tension. However, I'm not sure you need it now."

All four occupants of the automobile laughed, including Lorena.

"Why don't you drop us off at my place?" Franklin told the other couple. "I'll be happy to take Lorena home."

Everyone nodded in agreement, although Lorena did experience some sort of mild stabbing in her solar plexus.

After they arrived back at Franklin's apartment building garage, Miranda and her husband waited until Lorena was safely buckled into his sleek sports car.

"I'll call you tomorrow to check on you," Miranda said as they prepared to drive off. "Are you sure you'll be OK".

Lorena nodded affirmatively and the couple departed, leaving her alone with Franklin.

What have I gotten myself into with this guy? she asked herself.

By the next morning, the answer to that question would be irrelevant.

Within 10 minutes after Lorena and Franklin arrived back at her condo, the serious lovemaking began. For her, she started finding out what sex was all about. Her first two marriages had not provided much of a clue. Her few affairs outside of marriage were not much better. No man had ever been able to last beyond a few minutes. Lorena now found herself enthralled by the wonder of sustained passion, Franklin had sheer size and staying power beyond anything she had ever experienced before. She was swept into an indescribable and glorious ecstasy.

I hope this pleasure never ends, she found herself wishing.

But it did end. Franklin arose early the next morning and mumbled something about a business trip to Toronto that night. He had invited Lorena to join him and she had nodded yes without giving it much thought. At this point, if Franklin had proposed marriage, it would have been a "yes".

A few minutes after his departure, Lorena remembered something important. She had an appointment with the messenger angel in less than an hour.

I wonder if Seth will know about last night, she thought.

At this point, she could care less.

5

Seth's Message From God

The old bum had cleaned himself up.

Remarkably so, Lorena marveled, I almost didn't recognize him at first.

The angel was attired in a Burberry navy sports jacket and a tailored white dress shirt with an open collar. His khaki pants were clean, pressed and neatly creased. He also sported a pair of dark brown Bruno Magli penny loafers. His facial look included a trimmed salt and pepper beard and a pair of stylish reading glasses. Evidently, Seth had also been to the dentist. His jagged and stained teeth from yesterday were now replaced with a dazzling and perfect set of implants.

What a miraculous transformation, she mused, especially the choppers.

"Wow," she said, "You look great. How could you do all that in less than 24 hours?"

"I just wanted to keep you on your toes," Seth replied, "Even though you spent most of last night on your back."

The angel's direct reference to the tryst with Franklin stopped her short.

"How did you know about that already?

"I know just about everything about you," Seth confirmed. "That's my job. By the way, let me mention something about my improved appearance today. God warns us about judging by outer appearances. Spirit enjoys presenting some of Its top angels in ragged grab just to see if people will pay attention to them. Most human beings want zero contact with somebody who looks like a bum. Many of our best angels now live among the homeless and mentally challenged. That's where the action is right now. Lorena, never judge anybody by how much money they seem to possess. You can drive an expensive car and be six months behind on the payments. You might live in a huge mansion today and face foreclosure tomorrow. God understands that the human ego demands a big front. But many of the highest profile people are faking it from one minute to the next. So, my dear, God wanted to give you a little test. She wanted to see if my outside looks affected you. You nearly flunked, but then you decided to hear me out for 15 minutes. I'm sure that offering to pay off your car loan helped a little. You did pay it off, right?"

"Right," Lorena confirmed.

He's correct, she agreed internally. Without that cashier's check, he would not have gotten very far with me.

"Of course, I know what happened last night with Franklin," Seth said. "The other side didn't waste any time with you."

"What do you mean?" she asked.

"Let me explain something," Seth explained, "You just received your first "temptation". Do you remember in the New Testament how the Devil tempted Jesus three times? Last night was "Temptation #1" for you. "Sex" ranks as one of Satan's most effective tools. That's because it usually works. Most spiritual newbies are susceptible to being derailed by a little sex. Or, in your case last night, you were hit with a lot of sex. It hard to think spiritually when great sex happens along. That's understandable."

"That's true," Lorena agreed, "It's still on my mind right now."

"Well, don't get too caught up in it," Seth warned, "Temptations #2 and #3 are headed your way as we speak."

"What are the other two temptations?" Lorena inquired, "Surely they can't be as much fun."

"Maybe they won't be as much physical fun, but they are both strong incentives to throw you off the spiritual path. Don't worry, you'll recognize them both right away. Now, let's get cranking on today's business."

"Hey!" Lorena said, "What makes you think that I'm on any kind of "spiritual path"? I rarely even go to church anymore."

"Don't confuse religion with spirituality," the angel said, "Remember what I said earlier about "appearances". Some of the most spiritual beings among you never darken the doors of a church, cathedral, mosque or synagogue. Conversely, some of those do-gooders sitting in the front pews are devils in disguise. Until you really get to know somebody, you can't tell what evil may reside in their hearts. Going to church has nothing to do with traveling on God's sacred Path. Only He knows the Truth about what's in your heart."

"Let me ask you a quick question," Lorena said, "Why do you call God "He" at times, "She" at other times and occasionally even "It"? What gender is God? In Sunday School, God was always "He" and "Father"."

"Spirit is genderless," the angel replied. ""It" is probably the correct and purest answer. God is omnipresent, omniscient and omnipotent. It is everywhere present, all knowing and all powerful. Spirit is far larger than just a gender. It's true that most human beings use the "masculine" when speaking about God. However, I can assure you that the Spirit I know has an equal amount of both masculine and feminine characteristics."

"No matter what gender God may be," she interjected, "I find it hard to believe that God is so angry with us that He, She, or

It would destroy the planet and every living thing. That's drastic!"

"Yes," Seth said, "I do agree with you. Please let me explain. Spirit is a patient God. She understands that human sin has always been around. Disobedience must get bad before God deals out the Old Testament discipline. The world has already felt some of Her wrath. Tornadoes, earthquakes, wildfires, typhoons, tsunamis, floods, mudslides and even volcanic eruptions have plagued the world in recent years. Without a doubt, some of these disasters relate to climate change. However, His anger has been exacerbated in the last decade. When your scientists began creating human life, that was the proverbial last straw. God now sees no other option but to destroy everything, including the physical earth".

"How will it happen?" Lorena asked.

"Although only a few scientists are aware of the phenomenon, the general public has no idea that certain magnetic poles are now shifting bigtime. The ones who do know have been sworn to secrecy. Otherwise, a worldwide panic would take place. I will share the truth with you, but you must agree to complete secrecy. Promise me that you won't tell anyone, even your mother and father."

"Wow," Lorena said. "It must be bad. O. K., I promise."

"The end of the world is almost here," Seth explained, "If God does not intervene, the sun soon begins pulling the earth toward its flames. As you are sucked ever closer to the sun, the overwhelming heat starts consuming all life. The oceans and seas dry up. The heat also serves as a trigger to your weapons of mass destruction. They begin detonating world-wide. The results of those blasts are catastrophic for every living thing. The last time God disciplined the entire world, water acted as the cleansing agent. Now the fire destroys everything in a more permanent way. At the end, the sun's liquid gasses will cremate your planet. Only an emptiness will remain where the earth once spun. It's not a pretty picture. Oh yes, God refers to this scenario as a "Solaster". That represents the sun creating the ultimate disaster."

Lorena's jaw dropped. She felt shaken. Even if she doubted the enormity of what Seth described, the image of planet earth being consumed by the sun horrified her. It was an unimaginable finale to life as she knew it.

"That's terrible!" she almost shouted, "What would happen to the six billion people? What about the animals? I can't even imagine it."

"I agree it's a horrible outcome," the angel said. "Of course, every soul always returns to Heaven when the physical body dies. Your soul lives forever in eternity. But the earth's rich history would disappear, along with its physical beauty. I love your mountains and oceans. All of that would disappear. What a loss!"

"Can anything be done to keep that from happening?" Lorena asked.

"That's what part of my visit with you—and others—is all about," Seth said. "God has not made a final decision on anything yet. Spirit wants to give the world one last chance for redemption. THE 7 PUZZLES OF LIFE is part of a plan to save the world. God believes "The Puzzles" might get people interested in spirituality again. He also realizes it will take more than working on a few puzzles to turn things around. As they say, the genie is already out of the bottle. Artificial Intelligence and technology are not going away. However, people can still alter their attitudes about where God fits into everything. It won't be easy. Self-centeredness and the worship of money are powerful idols, along with a multitude of addictions, especially illicit drugs and pornography. It will be an uphill climb. Yet the threat of complete destruction might be a strong incentive to turn things around. I would hope so."

"Where do I fit into all of this?" Lorena inquired. "What can I do to change God's mind? I'm just one little real estate person."

"That's the subject of our next meeting," Seth smiled. "I'll tell you the specific thing that God has in mind for you. It's an assignment that She believes would be perfect for your skill set and soul history."

"Soul history? What does that mean?"

"Your soul has experienced many things over the years," Seth answered. "You have been prepared for spiritual service at a crucial time in world history. Are you ready to hear about it? If so, I'll meet you at the same time and same place tomorrow. I hope you say 'yes', Lorena. Will you?"

"I guess one more meeting won't hurt anything," she responded.

"Now I must go to work. The last time I heard, people were still buying and selling houses. That's how I make my living. It's called real estate."

6

Real Estate

Peter Thompson and Sallye Harland were among the top real estate producers in the area. Their office always seemed to snag desirable residential listings. Thompson and Harland had grown steadily, if not spectacularly. The couple had been together romantically and professionally for 15 years. They employed nine full-time and six part-time agents. They had just promoted newbie Lorena Mae Johnson from part-time to full-time.

"I believe in you," Sallye had told her. "You're smart, motivated, hard working and people like and trust you. That's a perfect combination for real estate success."

When Lorena popped into the office after her session with Seth, one of her associates hailed her.

"Hey, Lee," she said, "Sallye wants to see you as soon as possible in her office. By the way, who was that distinguished gentleman with you on the bench? He looks like an older version of that news anchor on Channel 7."

"Oh, he's just a friend and possible client," Lorena answered. "Is Sallye in her office right now?"

Her associate nodded yes. To prevent any more discussion of her bench partner, Lorena immediately headed toward her boss's corner office. She tapped lightly on the half-open door.

"Come," Sallye Harland called out. She motioned for Lorena to sit at her conference table. "Have a seat over there," she said in a friendly manner.

"First," Sallye smiled, "Who was that handsome man I saw you with on the bench? He reminds me of my father before he passed. He was a state senator, you know. I'm glad that nice looking guy was there today instead of the filthy bum I saw yesterday. I almost called a cop to shoo him off. Yuk!"

Lorena geared up for Lie #2.

"Oh, he's an old friend of my parents," she replied. "He plans to downsize from a house to a condo. He's looking for a place near the beach."

"Well, I may need more information," Sallye said, "My dear widowed mother is finally getting lonesome. Daddy's been gone 10 years now. I think she might be open to a good-looking man in her life. Does this guy have any resources? Mama doesn't do broke."

"Matter of fact," Lorena answered, "His net worth is heavenly. Now, I heard you needed to see me right away. What's up?"

"Peter and I like you, Lorena," Sallye said. "You've made good progress here. We think you have the potential to become a big producer."

"Thank you," Lorena replied, "I feel good about the future."

"Peter and I want to speed up your progress by throwing something big your way. That is, if you are interested.

"What's that?" Lorena inquired with a sudden anticipation.

"We just had a couple of unexpected listings fall into our lap. They're bigger than anything you've handled so far. One home belongs to that baseball player who was just traded to the Yankees. He's got a real gem right on the ocean. The comps in the neighborhood say we could easily list it at five-point-nine. The other listing is two blocks from the water. It's owned by a neurosurgeon and his heiress wife. He just got recruited by the Mayo Clinic in Scottsdale. This beauty has a few more square feet but would probably retail a little less, around 5.6 mil, because of not being right on the beach. The doc is a motivated seller, so we might get him to accept a little less. Anyway, Peter and I want to assign them both to you. We think you're ready for a bigger taste. The commissions would be around $300K. What do you think?"

What do I think? Ka-ching and Ka-ching again!

Lorena stared hard at Sallye. This was more than she could have hoped for, given her newbie status.

Suddenly, her vision began to blur.

"Hon, are you O. K.?" her boss inquired, "You look a bit pale."

"No, I'm just fine," Lorena replied.

"Let me fetch you a cup of water," Sallye said, "I hope this news isn't too much for you."

"I'm really OK," Lorena protested, "It's just a lot for me to digest. I want to thank you and Peter for having this much confidence in my abilities. I won't disappoint either one of you."

After uttering her appreciation, Lorena pitched forward in a dead faint. She rolled out of her chair in Sallye's office and hit the carpeting with a loud thud.

For a few seconds, Sallye was shocked speechless. Then, she called out in a loud voice: "Somebody call 9-1-1.!"

When Lorena opened her eyes, the office was filled with people. Besides Sallye and a few real estate agents and other employees, there were two EMT's and three police officers. One of the EMTs had propped Lorena up against Sally's large couch. Another first responder was swabbing her face with a towel.

"What happened?" Lorena asked, "How long was I out?"

"Long enough for help to arrive," Sallye responded, "Are you all right?"

Just then three firemen showed up and wedged themselves into Sallye's office. Right behind them, Peter Thompson strode in.

"What the heck is going on?" Peter said, "Is everything OK? Lorena, you look awful. What happened to you?"

I'm so embarrassed, Lorena sighed. How will I ever live this down with Sallye and Peter? What will they think about me? They present me with two listings and I react by passing out. First, it was at the restaurant with Franklin. Now, it's here in the office. What's wrong with me?

After the EMTs checked her vitals one more time, they backed up and departed. The police and fire personnel were right behind them.

Soon it was just Sallye, Peter and Lorena alone in Sallye's office.

"What happened with you?" Sallye asked, "Did me giving those two listings trigger that episode? Be honest with me, Lorena. We can always reconsider. I don't want to put any unnecessary stress on you. Is there anything else going on with you that Peter and I should know about?"

"I'm not sure," Lorena answered honestly.

"I want you to really think about this," Sallye continued, "If you take these two properties on, it will require more of your time and energy. Are you willing to make that kind of commitment? Peter and I are offering you the chance for some big money. It will really jump start your real estate career. We think you could be a big star for us. If everything works out, you might be on your way to some seven-figure years. The future is now for you, honey. Do you want it or not? Is there anything that might keep you from taking this opportunity and running with it. If so, please tell us now."

Lorena did not pause before answering.

"Absolutely not," she said, "I'm all in. Let's go to work!"

7

The Assault

In the confusion of the day, Lorena had forgotten her semi-commitment to accompany Franklin on the Toronto trip. She texted him that it might be best to cancel, given her second fainting spell. Lorena hoped he would understand. However, he sent back a surprisingly angry text. Franklin accused of her of leading him on after their night of great sex. Lorena just shook her head at the unexpected reaction. Then, about an hour later, her doorbell rang. She looked through the peep hole and saw Franklin. He looked agitated.

Uh-oh, she thought. What's this all about?

Lorena opened the door.

"Oh, Franklin," she said, "You didn't have to come over."

He brushed past her, then turned in an aggressive and confrontive manner.

"I thought we had a date," he said, "You let me down. I don't like it when people disappoint me!"

Then, without warning, he slapped her hard across the face. Lorena's knees buckled with pain and surprise.

"What the hell!" she shouted, "Why did you hit me? I think you better leave now."

What should I do? He seems out of control, she told herself. Should I call the police? Maybe he'll hit me again. I'm afraid of this guy. Help me, God.

Franklin raised his hand, this time in a fist. Lorena cringed, closed her eyes and waited for the blow to land.

Just then, she heard her front door swing open. Lorena sensed the presence of someone or something noisily arriving in the front hallway.

She opened her eyes and saw a huge form, much larger and more muscular than Franklin. The "thing" grabbed Franklin's arm in mid-air and violently spun his whole body around. Then it lifted the surprised man two feet off the floor, shook him violently and tossed him unceremoniously into a corner. The monster walked over, fetched Franklin's limp body by the scruff of his neck and gave him another hard shake. Then he raised Franklin to his feet, manhandled him to the still open front door and tossed him on Lorena's front steps. The "form" followed the disheveled man outside, gathered him up once again and delivered a hard kick to his rear end.

"And don't come back!" the monster shouted. Lorena peered out and saw a chastened Franklin slinking away into the darkness.

It was then that Lorena recognized her protector.

I'm certain that's the all-pro linebacker who played for our NFL team. I went to a game once with my dad and saw him play. I believe he passed away a few years ago. Whoever he was, I'm grateful that he showed up when he did. I've probably seen the last of Franklin. He seemed almost possessed. My face is still stinging. Strange things are happening. What have I gotten myself into? I'm not sure that I want to know. Oh well, I'll meet with Seth one more time tomorrow and then I'm doing real estate after that. I need to make some money. Ka-jing!

8

Puzzle #1 — Free Will

Seth greeted Lorena with a smile and wave as she approached the bench. He again looked spiffy, but a little more casual than the previous time.

"I hear you had an interesting experience last night," he said. "All is well, I presume?"

"I did get rescued, if that's what you mean," she replied.

"I'll bet it was something to see. That guy was quite a football player in his day."

"I guess that's the end of my relationship with Franklin," Lorena said.

"I wouldn't be too sure about that," Seth cautioned. "That's all I can say on that subject for now. Now. Let's get down to business. I have a big surprise for you this morning."

"What's that?"

"I have your first puzzle box," he smiled, "Free Will". I think you'll find it most interesting. It sets the stage for everything else."

The angel reached down to fetch a large leather briefcase. Lorena had not noticed it before.

"That's an impressive piece of luggage," Lorena observed.

"It's the best Heaven can afford," Seth smiled.

He loosened the buckles on the base and extracted a colorful box about 15 inches wide and 6 inches deep. He held the box up for Lorena to inspect. She was immediately enthralled by the spectacular beauty of the cover. It featured vivid colors that reminded Lorena of a rainbow. There was a collection of pictures strewn across the cover, both artist renderings and actual photographs. The words "FREE WILL" identified the puzzle contained in the box.

On the cover, she spied a photo taken at her parent's 25th anniversary celebration. There was an artist's illustration of the house where she had lived during her elementary and middle school days. Lorena also saw a photo of her favorite dog "Callie", a Shetland Sheep Dog. There were two small pictures of both ex-husbands without her presence. She noticed two somewhat larger likenesses of two other men. She did not recognize either one. Her recent lover Franklin was nowhere to be seen. One image that caught her attention was an artist's depiction of a large mountain. A bright red balloon floated over its top. The words "Pikes Peak" identified the mountain.

It's in Colorado, Lorena thought. Near Colorado Springs, I believe. I've never been there, but it looks lovely. There was one image that grabbed her attention. It was an artist's portrait of a winsome young girl, probably in her mid-teens. The serene countenance on the girl's face had been strikingly captured by the artist. Lorena stared at the image with an admiring awe.

She looks so at peace, Lorena decided. Whoever did the painting really captured the girl's innate beauty and serenity. She also looks a lot like me at that age, but I can tell that it's not me. I was never that peaceful in my teenage years.

"Could that be my daughter sometime in the future?" Lorena asked Seth.

"That depends on your free will choices," the angel answered, "But, yes, it could be. Again, everything rests on your future decisions. The pieces in this box depict both actual things that have occurred in your past and what may happen in the future. You, and everybody, get to decide what the future holds for you. The box cover is a mixture of past, present and future events and people."

"This makes the 7 Puzzles concept more interesting for me," Lorena said. "Please tell me more."

"The Free Will puzzle really explains your life journey," the angel told her. "It is the triggering device for the entire human adventure. When you are born, you are presented with a "clean slate". You don't make many decisions for a while. Your parents or some other authority figure controls your life. But sooner than you might think, you take over the decision-making process. Let's say that you live 80 years, which is now on the low side. You'll probably average 100 decisions a day at a minimum. Eighty years times 365 days is 29,700. That number multiplied by 100 equals 2,920,000. That means you will make nearly three million decisions in your lifetime. Most of these decisions or choices will be routine. However, they all add up and combine to create your history. When and what you will eat, even where you eat, are daily choices. Of course, some of the decisions are real biggies. Whether or not to attend college (and where), getting married, going straight to work or maybe heading to the military are huge things to decide. What specific career should you pursue? That can be a major determinant of your future happiness. In addition, deciding if you should pick up that first drink or smoke your first joint could also be turning points. Or maybe not, depending on how everything else shakes out for you. Making a conscious decision to break the law often turns anyone's life upside-down. Deciding who to marry or pair up with can very much shape your journey one way or the other. Of course, a wrong love decision can often be corrected through separation or divorce. But that still means pain and lesson learning. Loving the wrong person can even be fatal in some cases. Deciding whether to drink and drive is another critical choice that people approach in a cavalier manner. I think you see how and why Free Will is such a big deal. There are also multiple decisions that bring joy and happiness. Deciding to write that book, learning to play the piano or becoming a whiz on the dance floor are choices that can enhance your life. So, my dear, I think you can see that Free Will has both its good and not so good sides. Every choice you make can play an important role in your life."

"Yes, I can see that," Lorena agreed.

"God installed Free Will into your human engineering for three specific reasons. First, it stands as the spiritual framework through which you process the "life lessons" prepared for you in this lifetime. You choose exactly how those lessons unfold. The main purposes of you being on earth in the first place are soul evolvement (from successfully completing the lessons) and service to God. With Free Will, God hands you the keys to a new car with zero mileage. You decide which roads to travel, and at what speed. While you begin with a clean slate, you do carry some family history with you. If Great-Grandpa was a Supreme Court justice, you might be predisposed to the law. But if Great-Great-Grandpa was a cattle rustler in the Wild West, it might cause you to consider stealing that car with the keys in the ignition. That may sound far-fetched, but I've seen those kinds of things play out thousands of times."

"I don't think we have any cattle thieves in the family," Lorena offered.

"The second reason that God gave human beings Free Will has to do with spirituality. Every human being is born with a spiritual nature. However, sometimes it stays untapped for a lifetime. Spirit gives you the freedom to hide your inner essence from birth to death. The materiality of the secular world wants you to keep your love and compassion out of sight. Do you remember that famous book from years ago entitled "LOOKING OUT FOR NUMBER ONE"? That replaced the Holy Bible for many people. Focusing on "self" made sense to lots of folks. Putting themselves ahead of others has now become a way of life. God and spirituality are always under attack. The material world uses many idols to turn your head. Money, sex, power and celebrity seem far more exciting than quiet devotion to a Higher Power. To express your spiritual tendencies publicly often brings ridicule and scorn. However, mocking and disobeying Spirit are always bad uses of Free Will. God loves you and wants only the best for you. It hopes you someday discover the spiritual power located at the core of your being. It wants you to perform miracles. God can use you as a holy instrument to perform the greater works. Your job is to let God live God's life through you. You are Spirit's hands and feet. God wants you to speak and act on Its behalf. You become a blessing to humankind when the power and love of God flows through you."

"What's the third reason why God gave human beings Free Will?", Lorena asked the angel.

"It can be summarized in one word: TRUST. You can use your Free Will to trust or not to trust God. The LORD wants a working relationship with every human being. People have three choices when it comes to "trust". They can trust their own wisdom and abilities, which most people do. They might choose to put their trust in others, which can be problematical. Or they can decide to trust God. That is always the best and surest choice. One of the greatest Bible verses ever is "My Grace is your sufficiency in all things". God is telling you to trust Him with everything. That means your health, wealth, happiness, relationships—everything. Most human beings won't trust anything they cannot see, hear, touch, taste or feel. Trusting the invisible requires faith. When you put your supreme trust in God, you are exhibiting faith. There are millions of testimonials available from people who trusted

God and it all worked out for the best. But people are still skeptical. Human beings seek control. They want to dictate their own destiny. God wants people to make the Free Will decision to trust Him. Therein lies the real secret of life: Trusting God.

Lorena nodded, although the idea of letting an invisible spirit make life decisions for her was hard to grasp.

I don't know, she thought. Whenever somebody starts telling me about hearing invisible voices, I get suspicious. How can you really trust someone or something that you can't see? I want to trust God. It's just not a comfortable thing to do. But, I'm here to learn. I'll stay open at this point.

"I just want to add something about trust," Seth said, "It's easier to trust when you feel a Oneness with Spirit. A huge number of people see God as "punishing". If you have that negative idea implanted in your brain, it becomes almost impossible to trust in a benevolent Higher Power. Addictions of any kind also discourage human beings from trusting God. When you are addicted, the drug of choice becomes your Higher Power. It then controls you. God is cast aside, along with everything else. Addiction derails spirituality. The path to recovery for any addiction lies in restoring your Oneness with God. Nothing else really works."

"That makes sense," Lorena agreed, "But it's still hard to do."

"Let me share a bit more about Free Will and then I'll tell you a story," the angel said. "Free Will represents the "x-factor" in every human life. Just as there can be no identical fingerprints, no two mortal lives ever turn out the same. The diversity of experiences stands as a unique feature of human life. Identical twins born minutes apart can have radically different lives. Lorena, there is no other person on earth who will have the exact same past experiences or future outcomes as you. God created you as a unique individual. That's one thing that troubles Spirit about Artificial Intelligence. It tosses aside the entire principle of God as Creator of the Universe. That's just one of the reasons it cannot stand. Science will never be able to manufacture a machine with a soul. A robot may be 10 or 100 times smarter than a human being. But real compassion and love will be far beyond its capabilities."

"What story do you want to share? Lorena inquired, "I'm due at work."

"Settle back for a minute," Seth said, "I want to share a story about Free Will and its importance in everyone's life.

Some years ago, there were four teenage boys living in the same neighborhood. They were all about 16 years old and sophomores in high school. One of the boys had recently passed his driver's license exam. To celebrate, his parents had gifted him with a used pickup truck with an open flatbed in the back. On the afternoon in question, the boys decided to hang out together. They wanted to enjoy the freedom of just riding around. Two of the boys rode in front while the other two teenagers hoisted themselves up onto the back of the vehicle. One of the boys in the flatbed spotted a couple of old straw brooms. He yelled out to the others: "Hey, I've got a cool idea. Let's drive over to the poor side of town. We can scare some kids out riding their bikes. You all drive up real close and then we'll give them a swat with our brooms." The other three boys laughed and agreed. They drove over to "the other side of the tracks". Sure enough, they soon spied a young Hispanic boy out riding his bicycle. The driver of the pickup swerved to within a couple of feet from the youngster. One of the teens riding in the back took a hefty swing at the boy riding his bike. The youngster felt his bicycle suddenly wobble. Then the boy fell onto the pavement, along with his bike. The right rear tire of the speeding pickup passed within six inches of running over the boy. At the last possible second, the teenager on the passenger side of the pickup had reached over and turned the wheel hard left to avoid the boy's falling body. The older boy's free will choice had nearly led to a tragedy. The passenger in the pickup also made a free will choice to reach over and turn the wheel. It was a close call for everyone involved. Had the young boy died that day, many lives would have been impacted.

"How did you know that story?" Lorena asked.

"I was the angel that reached over and turned the wheel away," Seth told her.

9

More About Free Will

Lorena had a busy day in her real estate office. Most of time went to comparing comp sales for her two new real estate properties. She was excited that both sellers seemed realistic about their asking price. That could indicate a high motivation to close a deal sooner rather than later.

That's a highly positive sign, she thought. I've got appointments with both sellers later this week. Everybody wants to move ahead. I'm ready for that too.

She was surprised and even somewhat perplexed when she received a mid-afternoon text from Seth. It read: "Need to see you after work today. More about Free Will. I'll bring snacks. See you at the bench at 5:30 pm. Seth. P. S. Important!!

Lorena thought about texting the angel back saying she couldn't make it. However, she never got around to replying. At the appointed time, she headed over to the bench. Seth was already there, along with a couple of sandwiches from a nearby deli.

"I knew you liked pastrami on rye, so I got a sandwich for you," Seth told her, "And unsweetened iced tea with two funny sugars, right?" Lorena had ordered the exact same takeout from the same deli many times.

"You must have a thick file on me," she told the angel.

"We are quite efficient," he replied, "It's one Heaven's best features."

"What else did you need to share about Free Will?" she asked.

"When I reviewed our conversation from this morning, I decided that I had come across as too negative about Free Will. I wanted to give you a more balanced perspective. O. K.?"

"I guess," Lorena answered, "But I've had a long day. Can you get to the point?

"God wants human beings to make the world a better place," the angel said. "Choosing to grow spiritually makes that happen. Life is a wonderful gift. When you live by the Golden Rule instead of chasing the good times, you find real happiness and fulfillment. When you do for others, you vastly improve the quality of your time on earth. Each time you extend a kindness to someone, your angel wings really do grow a bit bigger."

"I can see that," Lorena said, "But that's not how the world operates. It's hunt or be hunted, eat or be eaten. Everything revolves around competition. I'm sure you know that real estate is the epitome of cut-throat competition. Some of my fellow agents would sacrifice their grandmother for a good listing."

"God doesn't expect people to spend 24/7 praying, meditating, reading the Bible, going to church or scouring the neighborhood for folks to help. Spirit just wants some balance. Right now, most people don't devote any time to growing spiritually or doing good deeds for others. God understands how stressful and complicated human life can be. Spirit never nags you for more attention. She hopes you'll make that Free Will choice yourself. However, people today think about their electronic devices and themselves. They don't understand that when you increase your spiritual life, good things happen."

"I don't think you (or God) are being realistic," Lorena opined, "Human beings are creatures of habit. If you've been in the habit of focusing on yourself, you can't change that tendency overnight. I still think there are some good people out there. A lot of them, actually."

"I agree there are some terrific individuals," Seth noted. "I'm speaking in overall terms. I think you'll admit self-centeredness is rampant. Everybody wants to know "What's in it for me?" Somebody praying for God's Will in their life does not happen much, except maybe during a 12-Step meeting."

He's right, Lorena silently agreed. I believe in God, but I can go days, weeks or even years without really thinking about Him. I have a mental picture of a benevolent (mostly) old guy with a beard, resting on a throne somewhere in the sky. He's got a hand-held calculator that keeps track of sins and sinners. I don't remember the last time I spoke with Him. I did pray (along with my family) before Thanksgiving dinner last year.

"I'm not trying to make anyone feel guilty," the angel said. "God simply wants everyone to become more spiritually aware. He and I want to remind you about your sacred heritage. You are a child of God, perfect in every way. There are no exceptions. Today's culture doesn't give a Big Rat's Tootie about where God fits into the scheme of things. Technology rules the day. False idols are everywhere. Addictions are rampant. The real God has gotten fed up waiting for positive Free Will to kick in. That's the bottom line."

"What can I do?" Lorena asked, "I'm just one person."

"You're doing something by sitting here and talking about God."

"Well, you did pay off my car," she commented, "I owe you a little something."

"Before you can do anything about a problem, you need to acknowledge that one exists. I'm helping you get past that first stage. The Al-Anon program talks about the three principles of "Awareness, Acceptance and Action." You're still at the beginning of the "Awareness" stage. You haven't moved the needle yet."

"But I'm still just one small person," Lorena protested.

"When a few souls begin stirring," the angel explained, "the whole world starts moving. However, Spirit also realizes that when one soul steps forward, 100 more rush headlong toward the other side. Those who oppose spirituality are cunning and baffling. The "culture" encourages and supports a Godless environment. Believe me, Satan knows every one of your weaknesses. You have already experienced one of evil's greatest lures — sex. That one shortcoming alone has snuffed out many of God's potential servants Let me tell you another story. I'll try to be quick."

"Please do," Lorena responded, "It's been a long day."

Once upon a time in Texas, there was a young minister. We'll call him Reverend Billy. He built a megachurch from scratch before he turned 30. One of his earliest congregants was an extremely wealthy woman. She founded what became a major corporation with thousands of employees. The woman was a multi-millionaire and she liked Reverend Billy. She decided to build a much bigger church for the young pastor. You know the saying "If you build it, they will come"? That is exactly what happened. Within a few years, thousands were flocking to hear the dynamic young preacher. He had become a religious phenomenon. People started comparing him to a more famous minister, also known as "Billy". However, the Devil soon began probing for weaknesses. The "ego" is the first place that Satan looks. Although blessed with a lovely wife and four darling young children, Billy enjoyed the attention of women. Many of his female congregants were young, beautiful and enthralled with the handsome minister. He soon began "counseling" nearly a dozen of these young women at a condominium owned by the church. One day, the husband of one "counselee" showed up at the church and demanded to see Reverend Billy. Word soon spread to the church *board and an investigation was launched. It uncovered that 26 separate women had received personal "counseling" from Billy over a two-year period. The board had no choice but to terminate their high-profile minister. He lost a $250,000 salary, many perks, a free parsonage worth $500,000 and his family in the months that followed. Billy made many wrong free will choices that brought him down. He lost just about everything and God lost an effective servant. It was a lose-lose situation for all. In that case, the devil prevailed. It's a cautionary tale, but one that is far too common among God's servants."*

"What happened to him?" Lorena inquired.

"He tried to make a religious comeback," Seth replied, "But it didn't work. Of course, his rich benefactor had long since cut her ties. He was also defrocked from his original denomination. The disgraced minister did start an independent church, but it failed within a few months. Reverend Billy eventually began selling life insurance. He passed away with a brain tumor before turning 50. His funeral was attended by less than two dozen people. It was a sad outcome, that's for sure. I know that God cried about it more than once."

"That's a sad story," she reiterated, "I feel bad for his wife and family."

"It's true," Seth agreed, "Negative free will choices can affect far more people than just the person involved."

"I need to head home," Lorena said, "But I have one more question. It's about the "Solaster". I've been told by my parents that God loves everybody. If that's true, and I believe it is, how can God even think about destroying the world and every living thing? It doesn't seem possible that He could be so mad at us."

"Good question, my dear," the angel responded. "However, if you read the Old Testament, God's judgement was on almost every page. He sent great and bountiful blessings to those who obeyed his laws. But He could also direct the locusts to devour the crops of others. What made the difference? One group paid heed to put Spirit first before all others. The locust group worshipped various idols, were amoral to the extreme and mocked God. When that happens, punishment is usually swift and merciless. However, today's world has far exceeded past misbehavior. When your scientists began creating "human" life, God decided "That's a bridge too far". It simply won't be tolerated. Many folks are rightfully worried about "global warming." That ranks far back compared to a "Solaster". We're talking about almost total extinction of life."

"What do you mean almost total extinction?", Lorena asked.

"God has a contingency plan," Seth replied. "He wants to take a small remnant of human life to a new home in the solar system. Only a few people will be chosen, along with some animals, birds and insects. It will be a space capsule likeness of "Noah's Ark". Even with His anger towards the current culture, God still refuses to completely give up on human beings. It's a token, albeit small, of His love for you."

"How will God decide which people get to go?"

"I've already seen your name on the manifesto," Seth said in a teasing manner.

"You're kidding!", she exclaimed.

"Yes, at this point I am," Seth smiled, "But that can always change. I hope it does. It's your Free Will choice. Everything is up to you."

10

The 2nd Puzzle Of Life — Family

As Lorena popped an English Muffin into the toaster before work, she received a text from her messenger angel.

It read: "Can u and i meet B4 work? Need 2 talk 2 u bout 2nd Puzzle — Family — S."

Oh well, she thought, why not? It might be interesting.

As usual, Seth beat her to the bench. He was dressed in a classy Under Armour running outfit with high grade Nike shoes. The shoe design featured angel wings.

"Going for a run afterwards?" Lorena teased, "I thought you probably flew everywhere."

"That's funny," the angel smiled, "I'm glad to see your sense of humor is still intact."

"Now, what's this about the "family" puzzle? I really should get into work at a decent time. I've got those two major residential listings that need some attention."

"Oh, I know all about the listings," Seth said, "In fact, that's your second temptation. First, it was sex. Now it's money. You'll get the third temptation before the day ends. Be ready."

"Since you know about the two listings, I'm sure you know what I told my bosses. I'm all in. Real estate is my livelihood. This is a big opportunity for me. I'm not going to pass it up. I'm sorry if that disappoints you."

"Oh, I'm not disappointed," the angel replied, "This is a predictable scenario. Once the LORD taps someone for a spiritual assignment, Satan gets busy. Temptations, distractions, threats and actual bad things begin happening. The principalities of evil are never passive. They jump right on people and situations. You're being targeted. Some folks are shocked when it happens. But our side can help. We've got resources, as you've already learned from the run-in with your friend Franklin and our angel linebacker. You saw how that one turned out."

"I wanted to talk to you about that," Lorena said, "There is no need for anybody to target me. I'm getting off the train. This is my last stop."

"That's your Free Will choice," the angel answered. "But, since you came today, we may as well cover the second "Puzzle". As I said in the text, we call it "Family". It's a big part of who you are. Give me a few minutes to explain. I think I deserve that much for paying off your car."

"I'm sure I'll never hear the end of that," she offered, "Just keep it at 15 minutes and then we're done. Promise me?"

"Absolutely," the angel assured her.

Lorena folded her arms across her chest and sat upright on the bench, hoping the body language would also communicate a degree of finality.

"First, let me ask you a question," the angel said, "Do you think God placed you in your family for a reason?"

"I have no idea," she answered.

"I can assure you that God never does anything without a reason. There is a spiritual purpose for everything. "Family" placement is an integral part of your life journey. Even your birth order is chosen with care. You are an only child. That meant you received your parent's full attention. In your case, that was an incredible benefit. It has given you a feeling of uniqueness and importance. I know that you regret not having brothers and sisters. However, God has other plans for you in this lifetime. Your mother and father are both respected educators. That was also a blessing for you. You were instilled with an appreciation for learning. You possess a curiosity about the world around you. It's a bit of a wonder that you didn't follow in your parent's footsteps. However, that was not part of your life plan this time around. For your information, you were a teacher in a previous lifetime in India. But that's a story for another time. Being a "teacher" serves as one of the most important spiritual positions. Jesus was really a teaching rabbi. His three-year ministry was built around instructing others. Anyway, your mom and dad were always teaching you. And, my dear, you loved it. "Learning" has always been important to you."

"You know, I think you're right", Lorena agreed, "I got sidetracked by my first marriage, but then I eventually went back and got my degree."

"I'm glad you brought that up," Seth agreed, "You were always destined to finish college. People often get pulled away from their true path for a while. But if something is pre-destined, it will usually find a way to happen. Your mother and father know the importance of "education", so they encouraged you about college. Another family might have urged you to focus on getting a job and sticking with it. Your folks wanted you to have a college degree."

"What else about "family"? Lorena asked.

"Spirit puts everyone in a particular family for one or more reasons," the angel explained, "When a soul transitions to the material world, it incarnates to learn specific lessons. Usually there is one "lesson" that exceeds all others. I want to reveal your lesson now. Do you want to guess? Remember, it could be something like "forgiveness", "courage", "responsibility", "compassion", and so on and so forth. I'll give you a hint: your "life lesson" is none of those."

"I give up," Lorena said, "I don't have any idea."

"Your life lesson is "trust." Let me elaborate. "Trust" represents a common lesson for human beings. In many past lives, souls found they could not trust people and situations for one reason or the other. Many did not trust God to have their best interest at heart. In your case, you experienced lots of "past life" broken promises. One of the most spectacular involved an engagement to be married. Your future husband abandoned you the day before the wedding. In another lifetime, your parents left you with a relative for a weekend and never returned to retrieve you. That was especially traumatic. You were eight years old at the time. That abandonment helped ruin your life. Now, fast forward to this lifetime. You've been married twice and divorced twice. You wonder if you can trust your judgement about who to marry. In every lifetime, you receive countless opportunities to practice your designated "lesson". Will you be able to trust your judgement about the next "love" partner? Right now, you're not too confident. In this incarnation, you will hopefully learn the spiritual principles of trust. Then, you can make better decisions. Being able to "trust" is important in any human life."

"How many lifetimes have I experienced?" Lorena inquired.

"Your soul has lived 37 times," the angel told her, "We don't have enough time this morning to discuss them all. Here are some generalities about your past incarnations: you have lived as both a man and a woman. Your female trait is more dominant. Twenty-two of your lifetimes were female, 15 were lived as men. Sometimes, one gender is extremely dominant in a person's soul history. When that happens, human beings can become confused when they live a lifetime in their opposite gender. That can cause sexuality issues. You may see and sense masculine traits in a female-oriented soul, and vice versa. Now regarding skin color: you've experienced lifetimes in every color under the sun. So has every other "old" or even "new" soul. That is why being prejudiced against anyone because of skin color borders on the ridiculous. Anyway, let me tell you specifically about one of your past lives. A dozen or so generations ago, you were a Choctaw Indian princess in what is now the state of Oklahoma. Your Native American name was "Big Flower". Physically speaking, you were the largest woman in the tribe. Your husband was the tribal chief. He was known as Grey Eagle. He was killed in a battle with a rival tribe. Without hesitation, you assumed command of your people and defeated the enemies. After the battle, you were named as the new leader. Lorena, your soul ancestor was among the first female chiefs in Native American history. You became known for your physical strength and unflinching courage in battle. No other tribe or internal rival ever dared to challenge you. You served as chief for many moons, as they say. Her courageous blood flows in your veins right now. Let me quickly share about one more of your past lives. In that incarnation, you lived as a slave on a plantation in Virginia following the Revolutionary War. You were familiar with many of the "Founding Fathers", as your plantation owner was one of them. You knew and conversed with three separate men who would later become presidents of your country. They all called you by your first name and treated you with kindness and respect. When you passed, people of all colors gathered for your funeral. There were tributes from a host of dignitaries, as well as family members. One future president told how he had quietly asked for your counsel on many occasions. Your soul left a beautiful legacy that is still being passed down to others. Her blood flows in your veins as well. You carry the traits of these two strong women with you today. You possess a rich "soul" heritage."

"Wow!" Lorena reflected, "I honestly don't know if I believe in past lives, but it's certainly something to think about."

"Now, before we wrap up today, I want to share one more story about "family". I'll try to make it quick, but it contains an important message."

Just know I need to go soon," Lorena cautioned.

The angel shared this story:

This is about a boy named "Jose". For the purpose of this story, I'll call him "Joe". For most of his later life, he was known by that name. Joe came from a troubled family. Both his parents were brought into the country illegally by their respective families. The families resided in the Mexican border town of Piedras Negras on the Rio Grande River. They crossed into the U. S. at Del Rio, Texas. Joe's dad and mother met and married when both were 16 years old. Joe came along a year later, followed by three other brothers and two sisters. When Joe was 10 years old, his father was arrested for a burglary and deported back to Mexico. His mother gathered the family together and moved to Houston, where she had some cousins. Joe's family soon splintered, with his siblings being scattered into to the Texas Child Welfare system. He and His mother were left alone. Then they heard that Joe's father had become involved with a drug cartel in Mexico. He was later murdered by another cartel. Joe's mother was also now dealing with several health problems. To get her some medications, Joe robbed a drugstore. He brandished a knife and demanded the pharmacist give him the needed drugs. He was apprehended by the Houston PD in less than 30 minutes. Stick with me here, Lorena, because this is when Joe's life took an unexpected turn. When his case went to court, he found himself standing before a crusty old Texas judge. The wise judge presented Joe with two options. He could go to jail for three years for the drugstore robbery. Or, he could join a new government program for wayward youth. It featured 180 days in a quasi-military setting, going through "basic training" and learning discipline. If Joe successfully completed the six-month program, he would then have the option joining either the U. S. Army or the Marine Corps. His criminal record would also be expunged. His court appointed lawyer urged Joe to choose the military option. Rather than fighting the camp's rigid structure, the young man loved it. He enjoyed the daily regimen, three good meals every day and feeling a sense of belonging. He grew another three inches in height and added 30 pounds of hard muscle. While in camp, Joe was chosen as the "squad leader" of 12 other boys. Right before graduation, he became a "platoon" leader of four squads. When Joe was successfully "discharged" from the camp, Joe enlisted the next day in the Marines. Less than one year later, Joe found himself in Viet Nam in heavy combat near Da Nang. He and five other Marines were cut off from the rest of their company. They were surrounded by 150 regular North Vietnamese troops with automatic weapons and rocket launchers. Joe volunteered to try and hold off the enemy while his friends escaped. He was able to keep his position for nearly 30 minutes, although he had been wounded in three places. The North Vietnamese were within 20 feet of Joe's position when an air cavalry unit arrived to drive them away. For his gallantry that day, the young Marine was awarded both the Bronze Star and Purple Heart. The former wayward teenage now held two of the nation's highest decorations. Joe ended up making a career of the Marines. He retired as a Master Sergeant. He accumulated several other medals along the way, including a wife and three children. One of his sons, Jose, Jr., enlisted in the Marines one day after his high school graduation. While in the service, Joe became interested in his family's history. He discovered that a great-great grandfather on his mother's side had served with General Santa Ana at the battle of the Alamo. The General himself bestowed a battlefield commission on the young soldier. Another relative was among the brave Marines who hit the beaches at Iwo Jima in World War II. He was surprised to learn of the strong military tradition in his family. When he found the family "link" in his life, Joe saw that his life had real meaning. Lorena, there are no accidents in the spiritual universe. That especially includes "family".

"That was an interesting story," Lorena said, "But I must go to work."

"Give me two minutes to sum up the Puzzle of "Family", Seth countered, "I promise that I'll be brief."

"You're on the clock," she smiled, "Go!".

"Your family is the living laboratory where you experiment with life. It offers you access to everything—relationships, chaotic and happy events, attitudes toward life in general, and the good and bad behavior of human beings. Most everything in life happens in the context of family. Your family can be a joy or a never-ending nightmare. Family members may be your greatest booster or your most painful detractor. You may not believe this truth, Lorena, but there are no perfect families. Now, here is my last and final thought on families. Addictions of one kind or the other run in all families. No family is without problems, even if they may appear so on the outside. There is always an addiction lurking somewhere. For one family, Uncle Bill's addiction to ice cream was as bad as it got. In another family, alcohol and drug abuse was rampant in generation after generation. If negative addictions are a problem, the cycle can always be broken by a family member willing to change the direction. There is always "hope" for any family problem. That's the one word that I'll leave you with about family: hope."

"Amen," Lorena said, "that's a good place to end."

11

The Beauty Shop

Lorena buckled down and spent her real estate day researching comps for the two residential listings. She also had positive visits by phone with each seller. In-person meetings were scheduled with both. All in all, she felt the day had been productive.

About 4:30 p.m., Lorena realized she had a beauty shop appointment in about half an hour. She wrapped things up in the office and headed for the salon. After presenting herself to the receptionist, Lorena was disappointed to learn that her regular stylist had gone home ill. The shop had not notified Lorena because they planned to offer her a replacement.

"She's really fabulous," the receptionist told Lorena, "You'll love her."

Although slightly piqued, the real estate woman agreed to try the new girl.

I really do need some work done, Lorena thought. I've gone six weeks without a color or cut. I'll take a chance. Why not?

While she and the receptionist waited for the new stylist to appear, Lorena inquired about her work-history and qualifications.

"Tell me something about her," she asked.

"She's Jamaican," the receptionist said, "Her name is Shanise. I think it means "Queen" or "royalty". She has kind of a mysterious presence. I like her, but she's different from any other stylist we've ever had. But I don't think you'll be disappointed."

Just then, one of the most striking human beings in Lorena's memory appeared. Her color was an unusual light shade of black, but that was the least of her stunning persona. She measured six feet two and a half inches tall, but her upswept hair style and stiletto heels added several inches to her height. She projected a regal and majestic presence. However, a brilliant and friendly smile tossed off any hint of haughtiness. As a first impression, Shanise was unforgettable.

"I'm Shanise," she announced in a voice three octaves lower than what Lorena was expecting.

"Of course," Lorena said, extending her hand.

Shanise's handshake was strong and lasted five full seconds. Lorena finally extracted her hand from the death-like grip.

Whoa, Lorena thought.

Shanise leaned close to Lorena's right ear and whispered, "Come with me, my dear, I've been expecting you."

That was more a command than a request, Lorena thought. What have I gotten myself into now?

The tall woman turned and walked ahead of Lorena toward the back of the beauty shop. She moved with such long strides that it was hard to keep pace.

"The management of the salon has given me a private space for now," Shanise explained as they reached the rear of the small building. "I prefer a quiet area when I do my creative work," she added.

Lorena was a regular customer of the beauty salon. However, she hadn't noticed the room before. It was decorated in flaming streaks of hot red on a dark mahogany background.

This room gives me the chills. Lorena thought. Maybe I should rethink the appointment. This woman is bizarre..

"Sit down," Shanise again said in a commanding voice that offered no escape.

Lorena plopped down in the chair and the stylist immediately threw a heavy blanket-style cover over her. It was much weightier than the light cotton covering the shop usually used. Lorena felt smothered and trapped underneath the heavy blanket.

"Wow," the real estate woman said. "I'm not accustomed to this kind of heavy cover."

Shanise just smiled, then circled behind Lorena and pulled the blanket even tighter.

"You'll get used to it," the stylist said. She then emitted a strange laugh, almost like a cackle.

"Let me tell you how I want my hair cut," Lorena said, trying to establish a boundary with Shanise.

"Oh, not to worry," the unusual woman replied, "I know your needs. I'll make you happy. I promise it."

"Pardon Me?" Lorena inquired, "What do you mean by that?"

"I said that I know what you require in order to maintain your beautiful looks."

"And what is that?" the real estate woman asked.

"Eternal beauty, my dear," Shanise answered. "It's what every woman wants. You seek to defy time and aging. Women desire to remain forever youthful. The calendar is your merciless enemy. It exacts a frightful toll. But not to worry. This is where I come in."

"What are you talking about?"

"Most women would gladly mortgage their souls to stop the aging clock," Shanise smiled. "I can grant that wish."

The hair on the back of Lorena's neck reacted.

I'm getting chills, she thought. Maybe I leave before things get even weirder.

"Lorena, before you bolt out of the chair, let me show you something."

Shanise reached into her working table. She extracted two glossy-type photographs. She held them up in front of Lorena.

"Take a look," she instructed her client. "As you can see, these photos seem to depict two different women."

Lorena gazed at the two pictures. One showed an ancient woman of about 90, with severely wrinkled skin. Her hair was stringy and uncombed. The old woman's jaw sloped downward. Indicating either Bell's Palsy or a moderate stroke. Her mouth hung open, revealing a serious lack of teeth. She looked almost deranged.

Poor woman, Lorena frowned. I feel sorry for her.

"She's a mess," Shanise said, "Right?"

"I can't argue with that", Lorena admitted.

"That's you in 50 years," Shanise said, "Not a pretty sight, eh?"

"No, I guess not,"

"Now look closely at the other photo. Consider the difference".

The woman in the second photograph was beyond stunning. She radiated good health and beauty. Her hair and makeup were impeccable. Lorena finally recognized who the woman resembled: a new and improved version of herself.

"Is that me?

"Yes," Shanise answered, "That can be you 50 years from today."

"What?" Lorena asked, "How is that possible?"

"That's why I'm here," the stylist replied, "I can make that happen for you."

"How could you possibly do that?"

"Come on now," Shanise cackled, "How do you think?"

It suddenly became clear what the stylist was saying: eternal beauty in exchange for your soul.

"A fair trade," Shanise said. "Wouldn't you agree?"

Without a word, Lorena flung the heavy body cover aside and leaped from the chair. She flew out the back door of the beauty shop and ran towards her car.

In the background, she heard a loud cackle following her steps.

OMG, what have I gotten myself into?

12

The 3rd Puzzle Of Life — Love

Lorena drove back toward her real estate office the next morning. She saw that Seth was again perched on their bench. There he sat, as if waiting patiently for her arrival. With a sigh, she joined him. "I suppose you've already heard about the beauty shop," she said.

"Hello to you too," the angel smiled. "I warned you to expect the third temptation before the day ended. Let's see, you had the "sex" temptation a couple of nights ago. Then, "rnonev" reared its ugly head at your job. Shanise and her "eternal beauty" scam topped things off. You've had quite a time of it, my dear girl."

"What's next?" she asked with a frown.

"A lot depends on your Free Will choices," Seth replied. "In some ways, your three "temptations" were like a warning shot across your spiritual bow. It can get much worse when you make a commitment to God."

"I haven't committed to anybody or anything yet," the real estate woman said emphatically. "In fact, I doubt I will. I hope you and God won't be too unhappy with me."

"Why don't you reserve your judgment a tad longer?" Seth said, "I want to visit with you about the 3rd Puzzle of Life. That's "LOVE" and I think you might be interested."

"Well, I'll see. What do you have to say?"

"First, I want to begin with another true story," the angel smiled.

"Oh no," Lorena said, "I hope it's not too long."

"Bear with me," he grinned, "There's a terrific point at the end."

"All right. Go ahead. Pardon me if I start dozing off."

Once upon a time, there two young women in their mid-20s. Their names were Carol and Melinda. They had been roommates in college. The pair graduated with teaching credentials and both got jobs in the same elementary school. It seemed natural they would decide to lease an apartment together near the school. Neither had a steady boyfriend or girlfriend. They both preferred the male species, so they decided to join an online dating service. In a creative twist, the girls marketed themselves together as fake-sisters, looking for a pair of two eligible men (although not necessarily brothers). The response to their unique approach was beyond their expectations. They received contacts from brothers, cousins, bosom buddies, roommates, teammates on athletic teams and even veterans who served in the same military unit. Finally, after much deliberation, they chose two worthy candidates. Both were graduates of the college they had attended, although neither girl knew them. The men were working in the corporate world, but not at the same company. A time and place for the first date was arranged. The two girls arrived first at a popular mid-scale restaurant. Soon, the two men appeared. Carol and Melinda tried not to look shocked as they approached. However, Melinda visibly reacted as they introduced themselves. "Warren" was tall, ruggedly handsome, and crushed Mel's heart with a dazzling movie-star quality smile. He was also extremely confident, something that Melinda adored in a man. His charm and charisma easily exceeded his three companions combined. Mel was simply bowled over by the "first-sight" impression. The thought occurred to her that she would need to fight Carol for Warren's attention.

However, her friend seemed almost not to notice his obvious appearance and charm. In fact, Carol barely reacted to either man. Warren took control and introduced his friend "James" to the girls. He was the exact opposite of his more exciting companion. James was at least five inches shorter, wore horn rimmed glasses and sported a strange haircut that could have been self-inflicted. He showed no teeth when he barely smiled. Once the group was seated, Melinda focused her entire attention on Warren. She even ignored Carol. That was fine with Warren, because he seemed awed with Melinda. Meanwhile, Carol and James exchanged a few stiff words and studied their menus. The evening ended a little more than an hour later, with Warren swooping up the entire check for everyone. As the foursome departed the restaurant, Warren and Melinda hung back. They exchanged contact information and made plans to meet alone for a date the following night. Meanwhile, Carol and James shook hands almost formally. There was no exchange of information or talk of another meeting. That was that, or so it seemed.

"So, what's the point?" Lorena asked almost impatiently. "Melinda saw something she liked in Warren and went after him. Carol and the other guy didn't connect. No harm, no foul. I don't get it."

"I think you will "get it" when I tell you the rest of the story," Seth said.

"There's more? Please make it quick."

Warren and Melinda fell into a hot courtship. Their sex life was incredible. The couple soon began spending most of their free time together. Carol tried to convince Melinda to slow down, but the message was unwelcome. It even put a crimp into their previously close friendship. Mel responded by practically moving into Warren's small apartment. After six months living together, Warren and Melinda eloped to Las Vegas. Things got rocky on the honeymoon. Mel knew her new hubby liked to gamble. While they were in Vegas, Warren placed two $500 bets on a pair of upcoming NFL games. Melinda later remembered sitting in their hotel casino and *watching Warren lose both bets. He was angry one minute and acting guilty the next. This quickly became the pattern for the early weeks of their marriage. Then, Warren went all in on one big football weekend. He placed a $1,000 bet on each of 10 NFL games and lost them all. Melinda discovered he had taken out cash advances on her credit cards to finance the bet. Mel was forced to ask her parents for help in covering the advances. Within six months, Warren owed more than $25,000 to friendly neighborhood loan sharks. Soon, both she and her husband began getting verbal and physical threats. Her car was vandalized. Warren was knocked down one day on the street. The marriage ended nine months to the day of their elopement. Melinda was so traumatized by her marital experience that she never remarried. As for Warren, he eventually landed in federal prison for bank fraud. On his 40th birthday, he committed suicide by jumping off a famous bridge not too far from here.*

"Not a pleasant story," Lorena noted, "Now, I need to go."

"Wait a minute," Seth said, "You still need to hear about Carol and James. You do remember that they were the other couple on the blind date?"

"Oh, yes, can you sum them up for me?"

Carol did not hear from James for several months after their first meeting. They bumped into each other at a new church that had recently opened. They laughed about the double date and wondered how Melinda and Warren were getting along after their recent elopement. The pair decided to have coffee after church one Sunday. They soon became friends and even worked on a church project together. Carol liked James' quiet dependability. He thought her sense of humor kept him lighter. They soon began exploring a more serious relationship but did not have sexual relations for nearly six months. That's an eternity these days. One year more and they became engaged. Then, still another full year later, they married. James and Carol recently celebrated their 30th wedding anniversary, surrounded by their children and grandchildren. We've never been happier, they told everyone. Every now and then, Carol recalls her friendship with Melinda and the eventful blind date. "I got the best guy that day," she still tells her friends.

"That's certainly the better outcome," Lorena observed. "I guess the moral of that story is don't let good sex decide your love choices."

"Oh, it's more than that," the angel observed, "But there are several basic love lessons here. First, never make any love decision with long term consequences based on instant attraction. That includes outer beauty, a scintillating personality or that the other person possesses money, power, prestige or some other visible trapping. Young women are often attracted to a man's "ride", A fancy vehicle may exude wealth. However, it might also be a lease car whose payments are in arears. Never make love choices with input from your eyes alone. Here are two practical words that apply when it comes to evaluating love: due diligence. Secondly, search for any kind of a spiritual connection with your potential love interest. I'm not saying that you should only date people you meet at church. In fact, sometimes it can be quite the opposite. Some of the worst predators can be found sitting in the front pew of your neighborhood church. You must be an astute observer when it comes to love. Watch how your lover treats other people, especially his or her parents or siblings. If he isn't nice to those closest to him, get ready for similar mistreatment. Be careful about choosing addicts of any kind. Co-dependency is rampant among human beings. Many people search for somebody who they can "save", whether they admit it or not. Nobody can cure or control an addict. Don't think you can change those odds."

"You're starting to peach a little now," Lorena smiled, "I know for sure it's time for me to go.

"Please give me a few minutes after work tomorrow," Seth requested, 'The next thing I share about The Love Puzzle you'll want to hear. I promise it."

"I'll think about it," she answered.

What the hey, Lorena thought. Maybe I'll hear something worth-while about "love" before I terminate our relationship.

13

More About The Love Puzzle

Lorena wrapped up her day at the real estate office shortly before 5:30 p.m.

When she left the building, Seth was waiting dutifully. He was even smiling.

"You're looking chipper," she said. "Did you spend the day doing good?"

"Actually, I was on traffic duty today," Seth answered. "Since texting while driving has become so prevalent, our collision prevention work has nearly doubled. I mean it, Lorena. I stopped two potential head-on crashes that would have injured or killed eight people. It's a real mess out there. In those states that legalized marijuana, it's even worse. I don't understand what human beings are thinking. Or not thinking. Anyway, I'm glad you showed up. I've got more about information about the Love Puzzle for you."

"My time is limited," Lorena shrugged, "I'm really tired."

"I'll get to the point, but I have one digression if you will allow me."

"Do I have a choice?"

"It's about a valuable resource for living that most people shun. I'll bet you haven't used it for weeks, months or even years."

"Let me guess," she mused, "The Bible?"

"You're smarter than you look," Seth said, "Wait. I'm kidding. I know you have great intelligence. You just proved it. God's Word is the premier guidebook for navigating human life. It's also the most important book about love ever written."

"How is that?"

"Do you remember your second wedding? Of course, you do. The officiating minister read from First Corinthians, Chapter 13. It's a brilliant discourse about "love". Do you recall the words "Love is patient, love is kind" and the concluding section about "faith, hope and love, but the greatest of these is love? That about sums it up. "Love" stands at the pinnacle of any human relationship. The Power of Love can overcome the greatest obstacles. It scales the highest mountain of negativity and endures the sharpest pain of neglect. Love survives the passing of time and the disappearance of outer beauty. True love never fails to inspire, advance and restore the human spirit. It creates a healthy heart and nourishes a withered soul. God has placed "Love" at the center of your being. You can activate it at any time. Love always awaits your summons. When you release love, it soars like a freed balloon toward the closest rainbow. And, it's all there in the Bible for you to read about and understand."

"I'm sure you're right," Lorena agreed, "I haven't read my Bible in weeks or months. Maybe even years."

"Living without some form of love can be the death knell for anyone," the angel observed. "You should always look for love everywhere. Your pets can be a wonderful source of love and acceptance. Cherish your pets! They exude unconditional love and can rescue their master's soul from depression and loneliness. You should witness the daily reunions of pets and their masters at the Rainbow Bridge leading into Heaven. These precious moments of being reunited with a beloved pet are beyond description. However, "love" is not only available from pets. You can find in many places. Again, the Holy Bible describes love relationships between friends, associates, and even strangers. Jesus the Christ personified a special kind of love. Do you remember the story of "The Woman at the Well"? Jesus offered the Samaritan woman the "living water". He was projecting love out into the world with a perfect stranger. There are always people, places and things that need some love. When you extend your love, it always comes back to you."

Lorena nodded her approval for Seth's words about love.

I've always known that my parents loved me, she thought. tt's true they are sometimes reluctant about showing it. I think its a generational thing. i've also gotten lots of love from qrandparents, aunts and uncles. My grandpa on my morn's side used. to tell me, "Lorena, remember one thing: you're great! Don't ever let anyone tell you differently. After all you're my favorite qranddauqhter." I would laugh and tell him, "But, qrandpa, I'm your only qranddauqhter!" He would always grin and hug me again. I've been blessed with so much love from my family. Not everybody gets that.

"Let's talk about your love relationships," the angel said, "What attracted you to your husbands?"

"Well, neither was that good-looking. However, both were big and sort of rugged. I always felt safe and protected when we were out somewhere. I married number one because I was ready to leave the nest. I wanted my freedom, I guess. Timing played a part as well. My friends were all getting married. That might have put pressure on me. With hubby #2, I wanted to prove that I could have a successful marriage. He also came along at the right time, just as I was feeling open to some male companionship. However, we just lost interest in each other. I think he preferred his male buddies over me. At the end, that didn't even bother me. But it made me extra cautious about any more marriages."

"What about the "love factor", Seth inquired, "I haven't heard you say anything about being "madly in love. What did love look like for you?"

"I don't think I knew what love was then" Lorena replied. "I'm not sure that I do today. I'll admit to feeling some passion for Franklin. It was the best sex I've ever had. Maybe it was more lust than love."

"A strong physical attraction can be an important part of the love equation," the angel agreed. "True love and hot sex can complement each other. Problems arise when the sex becomes routine, which it usually does sooner or later. Part of the sexual allure revolves around newness. That's what encourages infidelity on the part of both men and women. They still want that feeling you get with a new sexual partner. Now, I understand that some old married couples can still get steamy about each other. But for every pair still having hot sex after 20 years, there are 100 others who've found other common interests. The good feelings that come with children and grandchildren, shared experiences, common goals, and mutual respect. If a couple gets lucky, they discover how much spirituality can add to their marriage. Did you ever explore the spiritual side of marriage with either one of your husbands?"

"Absolutely not," Lorena laughed, "I never went to church with either of them. We liked sleeping in on Sunday mornings. I don't think we ever prayed together, except maybe before Thanksgiving or Christmas dinner at my folks. Don't get me wrong. We never sat around and used God's name in vain. Neither of them ever used the f-word much, which I think has changed today. They weren't atheists or even agnostics. Spiritual stuff just didn't come up, if you know what I mean."

"Addictions can mess up relationships," Seth observed. "Did either one of your husbands have problems with alcohol or substance abuse?"

"Yes, to some degree." Number One liked to binge drink about every three or four months. He once disappeared for a week. After that, we were done. Hubby #2 liked to smoke grass on the weekend. He may not have been addicted, but it was close. I never cared for it."

"Would you believe it if I told you that addictions did indeed affect your marriages? In both cases, your husbands thought more of their addictions than they did of your relationship."

"Why do you say that" Lorena asked.

"No need for defensiveness", the angel said, "Virtuallv every human being arrives on earth with a pre-disposition to some particular addiction. Just as diseases and illnesses are handed down from generation to generation, addictions cycle through families as well. Science now knows that if a woman smokes, drinks or does drugs during pregnancy, the fetus can be impacted. But it goes far beyond that in passing down chemical predispositions. Your first husband came from a long line of alcoholics. The second guy had family members that abused substances for years before he even came along. Then, there is the matter of your DNA. Remember, my dear, this is incarnation #38 for you. Co-dependency was your drug of choice. You come from a long line of Native American healers. You have lived before as a nurse and caregiver. When you encounter an addiction, you want to rush in and "help". That feels familiar to you. So many families "cycle" behavior and professions. One family might possess generations of lawyers and judges. Another family could be filled with bankers and business types. Still others could have a collection of con men (and women), embezzlers, and relatives who engaged in various criminal activities. This may all sound like part of the "Family Puzzle", but it also can have major impact on love relationships."

"You make true love sound hopeless," Lorena complained.

"Not at all," Seth countered. You just need to understand what you're getting into when you make a commitment. You're also selecting their DNA and family history as well. The Love Puzzle demands that you go much deeper in exploring the other person. You should look for someone that brings out the best in you, an individual who brings out your strengths. This is one reason that same-sex relations are growing in popularity. Men sometimes bring out the best in other men, as do some women with other women. You should also never discount reconnecting in this incarnation with a person you loved many generations or even centuries ago. It happens more often than you think. There are many things to consider before marrying somebody. You must find a person that will stick by his or her commitment to you. Infidelity scuttles trust. The real test of love never comes during the good times. Anybody can be there for you when you're rich or in good health. It's when you're broke and receive a bad diagnosis from the doctor that people tend to leave. How many people today would sign up to push their partner's wheelchair from day one? Not too many, I'm afraid. I think you get the picture. True love can be the gift of a lifetime. But it can also be rare these days, given that you live in the selfie era."

"But how can you predict what will happen?" Lorena inquired. "Can you ever be sure about another person?"

"That's why you need information in the beginning of a serious relationship," Seth said, that isn't available when you first meet somebody. To find the right person, you must put together the "Puzzle of Love." That takes time and effort. It begins with asking God to guide you in your quest for love. That's always a good start."

"That does make sense," she nodded.

"You must understand what attracts you to someone else," Seth told her, "In many cases, opposites do attract. A person with a knack for making money often gravitates to someone who loves spending it. An outgoing life-of-the-party type may unconsciously seek out a quiet introvert as a balance. Physical differences also matter. How many extremely tall men do you see with tiny women? It can happen, but only if they connect intellectually and spiritually. Sexual proclivities play a role too; a wildly unfaithful partner may expect strict fidelity from his or her partner. They can be crushed if their significant other strays. Still, I keep coming back to the importance of placing God at the center of any relationship. Rarely have I seen a relationship fail when both parties place God #1 above all others. The odds for marital success improve dramatically when Spirit is at the center of things."

"I can see where religion would be important," Lorena said.

"It's really more than religion", Seth explained. "It's about two individual souls linking up to form an unbreakable spiritual bond. Being religious is certainly OK. However, it also can become too ritualized. Spirituality is more dynamic. It always focuses on direct access to God as the most important goal. Connecting to God without some kind of a go-between encourages spirituality. However, having a sensitive and caring priest or minister in your life never hurts. They can help a couple bond with God. Too many human beings want to go it alone, without any human or heavenly assistance. Spirit allows for that free will choice, as we learned in the first Puzzle. To me, however, that's like taking off your life preserver when you feel the ship starting to sink."

"What's my specific outlook for love?" Lorena asked.

"Much depends on the choices you will make in the not too distant future," the angel said. "However, please pay attention to these four basic principles: (1) Be wary of anyone who causes you to have an instant physical reaction, especially if "neediness" or "lust" could be contributing factors; (2) Explore inner qualities by gathering information based on personal observation and also trusting what your gut tells you; (3)

Notice how someone acts toward other people, especially those who serve them. Check out how they treat a waiter or waitress, or a clerk in a store. That attitude will demonstrate who they really are; and (4) If your potential love interest demonstrates addiction problems with alcohol, drugs, gambling, sex or physical abuse, you should probably back off until you gather more information. People are usually quite good at telling you who they are. Pay attention."

"You've given me a lot to think about," Lorena said. "It doesn't make my love future any clearer right now. But I guess that could change."

"Yes, it can," Seth agreed. "You could always meet the love of your life before the sun goes down tonight. With God, all things are possible. Be cautious, but also stay open to finding love. Where there is life, hope springs eternal. You have a lot to offer someone. Believe it."

14

Celestina

After she returned home to her condo, Lorena headed straight to bed. She flung herself down on her colorful bedspread, flipped over on her back and stared at the ceiling.

A few minutes passed. Her mind felt chaotic, jumbled and confused. Then she called out: "If you're out there, God, please help me. I'm messed up and scared. I need you. Please."

She became aware of another "presence" in the bedroom. It was standing at the foot of her bed.

Lorena sat up on her elbows. What she saw astonished her. In a flowing white robe, a beautiful young woman stood with her arms folded. Like the "thing" that saved her from Franklin's physical abuse, this "creature" was much larger than the average person. She had long red hair. A white orchid was pinned on her head.

"You called?" the form asked in a melodic voice. "You sent a call to Heaven and I was the next angel up. What can I do for you?" Her tone was strong, vibrant and authoritative. Yet it was not intimidating or threatening.

"Who are you?", a surprised Lorena inquired.

"I'm Celestina, a warrior angel. You called for spiritual assistance. I'm here. What do you need? I don't perceive a visible threat, at least not yet. What's troubling you, hon? Lay it on me."

I must be losing my mind, the real estate woman thought to herself. First, a linebacker angel throws Franklin out on his rear end. Now I've got his female counterpart standing at the foot of my bed.

"Are you for real?"

"You better believe it," Celestina responded. "I may the most real thing in your life right now. You gave a shout out to God. She heard your request and here I am. Now if this really isn't a spiritual 911 call, that's OK. No harm, no foul. But if you have a need, I'm here. I can listen, comfort, guide or fight for you. I think it could be the fighting part that you may require. I believe your friend Shanise just pulled up outside. She's not coming for tea. You ran out on her before she could get your answer about the "eternal beauty" temptation."

"What are you talking about?"

Just then, lorena heard a heavy pounding on her door.

"Let me in right now!" Shanise yelled, "We weren't finished. I need your answer right now. Open up, bitch!"

"Cool your jets, Shan," Celestina called out in a loud voice. The warrior angel flew to the front door and flung it open.

"I thought it might be you, the red headed whore angel," Shanise screamed.

"Don't think you can get away with sucker punching me again."

Lorena heard a fearsome altercation erupt from her bedroom. It sounded ferocious, even by spiritual standards. There was shouting, cursing and shrieking and that was just from Shanise. There were several discernible blows being struck. Then there was a heavy blow followed by a "thud" of something hitting her wooden floor in the entry way. Then there was only silence.

Finally, the red-haired angel stuck her head inside Lorena's bedroom.

"I'm going to drag her sorry ass outside," Celestina said, "I don't think she'll be bothering you any more tonight. Is there anything else? If not, I'm outta here."

"I guess I should thank you," Lorena called out.

"Just doing my job, babe. You take care now. Hear?"

15

The 4th Puzzle — Work

Lorena again thought of skipping a meeting with Seth, but the angel seemed eager for a visit as she strode by the bench.

"I'm ready to talk about the 4th Puzzle of Life", he called out. "It's about work. You might want to hear me out before heading to the office. I think you'll find it edifying. I'll be quick."

"That's what you always say," she chided. "Oh well, I'm here."

"I understand there was quite a showdown at your condo last night," Seth smiled. "That Celestina is a real warrior."

"Yes;" Lorena agreed, "She saved me from Shanise. I'm glad she came to my rescue. Shanise is a piece of work. She was yelling and screaming. I think Celestina drug her outside after the fight."

"I wouldn't worry about Shanise for a while," the angel observed. "I heard she didn't show up for work at the beauty salon today."

"I want to tell you again that I'm planning to focus on my real estate," Lorena stated, "That's my job and I need the money. I've got two great listings that will keep me busy for a while."

"At least you're here today," Seth replied, "We'll just go from there."

"Tell me about the "Puzzle of Work," she commented, "What should I know?"

"The "Work Puzzle" generally concerns how you earn a living." the angel said, "It's about how you spend much of your waking time. Suppose you live 80 years during this incarnation. That's nearly 700,000 hours. You'll be sleeping or resting about one-third of that time, or around 235,000 hours. That leaves you with 465,000 hours to manage. Being a child, going to school, working and retirement should consume another one-third. Any way you slice it, you spend a big percentage of your life "working". Most people see their work as a way of making money. Of course, it is that. However, Lorena, I want to share something about work that remains hidden. It represents the true factor in whatever job or career you may pursue."

"What's that?" Lorena asked.

"In God's mind, whatever your work may be, it's only preparation for "spiritual service.""

"What does that mean?"

"It means that your "work" is always preparing you to serve God."

"Do you mean my real estate career is getting me set up for another kind of work? I don't see how that could be."

"It's not only the specific job you're doing today," Seth explained, "The work you performed in past lives also figures into God's equation. In your case, there was one recent incarnation that has many ramifications now. Would you like to hear about it? It's an interesting story."

"Of course," she said.

"It was your most recent past life," the angel stated. "It happened as World War II was ending in Europe. The date in question was March 17, 1945. Germany was on the ropes. However, they were still attacking the United Kingdom with air assaults. On that date, one lone German Henkel 111 bomber hit the Yorkshire city of Kingston Upon Hull, located on the northern bank of the Humber Estuary. People on the ground that evening were stunned when the lone enemy plane started dropping its bombs. It didn't make any sense, just one bomber. The 111 unloaded its deadly cargo just as movie goers were leaving the Savoy Theatre after watching a film. Thirteen people died on the ground and 22 were injured.

You had attended the Savoy that night with your family. Your name then was Sarah Spencer. You were 44 years old and worked as a general nurse at the city's main hospital. You had been accompanied to the theatre by your husband George and your twin 13-year old daughters, Elizabeth and Margaret. Your girls were named for the two royal princesses. Anyway, as I mentioned, the bombs fell just as the people were exiting the theatre. You were tossed up in the air by the explosions. As your body flew above the carnage, you heard a distinct voice. It said "You must go back and help. You are a nurse. The injured ones need your attention." You suddenly found yourself back lying on the ground. There wasn't a mark on you. Then your nurse's training and healing instincts kicked in. Although you were concerned about your husband and two daughters, you began tending to the wounded. You toiled the entire night without a break. According to our celestial records, you directly saved 10 people from dying in the hours after the raid. Without your presence, the death toll would have been much higher. Unfortunately, your daughter Margaret perished in the attack. She was killed by flying debris. However, George and Elizabeth survived with only scratches and bruises. There is a plaque honoring the dead and wounded now located at the site where the bombs struck. On that awful night, your name was added to our "List of Heroes" in Heaven. It is from that eternal registry that you were selected for a sacred mission. By the way, your soul from that incarnation was welcomed back home in God's Kingdom in 1979 after you died from natural causes. You were 78 years old. Your husband George followed you a year later. I understand your daughter Elizabeth finally passed away several months ago in her late 80s. Your soul returned to earth in 1984, exactly five years to the day that Sarah entered Heaven. There are no accidents, Lorena. God's timing is always perfect. You are being asked to use your nurse's training again to heal a troubled world."

"WOW" was all Lorena could think to add when the angel finished his explanation of why she had been chosen to serve God.

"Oh wait," Seth continued, "I need to add a P. S. to the story. Do you remember those 10 people that you saved? Six were women. Among them, they had a total of 15 children born after that night. Those 15 kids produced 48 more children and so on and so forth. A minimum of 63 more human beings have experienced life on earth because of your heroic actions that night. You had a lasting impact, Lorena."

"I would like to believe that," she said. "Your story makes a good point about the importance of one person."

"Let me get to the crux about 'The Puzzle of Work", the angel told her. "It dovetails nicely with the World War II story. No matter what your job or profession, you always affect other people's lives besides your own. Being in the medical field, your contributions back then were a given. Your parents are teachers. Their presence and influence have impacted hundreds and even thousands. Millions of souls have served in the military. Their bravery during times of conflict have preserved freedom for your nation. Whatever work you perform on behalf of others demonstrates spiritual service. You are helping people find a suitable home. Although you aren't saving lives per se, you offer a blessing than can affect their happiness for years to come. In whatever job you may have, you will probably interact with other human beings. Your daily interactions can lift someone up or tear them down. I realize that many folks hate their job. For those people, I would suggest they look deeper at the job's spiritual possibilities. They might be surprised. Incidentally, most workers either "Like" or even "love" their jobs. Now, I know you are getting antsy again. However, indulge me one more time. I've got one more story about "work" that I think you'll like. I warm you that it's another story about a minister, but then I've had many dealings with the profession over the years. Anyway, here's the story:

Pastor Bob had served his small non-denominational church for 10 years. He rarely took a Sunday off. It was not a wealthy church. A small but steady stream of congregants came from a nearby rehab center for recovering addicts. He once figured that he had counseled at least 300 patients over the years. Many of those people continued as regular members after their time in rehab ended. However, it was not a glamorous ministry. The church constantly strained to achieve its annual budget. Bob had sought an assistant pastor for many years to help ease his work burden. However, the church elders pleaded a lack of available funds. Lately, attendance was trending downward. Several older members had passed away and they were not being replaced with fresh faces. He often thought of the verse in the book of Daniel about "the handwriting was on the wall". Pastor Bob prayed daily for God's direction. The response from the LORD was always the same: "Just keep on keeping on. I will never leave or forsake you." Bob admitted to himself that his faith was dropping. "God, I'm nearly 50 years old," he prayed one day, "Maybe it's time for me to do something else. Will you please give me a sign, one way or the other?" A few weeks later, he had been chatting with several people after the regular Sunday service. Bob noticed a woman standing alone near the front of the church. She was gazing up at the depiction of a forlorn Jesus hanging on the cross. The minister recognized the woman as a sporadic attendee. She usually showed up at Easter or Christmas. He walked over to her and said "Hi, Edna. I'm glad to see you here today. Then, Pastor Bob did something spontaneous. He gave the woman a friendly and non-sexual hug. She stiffened at first, but then relaxed into the brief greeting. Their embrace lasted four or five seconds. They exchanged a few more pleasantries and then Bob said "Edna, I hope I see you again next Sunday. I appreciate you being here." He noticed the woman looking at him in a strange way. Then she mumbled a soft goodbye and walked away. Bob returned briefly to the pulpit, gathered up his sermon notes and retreated to his office. That was the last time he thought about the encounter. Then, the following Sunday, the pastor noticed that Edna had returned for the second consecutive week. In fact, she had parked herself in the front row. At the beginning of the service, as the platform assistant read the usual announcements, Edna suddenly stood up. She turned to face the congregation. Bob looked up from his customary seat on the dais and thought "Uh oh. What's this about?" Edna began to speak. She said: "Before we get into the service today, I need to say something about Pastor Bob." On stage behind her, Bob gulped. What might be coming, he thought to himself. Edna continued: "I was standing at the front of the church last Sunday and our minister came up to greet me. I had thought it would be my last time at church. I was planning to go home and commit suicide. Then, Pastor Bob reached out and hugged me. He said that he enjoyed seeing me here. He also told me, "I hope I see you again next Sunday." When I got home that day, I thought about what he said. I decided that I couldn't let him down. So here I am. Thank you, Pastor Bob for giving me a reason to live." Soon everyone was on their feet, crying and applauding. Tears popped from Bob's eyes too. He had wanted a sign from God about his future. Edna was the messenger. Pastor Bob served that church for 20 more years until his retirement. He remembered the special day when Edna was elected president of the church board of trustees. He had cried that day too."

"That was quite a story," Lorena said, "Thank you for that."

"Now you go and have a productive day at work," the angel said.

Then, before she could respond, he disappeared into the ethers of a beautiful morning.

16

Peter and Sally

Lorena's real estate bosses, Peter Thompson and Sallye Harland, were puzzled.

They could not fathom why their young agent was so lackadaisical. They had bestowed two prime listings on her. For some reason, she seemed detached from the excitement that comes from the potential of a a rich commission.

Lorena seemed well-liked by everyone. They knew she would be accepted by people of color. That aspect of the firm's business was exploding. But Lorena was not limited in any way. Her two closest friends in the office were somewhat older Caucasian female agents. Sallye knew both these women well. They were long-time real estate pros and possessed hard edged and competitive personalities. They both adored Lorena and vied to work with her. Peter and Sallye had long employed two male African American listing agents. "Herman" had been their top agent for several years. The other black agent, "John", was third in closings the previous year. Both Peter and Sallye saw Lorena as a challenger for #1 producer in the entire office. The lack of fire from Lorena was surprising and concerning.

"Something is up with her," Sallye told Peter.

"I don't get it," he agreed. "We plopped the moon right on her plate and she barely thanked us."

"I'm wondering if it has anything to do with that older gentle-man on the bench," Sallye ventured. "She sits with him almost every morning and sometimes after work as well. Lorena claims the old guy is a possible client. I don't think there is anything romantically going on. He could be her grandpa."

"Maybe we should just ask her," Peter offered.

"Let's do that," Sallye agreed. 'I'll set something up."

There was a tap on the glass outside Sallye's office. It was Marianne, her administrative assistant. "Charles White, Jr. is here to see you," Marianne said, "He wants to speak with both of you."

Peter and Sallye looked at each other. Mr. White was a long-time attorney with deep ties in the African American commu-nity. In fact, Mr. White had been the original source for the two listings now residing on Lorena's desk. There had been no scheduled meeting, deepening the mystery of his visit.

"Show him in," Sallye told Marianne.

Mr. White had a commanding presence that demanded in-stant attention. He was tall, but not NBA tall. His suit and shoes were Italian, while his dress shirt and tie were English. The only thing American about him was an almost Southern courtliness. Charles White, Jr. had the best manners of anyone Peter and Sallye knew. "He has real class," Peter told Sallye.

"I hate bothering you without advance warning," Mr. White said, "But something unexpected has come up. I wanted to see you all as soon as possible."

"How can we help you?" Peter asked.

"I had a call yesterday from one of my most important cli-ents," Mr. White explained. "I can't share his name right now, but you would know it. He was the origination point for the two residential listings that I gave you. He has learned that you all assigned both properties to Miss Lorena Johnson. She evidently is an agent in your office. Is that correct?"

"Yes, it is," Sallye said. "ls something wrong?"

"Oh no," Mr. White said, "Just the opposite."

"How's that?" Peter asked.

"Mv client called and told me that he had two additional properties available for listing. They are commercial rather than residential. So, more money is involved. Both are good-sized office buildings near downtown. Each one is worth about $10 million. So, we're talking about a total of slightly over $20 million. Is that something your office and Ms. Johnson could also handle?"

Peter and Sallye exchanged glances.

"Do you all have a commercial division?" Mr. White inquired. "We had one a few years ago," Sallye said quickly, "But residential got so big, we let the paperwork for commercial slide. I'm sure it won't be a problem. Right, Peter?"

"Er, absolutely not!" her husband responded. "We absolutely can take care of both office buildings. No problem, sir. We're good to go."

"lt will only take a week or two to get the licenses renewed," Sallye added with a smile.

"Of course, my client wants Lorena Johnson as the listing agent on all four properties. Is that possible?"

"Yes, sir!" Sallye exclaimed.

"There is one more thing," Mr. White said, "My client would like to meet with Ms. Johnson in person. Could you all set something up in the next couple of days? A business lunch would be perfect, perhaps in a nice restaurant?"

"*Of* course," Peter said, "We'll get to work on it this afternoon. I don't see a problem. How about you, Sal?"

"None whatsoever," she echoed.

"Good," Mr. White said as he stood to leave, "My assistant will call at the end of the day to confirm."

As the attorney departed, Peter turned to Sallye and whispered: "I think we need to find Lorena. Now!"

17

Work Pressure

Both Peter and Sallye charged back toward Lorena's small office. As the pair came around a corner, they saw the real estate agent at her desk. She was studying comp pricing for the two residential listings.

"Oh, hey, good morning," she said as her bosses scurried into her space. "I was just going over some comps for the houses. Everything looks good. Both sellers seem realistic with their asking prices."

For a few seconds, Peter and Sallye did not respond.

"What's going on?" Lorena asked, "Is something wrong?"

"Not at all," Sallye replied. "In fact, Peter and I have fantastic news." "Really?" Lorena said, "You both look worried."

"First of all, Sallye and I were wondering if something was worrying you. You seem a little detached lately."

"Does it have anything to do with that older gentleman on the bench?" Sallye inquired.

"No," Lorena answered, "As I told you before, I think he might be a potential client. I'm still working him."

Lorena hoped they would drop any further questions about the angel. Usually, her lying was painfully inadequate.

"Have you ever heard of Charles White, Jr?" Peter asked, "He has law offices downtown."

"Yes," Lorena confirmed, "Mr. White is a big deal in the community. My Mom and Dad know him. His office drew up both of their wills a few years ago. I've met him a couple of times. He has a good reputation."

"One of Mr. White's clients provided the two listings that Peter and I gave you," Sallye explained. He was just in the office a few minutes ago. It seems that his client wants to give us two additional listings."

"That's great!" Lorena interrupted.

"It's better than great," Peter embellished, "We're talking two separate office buildings worth about ten mil each."

"I didn't know we did commercial", Lorena noted with some surprise.

"We do now, sweetie!" Sallye said, "We do now!"

"Here's the other great thing," Peter chimed in, "Mr. White's client specifically wants you to handle both new properties. Are you up for that?"

Lorena suddenly felt lightheaded.

She heard Sallye's concerned voice somewhere in the distance.

"Are you O.K? Are you about to pass out? Do you need some water? Take a couple of deep breaths, honey. We know this might be a shock for you."

As the deep breathing began to kick in, Lorena felt her head clearing.

I wonder how much I should share with them, Lorena pondered to herself. They might simply think I'm nuts. I could understand their viewpoint. This all seems strange to me too.

"Well, I'm having some kind of spiritual crisis right now," she said in a barely discernible voice.

Peter and Sallye looked dumbfounded. "What did you say?" Peter asked.

"Can you explain what you mean?" Sallye questioned. 'To Peter and me, a 'spiritual crisis' happens when we're not hearing "ka-jing" echoing down the halls."

"What kind of spiritual crisis?" Peter probed. "Could you elaborate? We're talking about millions of dollars in sales and commissions. A lot of that money would be flowing straight into your pocketbook."

I can tell by the way they're looking at me that I've gone too far, Lorena decided. If I tell them about talking to an angel every day, I may get put on a hold in some psych ward. Without a doubt, they would take my listings away. It's time to slam on the brakes before it's too late.

"Yes," she said while holding up the palm of her left hand as if to say: "Stop! I have a plausible explanation".

"It has to do with the old man on the bench," she began.

"I thought so," Sallye interrupted. "See Peter, I told you."

"It's a long story," Lorena began, "He offered to pay off my car if I would counsel him on a personal matter. I still owed nearly $9000 on the Toyota so I said OK. The old guy has a daughter about my age. They have been estranged for more than two years. No phone calls or any kind of contact. He has tried to call and text her, but she won't answer him. He went to the doctor recently and received a bad diagnosis. He's got Stage IV pancreatic cancer. The poor guy only has six months to live. He wants me to help him understand the situation better, and maybe even intercede with the daughter. He did pay off my car, so I feel obligated to listen. I do feel sorry for him. That's about the extent of it. I feel like I have a moral obligation at this point. However, I want to know from you all if I should drop him. Real estate comes first. I want you both to understand that."

Thot's quite a lie, Lorena admitted to *herself I don't know whether I should be happy or sad that I could invent it so quickly. Surely, God will understand.*

Peter and Sallye exchanged serious looks, but both seemed to relax a bit.

"I think we can understand your explanation, especially since he paid off your car," Sallye said, "But here is what Peter and I need to know. Are you all in on these four listings?"

"I'm all in," Lorena assured her bosses, "Let's go to work!"

18

Lorena Questions God

Lorena felt she dodged a bullet with her two bosses. As the meeting adjourned, they had provided her with the commercial listing information. They also explained the lunch request from Mr. White's client. She quickly agreed to a meeting the next day at a nearby restaurant. Everything seemed back on track.

Lorena was positive about most everything, especially the potential for a big payday from the four real estate listings. Yet, while lying in the bed, Lorena found herself staring at the ceiling. She found it ridiculous that God would choose her for any kind of spiritual assignment.

Why me; Lord? Who am I? I don't understand. There must be many people more qualified than me. I'm not a religious person. My personal life is choppy. I've failed twice at marriage. I'm still getting situated with my career. I'll be 40 in a few years. I don't have an Ivy League education. In fact nobody has ever accused me of being exceptional in any area. Why would you choose me for some big-time spiritual assignment? This is the first time I've even prayed this year. I don't get it. Why me?

For a couple of minutes, Lorena laid in the silence. She heard no response nor did she feel God's Presence. Then, from the deepest part of her being, Lorena discerned a still, small voice.

The Voice spoke in bold face.

"I will never leave or forsake you."

The real estate woman was startled. There was no doubt the voice had originated from deep within the core of her body. There was another moment of silence, and then the voice spoke again.

"Here is my basic answer to your question: why not you? I created your sacred soul in My image and likeness. I endowed you with certain unique talents. I blessed you with the riches of Heaven. I AM granting you every resource required to complete your divine mission. I personally prepared you for this moment. Now, may I share something else about Myself? I AM a God of peace, love and compassion. I breathed life into every living thing. I covered the earth with awesome beauty. I provided water to the oceans, lakes, rivers and streams. I made each hill to rise and caused every mountain to soar. I personally hand-crafted deep jungles and barren deserts. I painted the sky wide, so that the birds would have room to fly. Then I gave humankind dominion over it all. I handed you the keys to My Kingdom. But things have not worked out well. Your stewardship of our planet has deteriorated. You disappoint and anger Me. Humankind pollutes the earth, scars it with war after war, and now threatens its existence with weapons of mass destruction. However, your latest offense forms the most damning indictment yet. I AM accustomed to being forgotten, ignored and disrespected. But now your scientists are usurping My eternal role as Creator. You are literally replacing Me. You are mass producing human-like clones, but without souls. I AM have become unnecessary in the world's eyes. Or at least, that is what you think. You are seeking to render Me superfluous. Well, I have news for you! Human beings are the superfluous ones. The world was around millions of years before you appeared. Humankind is a recent addition. Your concept of My non-existence will not stand. I AM a forgiving and ever hopeful God. But My patience has reached a tipping point. I AM giving your

world one last chance before I act. I have chosen you, Lorena Mae Johnson, as one of My Heavenly agents. Along with others, I AM commissioning you as a Messenger Prophet to alert the earth to its approaching doom. Will anyone listen to you? Who knows? The verdict on human awareness is still out. I hope you can save your brothers and sisters and all living things from destruction. Human beings have the Free Will choice to ignore you. However, I hope they do pay attention. The future of the world depends on it."

Then, without a waning, the voice ceased to speak. After nearly a minute, Lorena felt alone again. For some reason, despite the warnings of final judgement, she felt more at peace. At least she had an answer to her question.

19

More About The Work Puzzle

As Lorena approached her office the next day, she spied Seth sitting on his usual perch. She thought about waving and just walking on by. If she stopped, Peter and Sallye would surely notice and not be pleased.

Even though I've decided to *focus on real estate, she thought. It doesn't seem right* to *keep avoiding an official goodbye. I like Seth. I don't doubt that he has angelic tendencies. I'll try to make it quick and painless.*

She abruptly changed her trajectory and plopped down on the bench.

"I'm glad you're here," Lorena lied, "I have something to tell you."

"What?" Seth asked, "About your visit last night from the LORD? Or could it be that you want to tell me goodbye? Which one is it?"

"Both, I guess", she confessed. "This day had to come some-time," she said.

"At least you're being honest," the angel smiled, "for now anyway. So, how was your visit with "The Father" last night?"

"I'm not sure He didn't tell me anything new," Lorena responded, "He's very unhappy with how the world is disrespecting Him. I mainly asked God "Why Me?". I'm still confused about His answer. I don't understand what I offer spiritually."

"Heaven doesn't make mistakes," Seth commented, "Most people tapped by God don't feel worthy or capable. We've talked about Moses and the "burning bush". Nobody argued with God more than Mo. He lost the argument and did some of the most powerful things in history. Who says that you, Lorena Mae Johnson, would be any different?"

"Well, you know how committed I am to real estate," she argued, "I got two additional listings yesterday. We're talking 'big-bucks'. I just can't pass up the opportunity. Surely you and God can understand. This is my big chance."

"Of course, We understand," the angel said, "Financial temptations rank as a top lure for the other side. Countless human beings have chosen money over God. You are not the first and certainly won't be the last. Unfortunately, the world may be coming to a place where material things will have zero meaning. Think about it, my dear. Someone devotes his or her entire life to accumulating money. Then, before you can say "Ka-jing", none of it matters. Anyway, my dear, indulge me one more day. I've got a story this morning about "The Puzzle of Work" that you might want to hear. It also includes an important comment on "The Puzzle of Family." "I'll try to keep it succinct."

Oh well Lorena mused. Since this is my *last time, I may as well listen. She nodded for the angel to continue.*

"Good," Seth said, "You won't be sorry."

Jimmy, I'll call him Jimmy, was a superstar in many ways. He was valedictorian of his high school graduating class. He played the lead in the senior play "Father Knows Best" and won raves for an 18-year old kid. Jimmy also was movie star handsome as a teenager. Besides receiving numerous accolades, he remained a super nice guy. He was approachable and everyone considered him a friend.

Jimmy's controlling mother doted on her son. She had one overriding goal for his future. His mother wanted Jimmy to become a "doctor", specifically a surgeon. She saw him rich and successful, while building world-wide recognition as a brain surgeon. His mother kept her son laser-focused on medicine as a career. When he casually mentioned that he planned to join the drama club in college, Jimmy's mother threw a fit. Labeling his interest in theatre as a "distraction", she persuaded her son to drop any idea of diluting his focus. Jimmy didn't want to upset his high-strung mother, who he felt had sacrificed so much for him. So, he reluctantly agreed not to join the drama club. After graduation with honors from the university, he applied to a prestigious medical school and was accepted. Jimmy completed his freshman year with excellent grades. There was some slippage in the last part of the year, but nothing seemed amiss. However, in the fall of the second year, something happened. Jimmy began skipping class, something that baffled his instructors and raised some alarms. Then, at Christmas vacation from med school, he failed to show up at home for the holidays. His family was panicked. Through a friend, they tracked Jimmy down to a motel near the campus. He had been drunk for several days. It was the beginning of a downhill slide that ended with him in a lock-down alcohol and drug rehab for six months. He dropped out of medical school, never to return. His mother was devastated. She could not comprehend what might have happened to her beloved son. Later, she told everyone that he had experienced a "nervous breakdown". Jimmy slid off the radar for a couple of decades. Then, he resurfaced as an English and drama instructor at a community college in a small city of 10,000 people. Then came a tragic announcement from Jimmy's family. He had died of a self-inflicted gunshot wound on his 50th birthday. Adding to the family tragedy, Jimmy's mother passed two months later. People said she died of a broken heart. Unfortunately, it was true. Sometime later, a letter from Jimmy surfaced. It had been written to his mother many years earlier but never mailed. "I'm sorry I disappointed you." he wrote, "I wanted to be an actor. Being in the senior play was the highlight of my life. I'm sorry I let you down."

"Wow," Lorena said, "That's a super sad story. I may need a Kleenex. But I get the message: People should do the work their heart tells them to do."

"You got it," the angel agreed. "Don't ever let anyone dictate your destiny. You've only got one life. Make it about what you want, not what somebody else may want for you. Know that you're not being selfish, just realistic. Sooner or later, you'll find a way to do what you want. If your choices disappoint or anger someone else, so be it. Now, I know you'll be mad at me. However, I have one additional short example about following your heart (and God's) wisdom about work. I think you'll want to hear it."

"Oh well," Lorena responded, "I may as well not fight it. But you must understand this is our last time together."

"Agreed", Seth replied. Here's the last story:

Marianne was a beautiful, intelligent and talented young woman. She seemingly had it all. She was the daughter of wealthy and respectable parents. Marianne lived in the Highland Park section of Dallas, Texas. She attended the famous Hockaday School, just up the road. Her parents were old Texas money and well connected. She remembered visiting Washington DC. during her senior trip and being invited to the oval office for a personal meeting with the Texan president. After Hockadov, Marianne rode a parental legacy to Stanford undergrad and on to Harvard Business School for her MBA. While studying in California, she ran with the high-tech crowd. Three of her classmates ended up becoming billionaires before they were 30. All three tried to recruit her for their companies. Marianne chose the one with the highest salary and best stock options. Within five years, she was a millionaire several times over. On her 30th birthday, she celebrated at the company estate in Cuernavaca, Mexico. She was alone on the patio when a vision came to her. Marianne was visited by the blessed soul of Mother Theresa. The famous nun spoke to her in both a confidential and comfortable manner. The young business executive was awed by Mother's presence, sincerity and wisdom. She sat enthralled as the sainted spirit both encouraged and challenged her to answer the call to spiritual service. Marianne didn't respond at the time. She went back to her corporate job and contemplated the future. Within a few months, she cashed in her stock options and applied to a famous convent in California for training as a blessed Sister. She became a nun and applied for service in Mumbai in the same slums where Mother had worked. You haven't heard about Sister Marianne yet, but you will. She's the next Saint Teresa."

"Well, thank you for that story. It was a good one."

"Yes," Seth said, "But I need to put a quick addendum on it. This was not a random incident without any predicate. Marianne's soul already had a history with Mother Teresa. In an earlier incarnation, she was one of Mother's beloved teachers at Loreto many years before. The two souls managed to reconnect in Marianne's current lifetime. The young woman of today received the material success that allowed her to come full circle with the poverty and lack of yesterday. The result will have positive consequences for everyone concerned. It also demonstrates how the "5th Puzzle of Life: "Spiritual Service" operates. But perhaps that might be a topic we could pursue later."

20

The 5th Puzzle — Spiritual Service

"Tell me about the "5th Puzzle of Spiritual Service," Lorena inquired.

"Thank you for having the interest enough to ask about it," the angel replied, "Service to God provides real meaning to your life. Spirit is always seeking volunteers, but most people have better things to do. Everybody gets a chance to serve, if they so desire. Deciding whether to answer the call is another free will choice. God allows you to make the final decision."

"Why doesn't He just demand that people serve?" she asked.

"Demanding or forcing anyone against their will just doesn't work," Seth answered, "People always revert back to doing what they want to do. Of course, I won't deny that the LORD sometimes uses a cosmic 2 by 4 to get somebody's attention. If the person involved still doesn't respond or get the message, the opportunity for spiritual service eventually passes by."

"What types of service does God offer?" Lorena probed.

"Excellent question," Seth said, "There are six levels of service, distinguished by color. The lowest level is "Green". That one includes the people who might be given only one specific spiritual assignment during their lifetime. It could be something like changing a flat tire for an elderly couple during a snowstorm. That might seem a simple task over an entire lifetime, but many folks just can't be bothered. However, the

"Green" level could also include something more serious. The highest level of that service is directly preventing someone from being injured or killed. The next level of service is "Brown". These are the "encouragers" and "supporters" who uplift humankind. The "teachers" in your midst practically own this category of service. Your mother and father attained the "Brown" level through their teaching careers. Medical personnel fall into this group, especially doctors, nurses and those who serve at physical rehab centers. Next highest "color" are the "Blue" servers. These are your military, law enforcement, firefighters and first responder heroes who risk their lives to protect and serve society. Then, the next level up is designated by the color "Red". These are the more institutional types that can impact humankind on a large scale by their actions. Maybe surprisingly, workers at large corporations fall into this category. They often lead the way in discovering or inventing better ways human beings can be served. Powerful corporations possess the financial and human capital necessary to get big things accomplished. Another crucial "Red" service area includes the "News and Communications" media types. The "Press" gets a lot of negative attention these days, but it can be a hugely important servant of the people. The next level of service is "Gold." This is reserved for the "golden hearted" people among you. It has nothing to do with wealth, status, power, educational achievements or anything in the material world. Virtually anyone can aspire to the "gold standard" of service. It usually happens with those human beings who live by the "golden rule." They define the real spirituality of your planet. They are the "angels in waiting" for God's Kingdom. Without them, the society can become a real "hell on earth" where people are constantly at each other's throats. By the way, evil attacks the "Gold" group more than any others."

"Are there any other "levels" of spiritual service?" Lorena asked. "This is very interesting, but I really do need to get into work."

"I'm almost done," the angel answered, "but there is one more. The highest level of service is "Purple". These are the true giants of the spiritual world. They are the souls that found major religions, lead spiritual movements, act as prophets for The LORD and lead the world to a higher consciousness. They also produce the books, art, theatre and music that can transform a culture or change society for the better. They are "Change Agents" of the highest order. Only a few are summoned to wear the Purple Robe."

"I wonder what "color" of service a real estate agent might reach," Lorena mused.

"I already know your potential," the angel smiled, "I think you'll look good in a Purple Robe."

"No way," Lorena literally screamed.

"Oh yes," Seth beamed, "Way."

21

The Office Visitor

"Sallye is looking for you again," the receptionist called out as Lorena breezed by her desk. "You never seem to be around much anymore", she added without a smile.

"Where is Sallye?"

"She and some good-looking black dude are waiting for you in the conference room. She wants to see you ASAP."

Lorena walked down the hall and looked inside the glass-lined conference room before entering. Her boss was sitting at the big table, flanked by a handsome 40-something black man dressed in business casual. As she entered, Sallye motioned for her to come closer.

"Before you sit, Lorena, I want you to meet Reginald Jones. He's a special client of our friend Mr. White. Reggie personally supplied the four listings you're now working on."

Reggie did not stand when introduced, nor did he offer a handshake. He gave Lorena kind of a half-hearted dismissive wave.

"I've been waiting on you for half an hour, but at least you're here now," he said. "I thought I would come by and get acquainted before we had lunch today. But, yes, I should have called."

Lorena almost repeated "Yes, you should have called," but the stern look from her boss communicated "Back off!"

"I'm sorry I kept you waiting," she said instead. "It's a pleasure to meet you, Mr. Jones. I'm looking forward to working with you. All four of the properties look like real winners."

"Oh, they are" Reggie said, "And, if you and I reach a positive understanding, more business will be headed your way." Then, Reggie openly leered at Lorena with a look that induced chills throughout her body. Sallye's face also mirrored surprise at his aggressiveness.

OMG~Lorena thought. This guy is a dirty old man and he's not that old. And this is the dude that holds my *financial future in his hands. I don't know what* to *think.*

I wonder whether Sallye thinks we *might have made a mistake taking any listings from this creep. No, I guess not. There is too much money involved.*

Then, Reggie reached across the table. He put his right hand directly over both of Lorena's folded hands. His palm was sweaty. She reacted instinctively by pulling her hands away.

There was a moment of awkward silence.

"Er," Sallye offered, "Would anyone like something to drink. Water or coffee?" Reggie did not respond, but he gazed intently at Lorena.

"No, thank you," he finally said, "I think I'm ready to leave for the restaurant if that's O. K. with Ms. Johnson."

"Yes, it's fine with me," Lorena replied. "Boss, would you like to come with us?" she said to Sallye. Her look was almost pleading.

There was a pause and then Sallye answered, "I already have plans today. I'm sorry if that's a problem."

"No problem at all," Reggie said, "I was hoping that I might get Lorena to myself."

A sudden thought flashed into Lorena's mind. Who is this guy? I wonder if I'm about to have lunch with the devil himself.

22

Lunch With Lucifer

The restaurant wasn't crowded. In fact, she and Reggie were the only diners.

Lorena's companion still requested seating in the rear of the main dining area.

"A booth in the back will guarantee our privacy," Reggie whispered to Lorena as they were being seated by a tuxedoed host.

"I think you both will be happy back here," he said, "However, you all make such a handsome and dramatic looking couple. I personally would have sat you in the front. Then, the clientele could observe what outstanding people choose to dine with us."

That comment strikes me not as a compliment, Lorena thought. It really seems unprofessional. This is a strange looking restaurant anyway. It has lots of dark colors. The decor seems exotic and evil at the same time. Oh well, this creepo is still a big client. I'll try to make the best of it.

A waiter appeared and offered to bring a cocktail or some wine. Reggie's countenance brightened.

"We'll have champagne," he said, "Mv friend and I are celebrating. Do you have a bottle of Dom Perignon Vintage 2009 in stock?"

"Of course," the waiter replied, impressed by the customer's knowledge of the most expensive wine the restaurant offered. At $2,400 per bottle, there was little demand.

After the waiter departed, Lorena said "I don't drink much bubbly."

"You will from now on," Reggie smiled. He again leered openly, causing Lorena to slide a couple of inches away from him.

"Now, now, don't run," he said. "I'll have to catch you."

I'm getting a chill, Lorena thought. This dude is weird with a capital "W".

"I'll be honest with *you*, honey," Reggie said. "I'm having lots of digestive problems lately. Too much traveling and rich food is causing me a few problems. I'm having lots of gas."

Then, to prove his point, Reggie passed the longest and loudest fart she had ever heard-or smelled.

"You're smelling it but I'm sitting in it," Reggie laughed out loud.

"Maybe we should order," Lorena said with a frown.

"That last toot felt so good, I might have to do it again. I hope I'm not embarrassing you. We have a lot to discuss. I don't think you understand what's going on here. Do you know what's at stake for you?"

"What's that?" Lorena asked, becoming quite uncomfortable.

"Whether you live or die," Reggie said, showing zero emotion.

With that *comment*, Lorena's instincts took over. She bolted from her chair.

"I'll be back in a minute," she told Reggie as she hurried away, "I've got to call the office — right now."

"Don't be gone too long," Reggie called after her, "The champagne is on the way."

23

Reggie Gets Serious

Lorena wanted to tell Sallye about Reggie's bizarre behavior, but her boss was tied up in a meeting.

The realtor was forced to trundle back to her table, not knowing what to expect next.

Reggie, or whatever his name might be, sat in somewhat of a formal and dignified pose. There seemed no hint of his previous crude behavior.

"We need to get down to business, Ms. Johnson," he said with a firm authority.

"Fine with me," Lorena answered.

"I need to be straight with you," Reggie said. "I want you to work for me. I would like for you to quit the real estate company. The residential and commercial properties I've given you so far? They are just a taste of what I can offer you. I'll boggle your mind with opportunities beyond your wildest dreams. What do you say? How about switching horses? That also includes losing any notion of throwing in with your worthless friend on the bench. I want you to dump his feathered butt, once and for all."

Lorena felt blindsided by Reggie's direct approach.

"Whoa!" she said. "Where did that come from?"

"I'm being straight with you, Lorena. "I don't kid around. I am being deadly serious. And I do mean deadly."

"What does that mean?" Lorena inquired.

"Wait a minute now, we're getting off on the wrong foot. I want to stay positive. I'm offering you the deal of a lifetime. Throw in with me and watch what happens. You'll get rich. You know how the world loves a wealthy person. You'll have your pick of studs. What does the goody-too-shoes other side offer you? They are all stick-in-the-muds. They never shoot up or snort anything stronger than kale. They are not big on champagne either, like this fine 2009 we're sipping on. I have one word for the "God Squad": "Boring". You know I'm right. Has Seth ever cracked a joke or made any kind of "off-color" remark? He's a tight-ass and you know it. Go where the fun is! Get in on the action! They want to retire at 8:30 p.m. every night. My people don't even think of partying until after midnight."

"I'm confused," Lorena stated, "I don't even know what to say. You're putting me in an awkward spot here. I'm sure Peter and Sallye would be upset if you pulled those four listings. It's a lot of money."

"Face it, Babe, you're a hot ticket now. I'm not sure how long the demand for your services will last. You better grab the golden rung on the ladder while it's being offered. It might all be gone tomorrow. What do you say?"

"I really can't make a decision right now," Lorena said. "I need some time to think about everything. Can't you understand that?"

"What's so hard to understand?" Reggie said with a bit of snarl in his tone. "I want you to change sides. I'm asking you to defect from your current employer, set aside this spiritual baloney and have fun again. Besides that, I promise you'll rake in some serious dough. What's not to like? Do you comprehend what I'm saying? Can I spell it out more clearly?"

"I don't know anything about you," Lorena protested, "You could be Satan himself. In fact, you probably are the Devil or someone speaking for him. Are you?"

"Am I who?", Reggie protested, "Let me tell you something, Missy. If you persist in this God business, there will be hell to pay. You'll be shunned, even by your family and friends. You can expect public and private ridicule. Get used to criticism, because I'll make sure you get more than your share. I'll tell social media to destroy you. You'll be labeled a "religious nutcase." Trust me, I can even manipulate your credit rating. That could be a nasty outcome for someone as pathetic as you. Believe me, I can make things go dark for you."

"Please stop threatening me," Lorena said.

"I'm just telling you like it is," Reggie smiled. "If you don't do my bidding, I will make your life miserable."

"What is it that you want me to do?" Lorena asked Reggie.

"You can start by blowing off your meeting with Seth tomorrow. You've already spent too much time with that loser. I brought an employment contract with me today. I call it a "Letter of Evil Intent". Don't pay attention to the "evil" word. It's just a "boiler plate" term. Anyway, here are the conditions attached to the contract. First, you receive a "signing bonus" of $500,000 as soon as I have your signature. I have a cashier's check in my pocket as we speak. That's just for starters. You'll get a guaranteed commission of $2.5 million for the four properties I gave your old firm. Once your letter of resignation to Sallye and Peter is signed, I'll cancel those listings with them. I've got a new contract already drawn up with your name as the listing agent. That'll be a nice "ka-ching", don't you think? Once your other paperwork is done, you'll also go on the payroll with me at a guaranteed annual salary of $100,000 per annum, plus listing commissions. There is a company car involved too. It's a loaded Mercedes. Plus, if you are interested, I'll set you up with a Lexus convertible as a second car. Of course, you'll get a company housing allowance of $25,000 per month. I can offer stock options too. You'll get 5,000 shares free. The current NASDAQ price is $400 per share as of yesterday's close. That's another $2 million. You can buy a lot of happiness with that kind of money. We take care of your leisure time needs as well. You'll get a monthly stipend for cocaine and liquor. You'll also have a Platinum American Express card with a maximum limit of $25,000 per month. That can buy some nice vacations and the clothes and shoes you'll need. We help you with companionship requirements as well. We've got a stable of pro athletes that work exclusively for us. You name the sport and we'll find you the perfect fit, if you know what I mean. That's our package. How does it compare with what Seth has offered you as part of the "Loser" team? Don't tell me. I already know: zero perks, plus hardships."

"What do you get for all of this, besides my time?" she inquired.

"Not too much, honey," Reggie grinned, "Just your soul."

Uh-oh, Lorena thought, I was afraid of that. Reggie is staring at me intently, waiting for my reaction. What should I tell him?

"Oh, say," Lorena stated. "I forgot I have an appointment at the beauty shop. I need to see your friend Shanice. Is there anything you want me to tell her?"

"I can't think of a thing," Reggie answered.

As soon as Lorena departed, Reggie fetched his cell phone and speed-dialed Shanice.

"She's on her way over to you," he said. "Try to close the deal before she leaves the beauty shop. I don't know if I got through to her. Lorena's eyes got wide a couple of times when I talked about the money. I think that's her #1 weakness. You also might hit her again with the "eternal youth" ploy. With all those big bucks to play with, she'll want to look good. However, I just can't read her. Maybe you'll do better."

"I'll certainly die trying," Shanice replied.

24

Back To The Beauty Shop

Shanice was indeed perched at the front desk when Lorena arrived at the beauty shop.

"I've been waiting for you," she said with a twisted grin.

"I was afraid of that," Lorena answered, "I'm here against my better judgment. Let's get it over with. Be gentle with me. I don't want any more trouble."

Once she was seated in Shanice's private space at the rear of the shop, Lorena noticed that the air conditioner was not on. The room was already past 80 degrees.

"It's hot as, pardon the expression, hell in here. What happened to the a/c?"

"It stopped working an hour ago," Shanice stated.

"Then let's make it fast. I'll take a quick cut and be out of here. I don't even need a wash."

"Oh now," Shanice smiled, "Don't be so antsy. I've got a new digital feature that I want to show you. It refines what I showed you last time about eternal beauty. Sit back for a couple of minutes. You'll enjoy it."

Then, Shanice draped another shawl-like cover over Lorena. It had an unusually heavy feel. It reminded Lorena of a protective shield that might fend off radiation.

"Hey, that's really heavy," she protested, "What are you doing?"

"Chill out, you'll dig this!" Shanice exclaimed as she turned out the lights.

"Wait a minute," Lorena said with concern, "What are you up to now?"

Then, from somewhere, a computer projected an image on the wall. It showed a beach scene at a plush resort. A curvaceous and beautiful young black woman in a tiny bikini came strolling by. She was accompanied by a handsome and muscular man. The camera quickly zoomed in to the couple's attractive and handsome faces. They were a knockout couple.

"That's you four decades from now," Shanice informed Lorena. "That guy with you is the young stud-of-the-day. He's about 35 years younger than you, but he doesn't seem to mind. You guys are grabbing some rays on the beach before heading back to the room for a bit of afternoon delight. What do you think?"

Lorena was speechless. Of course, everything looked appealing.

"Keep watching," Shanice instructed her.

The next shot showed the outside of a dilapidated shanty in a poor part of town. There was some sort of hand-made old sign propped up against the front of the building. It read "Happy Times Nursing Home & Rehab". Then, the camera panned inside. There were elderly and incapacitated people strewn about. A man and woman in their respective wheelchairs were seated side-by-side in front of an ancient fish tank. Several small fish, some missing pieces from encounters with larger fish, swam lazily in the tank. The old couple just stared at the fish without speaking. The ancient woman was a decrepit mess. Around her neck hung a sign: "LORENA MAE ROOM4B". The withered man didn't look much better.

Around his wrinkled old neck also hung a sign: "CHARLIE ROOM 4A". Lorena couldn't help but notice that every couple of minutes or so, "Charlie" would reach over and fondle one of "Lorena's" breasts. This only lasted about five seconds or before she might notice and call out to an orderly.

OMG, Lorena cringed, that's not a pretty picture!

"Why are you showing me this," she shouted out to Shanice. "Turn on the damn lights and get this hood cover off me. Either cut my hair or I'm gone!"

"Cool your jets," Shanice said, switching on the lights and removing the heavy cover. "I just need to visit with you about that "Letter of Evil Intent" you forgot to sign at the restaurant. Reggie faxed me over a copy so you could sign it now. What about it?"

"Either cut my hair now or I'm gone."

"Reggie wanted me to go over a few things with you. He didn't think you understood all of the goodies involved."

"Oh, I think I understood," Lorena said.

"He wanted me to remind you of our specific expectations," Shanice stated, "I need to give you the details so that we don't have any misunderstandings."

"What do you mean?"

"You must renounce any future contact with God or any of his agents or angels. We can't have you sneaking around, meeting with some Deity rep. We don't allow for spiritual infidelity. We also don't want any meditating or praying. Stay the hell out of church too. That includes Bible study. We expect you to increase your use of profanity. You have a quota of 50 to 100 f-bombs every day. You should plan on hanging out at the local casinos at least two nights a week. Don't worry. We provide the chips. Talk it up with the drunks at the casino bars. They need reinforcement and a reason to be there. You absolutely must drink alcohol and smoke more weed. You've nearly quit both. We're disappointed in you. The straight lifestyle doesn't work for us. By the way, please try to do a little more shoplifting whenever possible. We just don't like "Dudley-do rights." You have such a boring life right now, Lorena. Spice it up a bit!"

"That all sounds awful," Lorena said, "I can't do any of that stuff. It's just not me."

"Come on!" Shanice suddenly shouted. "Sign the damn contract! Now!"

Without a word, Lorena bolted out of the chair and ran for the door. It was locked.

"Open this door right now or I'll kick your ass!"

Shanice fumbled for the keys, but she did unlock the door.

In a flash, Lorena was gone.

"That went well," Shanice mumbled to herself.

25

Another Look At Spiritual Service

"You look awful," Seth said when Lorena found him on the bench. "You must have had one hell of a night." "Literally", he quickly added.

"You already know about my encounters with Reggie and Shanice, right?"

"Of course," the angel chuckled. "For one thing, you need to find a new beauty shop."

"I agree," Lorena sighed. "As I'm sure you heard, those nuts are putting some big-time pressure on me. The money and perks are amazing! I wonder if it could all be true?"

"Yes, unfortunately for our side, it's accurate. Most human beings would give up the spiritual path in a heartbeat for a fraction of what you were offered yesterday. May I ask? Why didn't you take it?"

"I asked myself the same thing when I got up this morning," Lorena answered. "I don't have a good answer. Do you remember that old saying: 'If something looks too good to be true, it probably isn't (true)?" That just kept running through my mind. It's like "What's the catch here?" Then, I discovered the 'catch'. They take your soul. Call me naïve but that doesn't sound like an even exchange."

"Again, Lorena, most people would have cashed it in for a lot less. I must tell you that my respect for you is growing. You've got real "Balls". Well, not really. But you know what I mean."

 "I either have a strong set of female balls or maybe I'm just stupid," Lorena smiled, "I'm turning down millions for a spiritual concept that I don't really understand. Why would I do that? What makes people stay on "The Path" when it seems to have such few advantages? I'm being serious in asking that."

"I can understand what you are saying," Seth replied. "But that's a perfect lead-in to a discussion about the 5th Puzzle: "Spiritual Service." Maybe I can explain it to you with another story.

"Sure," Lorena answered, "Then I have a couple of questions for you."

"Well, get comfortable while I tell you the story of "Frank". I think it can best explain God's concept of "Spiritual Service".

Frank was 50 when he felt this strange pull. He had enjoyed a successful 25-year corporate career. He was one of only 20 VP's in an international corporation with 60,000 employees. But he had begun to feel that it was time for a change. He was not unhappy in his high-profile job as head of PR for a company that everyone knew. To the contrary, the corporation had several high-profile charitable causes that gave him much positive exposure. However, Frank's company also had a special retirement deal. If your age, plus years of service equaled 70, you could retire with full benefits. So, Frank set up a private meeting with the CEO and told him: "I've decided to retire." The top executive was shocked. He began talking about the company making a counteroffer."No," Bill told him, "It's not the money and I don't have another job. I just think it's time for me to go." Then, the long-time employee did something quite unplanned. He asked the CEO for a two-year salary continuation after retire-ment. This was something the company had never done with anyone. After thinking it over for a few hours, Frank's request was granted. The retirement package was worth about $200,000, plus all medical *benefits. In those days, that represented a generous goodbye gift. At the end of the calendar year, Frank took his leave. After being gone from the company for about four months, he had no other job or project in sight. In fact, he wondered if perhaps retiring had been a mistake. It seemed almost like he was "marking time" while waiting for his next "assignment". In fact, that was exactly the case. Frank decided to have an adventure for a few weeks. He had been divorced for several years and didn't have anything holding him back. He drove alone to a major city about a thousand miles away. He secured a short-term lease for a small apartment and just began exploring his surroundings. Frank felt a tremendous freedom, something unusual for him. One day, he walked by a large church in the downtown area. It was open every day for prayer. He went inside and took a seat near the back of the sanctuary. He bowed his head in prayer. After a minute or two, Frank discerned a voice coming from somewhere. It only said 10 words:*

"I will never leave you. I will never forsake you."

He looked around but the sanctuary was empty. Then, he heard the voice one more time:

"I will never leave you. I will never forsake you."

Sitting in prayer for a few more minutes, Frank had the distinct feeling that God was calling him into service. After a few twists and turns, he was ordained six years later at a famous seminary. For the next 25 years, Frank served in several cities as a senior pastor. Then, he retired as a pulpit minister and began another career as an author of spiritual books. He had answered God's call by deciding to retire from the corporate world. That decision opened the spiritual path. He then spent the next thirty-plus years being of service to the LORD. When he finally passed, Frank died a happy and fulfilled person."

"That's a nice story," Lorena said. "Did Frank ever remarry?"

"Yes," Seth replied. "He and his new wife became a great team and were well-regarded at every church they served. She preceded him in death by a few years. When Frank arrived in

Heaven, his dear wife was the first one to greet him. Now, let me explain how "Spiritual Service" works."

"I'm listening," Lorena said.

"First of all, you don't choose to serve God. God chooses you for service. You may think it's your idea, but it's not. Somewhere in your life, you have done something or become someone worthy of receiving a call. A past life can also qualify you. In your case, your service as a nurse during World War II had a big impact. You've also probably heard the old saying: "Many are called, but few are chosen." That is right on target. For every 100 called by Spirit, only one is selected. What happens with the others? Most de-select themselves. They are either tempted or threatened by the other side and the spiritual life just seems too hard. You've already experienced that aspect of the process. Some souls get weary and drop out. For others, they just don't have the passion necessary to succeed. Their hearts are not in it. The spiritual life can be hard. and simply not for everyone. It is tough, a real grind. Some declare for the spiritual Path and promptly experience huge setbacks and losses. This can be a real shock to your system. Many thought their problems would end when they tuned their lives over to God. When the challenges began multiplying, these folks started looking for an exit ramp. It doesn't take long to find one."

"That sounds sad," Lorena noted, "I'm sure they were disappointed."

"Actually," Seth responded, "Most of them were relieved."

"What happened to them?"

"Not anything, really," the angel told her, "They just went back to their regular lives. However, any time spent on God's Path isn't lost in the final accounting. It could add to your evolved consciousness in another lifetime. Soul journeys often require many incarnations before they become ready to serve God. You're ready in this lifetime."

"What else about the Puzzle of Spiritual Service?" Lorena asked.

"Here are the five essential Truths about Service to God. A couple of these Truths have already been mentioned: (1) You don't choose God, Spirit chooses you; (2) You did something at some point in your life that justified your call to go higher and further; (3) When you say "yes" to the LORD, every resource that you need is provided; (4) You can make the Free Will choice to end your call at any time. God will not judge, argue, nag or condemn you for your decision and (5) As you make your final soul ascension into God's Kingdom, this thought will accompany you into Heaven: "Yes, serving God was hard, but oh so worth it."

"That's good to hear," said Lorena.

"Now, allow me to add one last perspective about "Spiritual Service," the angel said. "When God calls you, it sometimes comes after you go through a "storm of life.""

"What does that mean, a "storm of life?""

"Every person goes through a stormy time at one time or another," the angel explained. "God often allows these personal storms for a reason. He might need to finally get your attention. Maybe the subtle attempts to make you notice Him haven't worked. So, God resorts to churning up a physical, emotional or spiritual crisis that stops you cold. Many people turn to religion and spirituality when a big crisis overwhelms them. That is exactly what Spirit wants you to do. You may have been putting off God's call. Then, a big-time crisis swoops down on you and you start looking for some godly answers. Whenever you see those storm clouds beginning to form around you, you could be receiving a message from God."

"I've seen a lot of storm clouds lately," Lorena noted.

"It all comes back to understanding the "Puzzle of Spiritual Service.", the angel explained. "There is a reason why you were incarnated during this time in world history. There comes the perfect moment when God reveals that reason. Of course, your soul is sent here originally to evolve. Remember, Lorena, there are always more "lessons" to learn. As your instruction unfolds, you should rise higher in consciousness. That new spiritual awareness should make you better equipped for your next lifetime."

"You mean that I have to come back again?"

"Most people do return, but not all."

"What happens to the souls that never return?"

"They go on to higher levels of service in Heaven," Seth said. "I never went back. I'll be in Angel Service for the rest of eternity. Speaking of the future, do you have time for a quick primer on the 6th Puzzle of Life — which is Death."

"That's sounds interesting, Lorena said, "If you can make it quick."

"Sometimes death is quick, sometimes it's slow. But physical death always comes, sooner or later. You just don't know when and where."

26

The 6ᵗʰ Puzzle — Death

"Let's talk about "Puzzle of Life #6," he said. "It was originally called "AGING AND DEATH", but God decided to shorten it to just "DEATH", Seth explained. "That's where all "AGING" is headed anyway. So, what I'll share first concerns the importance of the aging process before your physical death. A good "aging" can make a difference in the quality of your eventual moving on to Heaven."

"I'm ready to listen," Lorena said. "Maybe I'll learn something."

"Most people are concerned about living instead of dying," Seth said. "This is normal. The reality of getting older doesn't really hit you right away. One day, you're young. The next day, as you creak out of bed, you're old. You honestly don't know where the time went. For the first 50 or so years of your life, you're concerned about getting an education, finding a job, getting married, raising a family and building a business or career. Then you begin having various health challenges. As your body starts breaking down, life can become a real physical and mental struggle. Sometimes it happens sooner rather than later. You can be less only half-way to your life expectancy when things start to happen. You don't feel that much older, but aging has begun in earnest. Lorena, what I'm telling you today can be useful information for someone your age. It wouldn't mean quite as much to your parents, although some of it might apply. Here's the bottom line: the time to prepare yourself for aging and death is when you can still affect it. Your "Quality of Life" at 80 will probably be determined by how you handled your health from 30-60. If you started overeating, smoking, drinking and drugging at a young age and never stopped, the chances are good that physical death will claim you sooner rather than later. It also could be quite unpleasant. If you were a lifetime smoker, emphysema is a terrible condition. Trust me, you don't want it. Every breath is a struggle. If you are grossly overweight and become diabetic, that also can bring many health challenges. Obesity is a big-time crisis right now, but nobody wants to talk about it. Carrying too many pounds around can bring on high blood pressure, diabetes and heart disease. You could become incapacitated with a stroke or die off from a heart attack. Please don't underestimate the mental challenges that affect aging. There are many things that can put your brain at risk. For example, alcoholism and drug addiction are devastating to your brain. You can't drink a fifth of Scotch every 24 hours and smoke three packs of cigarettes a day and expect to hit your 50s or 60s with some semblance of good mental and physical health. On the flip side, if you've taken care of yourself with exercise, nutrition, controlling your weight and protecting your brain, you can expect a good aging process. But it's all determined by what you do now, when you're young. I'm not even talking about what stress and a chaotic lifestyle does to the aging process. Having a stressful work or personal life can bring on many debilitating and fatal illnesses, including cancer and heart disease. I realize that you can take perfect care of yourself and still die prematurely in a car accident or some other freakish event.I'm referring to the predictable health crises that will surely come for people who try and defy the odds. It's like going to Vegas and expecting to win every bet. Eventually, you are going to lose. That's the aging process in a nutshell. I see many folks already losing the battle. The life expectancy for people in their 50s is dropping.

That's a major health crisis and you rarely hear about it. By the way, health care costs could bankrupt your country in less than two decades. It's a much more imminent problem than even global warming. Typically, humankind is always in denial about a crisis. They think "I'll deal with it tomorrow." In this case, tomorrow is way too late. There is also another mental health problem flying under the radar. Don't laugh when I tell you."

"What is that?" Lorena asked.

"Pornography is corrupting millions, both young and old. It is messing with people's minds and lives in big-time negative ways. The internet has caused porn to explode. This may be one of the hardest habits to break for people of every age and gender. Twisted sexual fantasies often do lasting damage. Pornography is a major crisis that destroys lives daily. Because the internet can now bring pornography directly into the home at all hours, the mental health risk has increased dramatically. This problem is being exacerbated by the legalization of marijuana and other drugs which can act as mental enablers."

"You're painting a scary picture," Lorena reflected. "I'm getting depressed. I also think you're starting to preach. Nobody listens to a Bible-thumper. People are just human beings. They're made to behave badly in some situations. Nobody is an angel, like you, 24 hours every day. Maybe you need to lighten up."

"I hear you and understand your perspective," Seth said, "I'm talking mostly about long-term negative behavior that takes a real toll over time. But since you've accused me of "preaching", let me bring up the issue of growing old without a spiritual anchor. God knows that many folks don't begin searching for Him until their final days or maybe even right before the last breath. Spirit allows for human procrastination. It understands the lateness of seeking God's Presence. On the flip side, the people who built their spiritual house on "solid rock" early on are much more prepared for the end of human life. The fear of death has mostly been erased. Of course, the human condition guarantees that not every fear of death is eliminated. Most people go straight to the doctor if they encounter any kind of physical problem. For their peace of mind, they should do that. What I am talking about involves a constant and obsessive fear about death. Without God in your life as you get older, you can become paralyzed with anxiety and dread. Here's another true story that illustrates my point:

Arthur was an ordained minister in a retirement community. The average age of his congregation was 83. For them, getting sick and dying was an ever-present reality. One day, a long-time member of the church came to see Arthur. She told the pastor: "My 88-year old sister June has been in "hospice end of life" care now for over six months. That is past the time allowed. But, pastor, she won't die. The rest of the family has come to say "goodbye" several times. She just keeps on living. Her own doctor says June has already outlived his expectations by several months. Something must be troubling my sister about the next life. I think she really fears going to Hell instead of Heaven. Would you mind visiting her in Hospice? Maybe you can find out what is going on with her. I would appreciate your input." Arthur made an appointment to see "June" the next afternoon. He had no plan on how to approach her. Arthur prayed that God would speak through him. As he entered June's room, she reacted with a startled and fearful look. Her eyes opened wide with fear. The pastor walked over to the terrified lady's bed and placed his right hand on her arm. Then, he spoke these words: "June, I am here today on behalf of God. I have a message from Him to you. God wants me to reassure you that He loves you unconditionally. There is nothing you have ever done, said or been that could ever stop God from welcoming you into Heaven with open arms. You are God's beloved daughter. He is waiting for you in His Kingdom right this minute. You can decide the time when you are ready to receive His divine Love. But when you do let go, He will catch you. God is looking forward to that beautiful moment when you enter Paradise. He promises that you are already forgiven of anything and every-

thing. God loves you, dear June, now and forever." The expression on the woman's face had not changed during the pastor's comments. Then she smiled and said only three words "Thank you, God." Then she closed her eyes and slept. Arthur turned and left the room without another word. June passed away the next afternoon. The Duty Nurse said she had a peaceful transition. "She had the happiest look on her face," the nurse told everyone. The Spirit of the Lord had worked though Arthur to reassure June that God's forgiveness and under-standing were already in place. That was all she needed to hear in order to let go."

"That was another good story," Lorena told Seth. "But I'm already late for work. I guess we are down to the last "Puzzle of Life". That one is "God", am I right?"

"Yes," Seth confirmed. "We'll handle that one a little differently from the others."

"How's that?" Lorena asked.

"She'll contact you directly. You'll meet with God in person"

27

Real Estate Trouble

Both Peter and Sallye were waiting for Lorena when she arrived back at her real estate office. They were in obvious distress.

"I thought you had finished up with that old man on the bench," Sallye scolded.

"Come on in to Sallye's office right now," Peter said, "We've got a serious problem."

"What's going on?" Lorena asked.

"We received a text this morning from Reggie Miller III," Peter said. "He's accusing you of trying to bribe him to get those four listings. Then, he's also saying you extorted him. He said that when you two had dinner, you threatened to say he sexually harassed you. This is serious, Lorena. Reggie has already gone to the authorities about it. We understand that two detectives are due here any minute to question you about the complaints. This all sounds crazy to us, but what do you have to say for yourself? Can you clear it up? What happened with Reggie at dinner?"

So here we go, Lorena thought. Because I wouldn't sign that letter of evil intent, he's coming after me. I'm sure Reggie knows I'm still seeing Seth. He may think I've already made a spiritual commitment to God. Either way, somebody is trying to make my life difficult right now. The last thing Peter and Sallye want to hear is some crazy story about me being involved in spiritual warfare. They might just fire me on the spot. I better keep my mouth shut.

"I don't have the slightest idea of what he's talking about," Lorena said. "Reggie brought all of those listings to you all, not to me. I didn't know anything about the guy. He asked me out. Sallye, you were invited to come along. Nothing, and I mean nothing, happened between us. He did start acting strange at the restaurant. Sallye, I even tried to call you about it. I couldn't get through because you were in a meeting. But I would never come on to any client, much less him. I'm not sure why he is saying these things about me. I'm innocent of everything."

Lorena's passionate claim of innocence sounded like the person both Peter and Sallye knew. They seemed to relax a bit.

"Well, you've still got to straighten everything out with the detectives when they get here," Sallye commented. "Peter and I will back you up. Hopefully, we can sort it all out. Reggie hasn't officially pulled the listings, but that could happen. We must be prepared for anything. Are you certain you didn't say something that could have set him off?"

"No," Lorena lied, "I can't think of a single thing."

Two men in light grey suits lightly knocked on Sallye's office window. Peter motioned for them to step inside. The pair identified themselves as Detectives Curtis Brunson and James Holland, respectively, from the Larceny and Fraud section at police headquarters.

When Lorena was formally introduced to the detectives, she crossed her arms defiantly and asked: "Can I ask what this is all about?"

Both Peter and Sallye were surprised at her obvious indignation. Lorena had never displayed much of a temper around the office before now.

"Ahem," said Det. Brunson, "M'am, we had a man come by the station earlier today and swear out a complaint against you."

"His name was Mr. Reginald Miller III," Det. Holland added, referring to his notes. "He said you attempted to bribe him over some real estate listings. Mr. Miller also stated that you were threatening to charge him with sexual harassment if he refused to give you the listings. Does any of this sound familiar?"

"Absolutely not!" Lorena shouted indignantly, "If anything, he propositioned me. He began acting strangely so I left the restaurant to get away from him. I didn't even say goodbye. I was already late to a beauty shop appointment anyway. But nothing like what he is saying ever happened. The man is a 100% liar. I can't tell you why he said those things about me."

"So you admit to knowing Mr. Miller?" Det. Brunson said, stopping to write that fact down in his notebook. "How long have you known him?"

"I only met him here in this office about an hour before we had lunch," Lorena explained. "I don't think we exchanged 10 words before we sat down at the restaurant. By the way, he's the one who asked me out."

"What did you talk about at the restaurant?" Holland interjected.

I obviously can't tell these detectives the truth, Lorena thought to herself. They would lock me up.

"We talked about a couple of things regarding the listings," Lorena said, "Then he began acting weird. He caused a scene with some loud belching and farting. That's when I decided to separate myself from him. You can check my story with the staff at the restaurant. I was mortified."

"We'll do that," Detective Holland said, writing down more notes in his book.

"Why do you think he accused you of trying to bribe him?" Brunson asked Lorena.

Again, Lorena knew she couldn't give up the real reason for Reggie's behavior. Not wanting to sell your soul to the Devil was a great explanation from her standpoint, but only in a spiritual setting. Prudent discretion is the watchword, the real estate woman reminded herself. Reggie may have already told them I had a few bolts not screwed on properly. In fact, who knows what he told them?

"I don't have the vaguest idea," Lorena said, looking first at Peter and then glancing toward Sallye.

Then she directed a question at both of her bosses.

"Do either of you know why he could be saying these things about me?"

Both Peter and Sallye shook their heads no.

"Does Lorena need a lawyer?" Peter asked the detectives. "If so, the firm has one on retainer. He's mostly a real estate attorney, but he could probably help us deal with this "situation". Or whatever it is."

"You should do whatever you think is appropriate," Detective Brunson advised. "We were asked to look into the situation as a follow-up to Mr. Miller's complaint. It sounds like a classic "he said, she said." We're hearing two conflicting stories here. Without more digging, I don't think we have enough to charge anyone."

"I should hope not," Sallye agreed.

"Look, Ms. Johnson," Detective Holland interrupted, "How about we get back to Mr. Miller? But you're telling us for certain that you never tried to extort him about some real estate listings or threaten to accuse him of sexual harassment?"

"Certainly not!" Lorena repeated emphatically, "Never."

"Well, he did promise us that he has a tape recording of you doing just that. We haven't heard it yet. But we probably should review the tape, if it exists. That could give us a clue about who is telling the truth here. Are you up for that? Maybe you can come down to the station with us right now. We would like to close this case as soon as possible."

"I hear you," Lorena said some finality, "So would I."

Wait a minute, she thought, what's this about a tape? If Reggie is really the devil or working with Him, I'm sure Hell could create a damning tape. A fake recording could make me seem guilty, even when I'm not. These two detectives might even be part of the plot. This whole thing is sounding worse by the minute. Maybe I need to do something to protect myself. Now!

"Would you all mind if I powdered my nose first before we go?" Lorena asked.

"Sure," Detective Brunson said, "But please don't be too long. We need to track that tape down. In the meantime, we'll call Mr. Miller and have him meet us at the police station."

Lorena excused herself and headed toward the rear of the real estate building. Within 60 seconds, she was out the back door and sprinting toward her car. Another minute or so and Lorena was whipping around the front of the building with her tires burning rubber.

Peter looked up to see her speeding by, as did one of the detectives.

"My God, she's fleeing the scene," Brunson said.

"Quick, man, put out an APB, "Holland shouted, "This must be a bigger deal than we thought!"

"Listen you two," Brunson cautioned Peter and Sallye, "Don't leave this office until we say so. You all could have a rogue employee here or maybe you're both involved too. We need to find out what in hell is going on here. Stay put!"

28

Fighting The Law

What just happened? Lorena thought as she sped down the street. I've never even had a parking ticket before. Now, I'm fleeing from the law. I'm not sure this is the best decision. Where am I going anyway? I must be losing my mind.

Just then, her cell phone beeped. A text was coming in. Even in an agitated state, she knew better than to text and drive. She saw a 7-Eleven store coming up on her right. She activated her turn signal before sweeping into a parking spot in front of the store.

She looked at her cell and saw this text:

"Stay parked in front of 7-Eleven. Don't move. I'll be there in a minute. Keep calm. Seth."

Lorena had barely processed this information in her brain when she heard another beep. Another text! This time, she read:

"This is all a big mistake. I can explain. I'm headed your way now. Get yourself a Slurpee and wait in your car. Reggie III."

Within a few seconds, Lorena had backed out of the store parking lot and was on the road again.

I'm not about to get in the middle of those two, she told herself. I don't know where I'm headed, but I don't feel safe. Who can I trust anymore?

As she drove down the street, Lorena heard a distinct and clear voice coming from somewhere in the car. It spoke with firmness and clarity:

I WILL NEVER LEAVE YOU.

I WILL NEVER FORSAKE YOU.

YOU CAN TRUST ME. TURN INTO

THE NEXT CHURCH YOU SEE.

I WILL BE WAITING FOR YOU.

The message was unsigned. Lorena began scanning both sides of the street. Up ahead on her left, she spotted a sign. It was a mosque. Lorena pulled into the parking lot. She quickly remembered a head scarf in the glove compartment. She had stashed it there several weeks ago for reasons unknown. She donned the scarf and walked toward the building. As Lorena was about to reach the front door, an Imam suddenly appeared from inside the mosque.

"They told me you were coming," he said quietly. "We have made a private room available. Let me show you the way."

Lorena had quit seeking an explanation for anything. She followed the Iman at a respectful distance. He took her to a small conference-like room near the front door. There was a nondescript table in the room, covered by some type of beige shawl. There were two folding chairs, one on either side of the table.

This must be a private prayer room, she thought.

"Our regular prayers will be starting soon," the Imam told her, "But you won't be disturbed here." He backed out of the room, displaying a respect that Lorena found both gracious and curious.

I'm not asking any questions, she promised herself. It's better that way.

Lorena sat in the silence when her head bowed.

I feel so alone, she thought.

The door opened. A dark-haired woman, also in a head scarf, entered the room and slid into the opposite chair.

"I'm here for you," the woman said in a soft but strong voice.

In a natural gesture, she offered both of her hands with palms turned upward. Lorena felt at ease accepting the visitor's obvious friendliness. The two women sat for a moment in the silence with their hands lightly touching. Lorena felt a surge of love and caring unlike she had ever experienced before.

Now that's "communication", she thought. Who is this woman?

"I am Miriam," the woman stated matter-of-factly, "I am the sister of Moses, the servant leader of God's people. I am also the first female prophet."

"Whoever you are, thank you for coming," Lorena said, "I'm in big trouble. I just fled from the law. I'm sure they're looking for me right now. They'll probably find my car parked outside the mosque any minute."

"You are safe with me," Miriam said. "Nothing can harm you."

"I don't know what to do," Lorena said, releasing Miriam's hands.

"I know you feel stressed," Miriam stated, "The spiritual attacks can come thick and fast. You hardly catch your breath before another heavy blow arrives. But, for right now, try to relax. Rest in my care. Take a few deep breaths."

She sounds like my own mother, Lorena thought. I feel a little more comforted by that. She even reminds me of my mom.

"What should I do besides breathe?" Lorena asked. "Will these attacks ever stop? I'm confused and more than a little bit scared."

"You are under divine protection," Miriam said, "Try to accept that God watches over you at all times. I know this can be hard to process. However, it's true. Trust and believe what I tell you."

"Thank you for that," Lorena said with obvious gratitude.

There was a soft knock at the closed door.

"I want you to meet someone," Miriam said to Lorena. "Please come in, dear."

The door opened and a beautiful young girl African-American stepped into the room. She looked to be in her early teens.

"This is Ruth," Miriam told Lorena, "She's your daughter."

Lorena gasped.

"What did you say?"

"Hello, Mother," Ruth said with genuine affection and a winsome smile.

Lorena's frightened heart dissolved. She felt Ruth's warmth, goodness and love.

Oh my God, Lorena exclaimed silently to herself. Where on earth (or in Heaven) did this beautiful presence originate? She seems truly incredible. And she is my daughter? How is that even possible?

It was as if Miriam could read her thoughts, which she could.

"If the world survives, you and your soul mate will connect," she said. The two of you will conceive your soul child, the lovely Ruth."

"I am blessed to be your daughter," Ruth said with a smile.

Her voice seems so lyrical, Lorena thought. It sounds almost like a wind chime. She radiates a discernible goodness. There is something almost Holy about her demeanor. This girl is "somebody". I can even see a purplish aura around her.

"I hope you choose wisely," Ruth said, "I know you are facing many decisions. I'm praying for you."

"Thank you," Lorena replied. "I need some extra prayers right now."

"I must say goodbye for now," Ruth said. "I hope we meet again soon."

"As do I," Lorena said. Then, she spontaneously added an "I love you".

"I love you too," Ruth smiled again. Then she was gone.

"The stakes seem much greater now," Lorena told Miriam.

"Yes, indeed. Have you made a choice between God and the other side? I sense that you're leaning toward Heaven rather than Hell. Am I right?"

"I'm confused," Lorena said. "I have my doubts about all these "spiritual" challenges. The attacks are happening non-stop. They wear me out. Do they ever stop or slow down?"

"Unfortunately, no", Miriam replied. "We do have cases where human beings walk away from the first, second or even third call. Then, for some reason, everything starts to make sense. When that happens, they come pounding on the doors of Heaven. God always lets them back in. Many prodigal sons and prodigal daughters arrive, each asking for another chance. Our Father/Mother always grants their request. Of course, it saves a lot of time and trouble when someone answers "yes" in the beginning. However, we all know about the mysteries of Free Will."

"I know I need to make a decision soon," Lorena said. "I want to do the right thing. I'm just so into the material side of life. It's been my way forever. I'm not sure I can change."

"What can I do for you right now?" Miriam asked, "what do you need from me?"

"You've already calmed me down," Lorena said, "How about getting those two detectives off my back? I haven't done anything wrong. But I just can't say "the devil made me do it". They'll lock me up right quick."

"God's followers are regularly imprisoned," Miriam said, "Being sent to jail just made them stronger in their faith."

"I'm sure that's true," Lorena said, "But aren't there softer ways to toughen me up?"

"If you accept God's offer, you'll need lots of courage, stamina and toughness. Anyone who speaks for the spiritual side can expect a bullseye on their back. Nobody wants to hear what you're saying. Expect to get ridiculed, shamed and booed. The mocking may be the least of it. I would suggest you get fitted for the "whole armor of God."

"What's that?"

"Read Ephesians 6: 11. It explains everything."

Just then, Lorena heard a siren outside and the sound of more than a few cars pulling into the mosque parking lot.

When Lorena glanced toward where Miriam had been sitting, the first female prophet had vanished.

"Help me, LORD!" Lorena cried out to the Heavens.

"I will," she heard a deep voice say in response.

29

Arrested

Lorena stumbled out of the mosque to find her car blocked by two patrol cars. A total of four police officers with guns drawn were waiting for her.

"Lorena Mae Johnson?" a female police officer called out. "Step away from the building, ma'm."

As the real estate woman complied with the order, another officer slipped behind Lorena and handcuffed her wrists together. She was then directed to get into the backseat of one of the patrol cars.

"Why am I being arrested?" Lorena asked, although she full well knew the reason. She had fled from authorities.

"I think you know why," the female officer answered. "You ran. Don't act so innocent."

Lorena didn't say another word during the 10-minute ride to the closest police precinct. She was taken to the front desk.

"Your lawyer arrived a couple of minutes before you," the sergeant on duty informed her. "You must have the guy on speed dial. He's waiting for you in Interview Room #1, down the hall.

The handcuffs were removed by the female officer, who said: "You don't look like a hardened criminal, but don't run away from the cops again. OK? It's not a good plan. Haven't you ever watched 'COPS' on TV?"

"Yes ma'm, thank you," Lorena answered. Then she added, "I won't ever do it again."

She opened the door to Room #1 to meet her "lawyer".

It was Seth, the angel.

He was cast perfectly as an older attorney, complete with a polka-dot bowtie and a beaten-up briefcase.

"What were you thinking?" he asked.

"I guess I wasn't," she answered, not able to look him in the eye.

"I can get you released in a couple of hours, but you'll have to spend some time in lock up until the paperwork goes through. Please stay out of trouble while you're waiting. You can meet some tough characters in jail, you know. Now, after you get back home, stay there. You'll have a meeting tomorrow with either God or me. We'll let you know. But stay home tonight and be careful about answering your door. I heard that your friend Franklin is roaming around again. Be careful."

Seth stood up and excused himself.

One of the jailers entered and escorted Lorena to a holding cell, just inside the precinct's main entrance.

There were two other women in the cell when she arrived. One had long blond straight hair. Lorena thought she looked harmless. The woman had a relaxed, sweet and dreamy look about her. Lorena wondered if she might be high on something. Her other cellmate sported bright red hair and was clothed in black leotards and a blouse open to her navel. She had a long scar across her left cheek.

She must have been in a knife-fight, Lorena thought.

Lorena also noticed that one of the woman's eyes was blackened.

Somebody must have beaten the crap out of her, Lorena surmised. I better stay away from her. Maybe I'll cozy up to the sweet-looking one.

Without warning, the dreamy blonde walked up and slugged Lorena in the jaw with a right cross. The real estate woman saw instant stars and staggered backward.

"Do I have your attention now, cutie pie?" the blonde snarled in an evil voice.

Suddenly, the beaten-up red-haired woman hurled herself in front of Lorena. She wrapped the surprised blonde in a tight headlock. The redhead then slammed the blonde's unprotected nose upward in a violent motion using the palm of her hand. The flame-haired prisoner then dropped the unconscious blonde onto the floor of the cell.

"There you go, honey bun," she said to Lorena.

Hearing the fracas, two burly policemen rushed into the cell and unlocked it. One had his service weapon drawn.

"Stand back, all of you!" the other cop shouted.

Lorena didn't require a warning. She cowered in a corner, traumatized by the sudden violence.

"What happened here?" the desk sergeant yelled as he came into the cell.

Just then, a fourth officer joined the group.

"I saw everything on closed circuit," he announced. "The blonde walked up and clocked the dumb looking one. The redhead was on top of the hitter immediately. She jacked her with a karate move and that was the end of it. Somebody better check on the blonde. She really got clobbered."

Sure enough, Lorena's attacker was still unconscious. However, at least she was still alive. The officers emptied out the cell, with the blonde going to a hospital emergency room for medical attention. The redhead was put in a cell by herself. As for Lorena, she was ushered to the booking desk.

"Your paperwork came through," the desk sergeant informed her. "However, let me caution you, honey. Try to stay the hell out of trouble. You're lucky that the red-haired babe came to your defense. I know the blonde. She's evil. You could have gotten messed up bad. You seem like a decent enough young woman. You don't belong in a jail cell with these type people. Get yourself together. Square yourself up. Do you hear me?"

"Yes, sir," said a chastened Lorena.

With that, she headed to the door.

Let me out of here, she thought to herself, I can't get home quick enough.

30

The Accident

As Lorena was driving back to her condo, she stopped at a red light about three blocks from home.

When the signal flashed green, she automatically hit the gas pedal and her car leaped forward. She did not see a heavy-duty 4-door pickup running the red light. The big truck t-boned Lorena's car. The air bags deployed, violently jarring her.She felt the twin impacts of the crash and the bags. Her vehicle then made a third contact, striking a curb and flipping on its side. Lorena lost consciousness with the last blow.

In her sudden state of oblivion, Lorena's disrupted mind fluttered into an unfamiliar dimension. A strange dream overwhelmed her befuddled brain. In the dream, Lorena was traveling in the back of an open glider-type aircraft, soaring several thousand feet above a large city. She saw many clusters of lights illuminating the ground below. The glider had open canopies in the front and back. Lorena could not see who occupied the pilot's seat. She called out to the pilot: "Hey, what's happening?" When the pilot turned back toward her, Lorena was shocked. It was a mirror-image of herself, but wearing goggles and an ancient aviator's cap.Without warning, the glider nosedived toward the ground. Lorena felt terrified as the aircraft dipped underneath the clouds. She looked over the side and saw the ground rising ever closer. The noiseless glider was headed straight toward a dense forest.

At the last second, the tree line gave way to a beautiful valley. The glider touched down gently in a spacious and open clearing with barely a bump.

"We made it!" her mirror image shouted from the cockpit. "We should be right on time for lunch."

They both deplaned and began walking side-by-side into the clearing.

"Where are we?" the real estate woman asked.

"Look!" her twin exclaimed, "I see our table."

Sure enough, Lorena spied a pine-top table with bench-seating. Despite the picnic-style setting, there was a full complement of silverware and china on a festive table covering. Their two meals were already prepared and protected by a covering dish.

"Let's sit down," God said. "May we say Grace? Lorena, would you please do Me the honor of blessing our food?"

The real estate woman felt paralyzed. What words would suffice in the company of God? Her throat was frozen into silence.

Finally, she spoke a simple prayer from her childhood:

"God is great. God is good. Let us thank Her for this food. Amen."

"Short and sweet," God smiled. "I like it."

Their meal was simple, consisting of grilled salmon and stewed asparagus spears. There was a medium-size fruit cup beside each of their plates. It consisted of kiwi, strawberries and sliced peaches. Evian water was served as the lone beverage.

I could and should eat like this every day, Lorena heard herself thinking.

"This valley is a nice place for a picnic, don't you think?" God inquired.

"The best," Lorena heard herself reply.

She and Spirit ate in silence after that exchange, until the meal was finished.

"How do you like this part of My Kingdom?" God inquired.

"Is this valley a part of Heaven?" Lorena replied.

"Oh, yes," God answered. "I know when most souls come back to Heaven, many still yearn for the beauty of nature. They miss the oceans, mountains, lakes, rivers, and even the deserts. My Kingdom is a spectacular place, but I understand the awesome pull of the world's natural charms. So many human beings regard nature as their personal soulmate. So, we have set aside special areas in Heaven where everyone can relive the grandeur of nature again. I like to say that we think of everything in Heaven. Bringing replicas of the earth's natural beauty into eternity has worked out well for everyone. You know what else new souls still yearn for most from their time on earth?"

"What?" Lorena asked.

"Rain," God said, "Not hurricanes or other storms, just plain old rain. There is something comforting about it, don't you think?"

"Absolutely," Lorena agreed.

Suddenly, she sensed they were not alone.

"Some people wanted to stop by and say hello," God said.

Lorena looked up to see several people standing around the picnic table. She recognized both sets of her grandparents, a favorite aunt and her best friends from grade school, high school and college, respectively. She had gotten along well with others in school, but usually one friend had emerged as #1 in each venue. She also saw the little red-headed boy she had crushed on in the fourth grade. Everyone smiled and waved, but no words were exchanged. Then, they all disappeared as quickly as they had come.

"That was kind of weird," she said, "but nice."

"You'll have time to visit with them all in Heaven," Spirit said, "None of your school friends have arrived yet. By the way, the little red-headed boy still thinks about you occasionally. You must have made quite the impression."

There was a brief silence and then God stood up from the table.

"Walk with me," She instructed Lorena.

There was a path a few yards from the table. God offered her hand to Lorena. It was warm to the touch.

"You feel very human," Lorena offered.

"Well, I AM both fully human and fully divine," Spirit reminded her.

The two approached a peaceful pond.

"Let's sit for just a moment," Spirit said. "I was wondering if you had made your final decision about committing to My spiritual path. Will you allow Me to use you as an instrument of My Grace? Time is growing short now."

"I'm still conflicted," Lorena replied.

"Here is why I need an answer now," God explained. "You've just had a terrible car accident. That was real. Right now, you are vacillating between life and death. If you say "no" to My earthly Path for you, your human life will be over. I'll carry you back to Heaven with Me in the glider. If you still think you may say "yes" to My Path, you'll return to your life on earth. You have Free Will choice to decide either way. So, Lorena, which is it?"

"I want to go back," the real estate woman answered without a pause.

31

The Hospital

Lorena awoke in a hospital room. Every part of her body ached. She looked around. There were three people standing by the bed: her mother and the two real estate bosses Peter and Sallye. All three had a worried look. However, Lorena had been in enough medical settings to know that she wasn't in the ER or ICU. Her room was too standard.

That's a good thing, she thought. But man, am I sore!

"The air bag saved her," she heard Peter say.

"Yes, but those things can hurt people too," her mother opined.

"What about the guy in the pickup?" Sallye asked.

"I heard he walked away with a few scratches," Lorena's mother said, "He's lucky. They also said his breathalyzer test was negative. I think he was just trying to beat the light."

"That's always the way it is," Peter said, "The person who breaks the law is almost never the one who ends up in the hospital—or dead."

"It could have been worse," Lorena's mom added.

"Oh, I think she may be awake," Sallye said, "How are you feeling, honey?"

"Sore!" was all Lorena could manage.

"I'll bet," Peter commiserated.

"What happened to the other driver?" Lorena inquired.

"He's O. K.," her mom said, "He didn't have any real injuries. His big red pick-up is a mess though.

"I'm glad he's all right," Lorena said with sincerity. "I'm sure my car was totaled. And I just got it paid for."

"Don't worry," Peter said, "The company will pay for a rental until your insurance settles up. We're just glad you weren't seriously hurt."

"What about me?" Lorena asked, "Do I have any broken bones?"

"Bruised, yes, broken no," Sallye responded.

"The doctor told us you have two cracked ribs, probably from the air bag deploying," her mother said.

"I'm just grateful you were wearing your seat belt," Sallye said. "Otherwise, we would probably be talking to you in the ICU."

"When can I get out of here?" Lorena asked.

"Not for a couple of days, honey," her mom answered.

"Don't you worry about work," Peter assured Lorena. "With everything that's been happening lately, a few days off might be a good thing for everybody."

"By the way, sweetie, there is a gentleman in the lobby who wants to see you," her mother informed her.

"It's that guy from the bench outside our office," Sallye said, "You know, the one that looks like a bum one day and a well-dressed man-about-the-town the next. He told your nurse it was on an urgent manner. Are you well enough to see him? What should we tell him?"

"Tell him to come on down!" Lorena said with a smile.

I could tell them my angel is here, Lorena thought, but they probably wouldn't understand.

32

Angel Visit

"How are you feeling, girl," Seth asked when he entered the room. Everyone else had departed.

"How do you think I feel?" she answered, "I got t-boned by a big red pickup."

"I'm sorry about that," Seth acknowledged, "Many times we can do something about traffic accidents, but this one happened too fast."

"It sure did," Lorena lamented.

"I heard from Headquarters that you may be getting closer to choosing the spiritual Path," he said with a smile.

"I'm confused and conflicted," she replied.

"At least you're still considering it," the angel observed.

"To tell you the truth, I haven't had time to think much about anything. I just don't feel that great. Maybe I'll be more focused after I get out of the hospital. By the way, did Heaven or Hell have anything to do with my accident? It looks suspicious."

"What makes you think it was either one of us?" Seth asked. "Who really caused your accident? Personally, I think it was the guy who ran the red light. He made a "Free Will" choice, don't you know? However, I can assure you about our traffic angels. They do a good job of preventing thousands of accidents every day. But they don't stop all of them. Every one of the traffic angels died in a crash so they have a special interest in keeping all drivers safe. It isn't easy, with the texting, speeding and pot smoking going on these days. Personally, I would hesitate even being out on the road, especially at night. Anyway, having your seat belt fastened helped. You'll be home in two days."

"Good," Lorena said. "Now I'm sure you know that I spoke with God during the accident. Do I still need to see Her about the 7th Puzzle of Life?"

"Good question," the angel said. "I'm glad you remembered that God was the 7th Puzzle. Yes, you still need to complete that session with Her. Spirit has a lot more to share with you."

"When will I do that?" Lorena asked.

"The first day that you feel like it," Seth answered.

"Actually, I have a question or two for you now," Lorena said.

"Shoot!"

"These so-called spiritual attacks, do they ever stop?"

"I'm afraid not."

"Do they get worse?"

"Oh yes," the angel replied. "They can get worse and sometimes do. It's just the way things are arranged. Human souls travel back and forth between good and evil. You know about that. However, many people still live out their entire human lives without too much happening. But when people begin speaking out on God's behalf or simply doing good things that help others, trouble usually follows. A lot of folks on social media enjoy poking fun at God's people. In fact, they love it. You can get harassed, stalked and bullied online if you're perceived as being too self-righteous. The evil side knows how to scare people into submission. They are good at it. Your sanity will be questioned, sometimes even by your own family. You could be painted as a religious nut or as a disturbed person. The principalities of evil also go after anybody that dares defend you. No, Lorena, if you think it gets easier after you say "yes" to God, I hate to disappointment you."

"That doesn't sound very appetizing," Lorena frowned.

"It's not," Seth said. "But here's the good news. You draw extra courage from your relationship with Spirit. God represents your best resource in meeting spiritual assaults. When Heaven lines up next to you, the playing field tilts in your direction. Occasionally, things can get dicey. I don't want to mislead you. Evil is quite capable of kicking your butt sometimes. But Heaven is always on your side. God's Kingdom is excellent at lifting you up out of the muck and mire. We love restoration projects. Right now, you're still under the public radar. Expect that to change. When you put yourself out there, your critics start pouncing. The gloves come off. It's bare knuckles time. The "other side" searches for your vulnerabilities. If they find a weak spot, look out. These guys are cunning and baffling. They seek to cause you pain and make you doubt your decision. More than a few of God's men and woman end up scuttled and sunk in the Lake of Fire. It's not a pretty sight."

"You're almost convincing me that I made a mistake," Lorena commented. "I'm not sure I have the courage to withstand these big-time attacks. I'm a chicken at heart, a big chicken. I've never been keen on fighting anyone about anything."

"They would like to scare you off at the beginning," the angel said. "That saves them the time of planning attacks and carrying them out. You would be surprised how many people veer off the Path after they experience their first spiritual battle. It's scary."

"Would you go through with choosing God it if you were me?"

"First of all," Seth responded, "I'm not you. I've been fighting evil for a few thousand years, so I know how it goes. You're a newbie, especially in big-time spiritual warfare. I find these soul battles exhilarating. I love being on the winning side. Satan's fighters are such whiney losers. They love trying to change the rules when things start breaking against them."

"Does evil ever win in the long run?" Lorena queried.

"I must be honest," the angel answered, "It does happen. Anytime we lose the battle for a soul, I cry. I remember some beautiful spirits that didn't survive, for one reason or another. There are casualties in every war, even spiritual ones. Make that ESPECIALLY spiritual ones. Listen to me, Lorena. Evil spirits are out there, trying every minute to capture your soul. They will stop at nothing to succeed. But we won't be intimidated either. Stay strong! Never give up. You have a lot more courage than you think."

"I hope so," Lorena stated, "I guess I'll find out soon."

33

The "Doctor"

Lorena had begun drifting off when she felt a soft touch on her arm.

"How are you feeling?", she heard a male voice ask.

I know Seth has gone, so maybe this man is one of my doctors. That's good. I want to know when I can go home.

"Good afternoon," the "doctor" said, "I just wanted to check in with you. Are you doing OK?"

"I'm sore," Lorena responded, "Really sore".

"I understand," the "doc" stated, "You can expect lots of soreness from this type of accident. Your air bag deployed and gave you quite a jolt. However, you would have had much worse injuries without it. So, God bless air bags."

"When can I go home?" Lorena inquired.

"I'm sure you're anxious. Let's plan for the day after tomorrow. The neurosurgeon wants to see you one more time. She wants to make sure nothing else is going on with the brain. They did x-ray your head when you arrived and found nothing. That's a bad joke, Lorena. Pardon my feeble attempt at humor."

She opened her eyes wider to get a better look at the "doctor".

He was about six-two, with a dark complexion and even darker eyes. He looked a trifle foreign to her. Age-wise, he could have been about her age (35).However, his mannerisms made him seem younger.

"Are you a resident here?" she asked.

"Do I really look that young?" he responded. "No, I've been on staff here for seven years. I've been around for a while."

"Let me look into your eyes," he said, while bending over her.

Their eyes met and Lorena felt a distinct chill ripple through her body. His eyes were a harsh black. They seemed almost empty.

Uh-oh, she thought. I'm getting paranoid. Suddenly, every person I meet seems strange. I'm sure this guy is just fine.

"I didn't catch your name," she said, "You're doctor who?"

"Does my name really matter?" he inquired. He suddenly flashed a strange smile, revealing a set of jagged teeth.

At least I know that dentistry isn't one of his specialties, Lorena thought. Now where did I put that call button?

"Are you looking for your call button," the "doctor" asked. "I put it away. I need a few uninterrupted words with you alone."

"What do you want?" Lorena inquired in a slightly frightened voice.

"What do you think I want? I need to ask you about something. It won't take long."

"I can scream, you know."

"It won't do you any good. There's a Code Blue down the hall. Everybody is busy with that right now."

"What do you want with me? Who sent you?"

"I think you know, Lorena Mae," the "doctor" said, "You're a smart person. You can figure it out.That's one reason we want you on our side. You aren't one of them. Those do-gooders are big-time losers. Trust me. They have no fun at all."

"I don't know what you're talking about," Lorena semi-pro-tested.

"Oh yes you do," he said with a sudden snarl, "They're been recruiting you for weeks. They want you to declare for them and get on some spiritual "path". Forget about it. That "path" leads nowhere. Now, our side has a better plan.It's exciting, fun and can be worth big bucks. But then you know that. Right?"

"Yes," Lorena agreed, "I've heard it all before. But I still don't understand why you're here right now and posing as a doctor. Are you people everywhere?"

"I'm here to stop you, once and for all."

"What do you mean?" Lorena asked in a fearful tone.

Instead of answering her, the "doctor" reached inside his white coat and produced a long and menacing syringe. He grabbed Lorena by the elbow and began probing for a vein.

"No, no, no, no", she started wailing.

"Calm down, sweetheart," the man told her, "It won't hurt—much."

"Why are you doing this to me?" she shouted.

"It's nothing personal, just business," he said. "Relax! Don't fight it. It'll be over before you know it."

Lorena struggled to pull her arm away from the needle. The "doctor" stabbed at her flailing arm without success.

"Hold still!", he said in an irritated voice. "Help me out a little here!"

I'm the one who needs some help, Lorena shouted out silently. Help me, God!

She was suddenly aware of a third presence in the room. It was a huge black female nurse, clad in all-white. She was wearing an old-timey three-cornered nurse's cap on the top of her head.

"What can I do for you, baby?" the nurse inquired.

The doctor stopped his jabbing and just stood with his mouth gaping.

"Oh, yes, I see," she said.

WHAM! She hit the fake doc with a straight left hand to his nose. His needle dropped to the floor and the nurse kicked it away. From an inside pocket in her uniform, she then produced her own syringe. She slammed it hard into the man's neck. He sank to the floor with a loud moan.

"Thank you," Lorena managed to say.

"It's nothing, honey," the nurse smiled, "Now what will you be having for lunch? The meat loaf is always good."

34

Back On The Bench

It was four full days before Lorena made it back to her real estate office. She had not heard from Seth. However, she did wonder if he might be waiting for her as usual on their familiar bench.

The angel was there, dressed in a colorful Hawaiian shirt and blue walking shorts.

"Hi Lorena", he called out as she approached.

I wonder what he has in store for me today, she thought.

"Can you sit with me for just a few minutes?" he inquired in a friendly voice. "I won't keep you long."

"That's what you always say," she replied in a half-kidding tone. "I do need to get into work today."

"It won't take long. I just need to update you on the 7 PUZZLES. God has made a couple of changes."

Lorena walked over and sat down on the edge of the bench.

I want to make sure he understands that I don't have much time today.

"What's up with the Puzzles?" she asked the angel.

"Do you remember I told you that each one of the 7 Puzzles of Life has 500 pieces?"

"Yes," she responded.

"God has decided to reduce the number of pieces in each puzzle," he said, "Because time has become more critical, each puzzle will now have 365 pieces. That's basically one puzzle piece for each calendar day in the year, except for leap years."

"What's the reason for that?" Lorena inquired.

"Hopefully, fewer pieces won't seem as daunting to people," the angel replied. "God wants to get folks working on the Puzzles. He wants to decide soon about the earth's fate. The Puzzles could play a part in that decision. In a way, I see this as a big concession. God wants to avoid a "Solaster" as much we all do."

"I hope reducing the number of pieces works," Lorena said. "I just question how much people will actually do. We're all lazy, you know."

"God knows that She won't ever get a 100% buy-in on the Puzzles. Anything approaching full participation isn't going to happen. But who am I to rain on God's parade? Personally, I think the entire concept could be wishful thinking. Many people won't take the time to even look at the Puzzles, much less try to understand them. But this decision of cutting down the number of pieces may help. I guess it's worth a shot."

"What percentage of participation is acceptable to God," Lorena inquired.

"Good question. I've heard rumors that 10% would indicate an openness to change. That would be ample enough proof to spark some hope. However, you are still talking about 600 to 700 million people. That seems like a lot to me, considering the anti-God sentiment out there in the culture."

"I think that would be a fantastic beginning," Lorena observed, "I hope the rumors are right."

"I do too," Seth stated, "But for every 10 who begin the process, I think more than half will quit because of a loss of interest.

Some will start, quit and then start up again and then quit again. Human beings are erratic when it comes to learning new things. Still, I'm for anything that might prevent the "Solaster."

"Does God plan to tell people what will happen unless things change?" Lorena asked. "That might be a motivation for folk to take the puzzles more seriously."

"Yes," Seth said, "This is where the modern-day "prophets", like you, come in. You all will spread the word, just as the Biblical prophets did in the Old Testament. In this age of social media, it might have some real impact. I'm hoping you will emerge as one of our best new prophets. I think people will pay attention to you."

"Me?" Lorena said, "I hardly doubt it. I think I would be a terrible prophet."

"I hear you, Lorena. However, I can assure you that God has heard every excuse under the sun.You should see people scatter when She asks them to do something. You probably won't be any different. I remember when God approached Moses by the "burning bush". Moses protested to Spirit that he was inadequate to take on anything. Yet the old man proved that he was more than capable. Pay attention to your fears, but also try to balance them. God always provides every resource and talent you'll need to complete any sacred work. Some human beings opt-out of a challenge because they don't believe that Spirit will see them through to completion. Others will be in denial of a world-ending event. They'll just hunker down and hope for the best. Here's the thing: It's the Holy Spirit within you that does the work anyway."

"Are you saying that I would have to be on TV?" "Yes," the angel said, "You'll have to do all of the regular stuff and social media too. In fact, your voice will turn up in every avenue of human communication. Don't worry about it. You're just the instrument. When you open your mouth, the Holy Spirit does the talking. I'm sure you'll do fine."

"I appreciate what you're saying," Lorena protested, "But you won't change my mind. That kind of stuff isn't for me. I can't do it. Period. End of story."

"How about if we do a small test?" Seth suggested.

"What kind of test?"

"I know you have a Twitter account,", the angel said. "How about if we send out one Tweet in your account promoting the 7 Puzzles of Life? I'll write it. I promise it won't come across as weird or threatening. You can see how it feels. We can also gauge the response. How many "Followers" do you have?"

"I'm not sure," Lorena responded, "Maybe 60?".

"You also could also do one brief post in your Facebook account." That would really give you a taste of communicating on social media. How many Facebook friends do you have?"

"Not too many," Lorena answered, "Maybe 150 or so. Some are business friends related to real estate."

"I think Twitter and Facebook posts to your small accounts would be an excellent sample," Seth said. "What do you think?"

"And you would write the posts?" she said, "Subject to my approval?"

"Absolutely," the angel confirmed.

"When would this all happen?" Lorena asked.

"How about tonight?" Seth said, "Go on in to work for a while. I'll get the copy written and meet you back here at 6 p.m."

"Are you sure?"

"Absolutely." he said, "Just bring your personal laptop for sending out the Tweet and for the posting on Facebook. We don't need those electronic contraptions where I come from.

I'm doing good just to text. Technology frightens me. I don't understand it. I'm not sure most humans do either."

"O. K," Lorena sighed with some resignation, "Let's give it a try."

35

Real Estate News

Lorena had received several texts from Sallye while meeting with Seth. Therefore, it was no surprise when the receptionist greeted her with the standard news.

"Sallye is looking for you ASASP."

Lorena found both Peter and Sallye waiting for her in the conference room.

"We've been trying to find you," she said with some irritation.

"I've been right outside," Lorena replied, "I promise this will be one of my last meetings with the old guy. Well, at least until 6 o'clock tonight.

"What's going on at 6 p.m.?" Peter inquired.

"Oh nothing," she lied. "What's going on here?"

"Lorena, Sallye and I have been more than patient with you," Peter began, "But you've got to keep us clued in. What's going on with you? We're your bosses. We deserve to know what's happening. Is that too much to ask? If so, we've got a problem. We've got a business to run here. We're sure you can understand that."

"There have been some big developments," Peter continued, "We just got off the phone with Reggie Miller III.He called and was quite apologetic. After accusing you of bribery and sexual harassment and then getting you arrested, he now says it was all a big misunderstanding. He wants you to have dinner with him again. He wants to apologize and explain. By the way, the real estate listings are back on, all four of them. And Reggie insists that there is much more where those can from."

"Whoa, I'm puzzled," Lorena said.

And more than a little suspicious, she thought to herself.

"That's not all of the news either," Sallye added.

"What else?" Lorena asked.

I'm almost afraid to ask, she thought.

"There is some guy in a government-looking suit waiting in your office," Sallye said, "He won't tell me much, but he could be FBI, CIA or NSA. He did say they were trying to track down a nasty rumor someone is spreading."

"What kind of rumor?"

"It's some crazy story about the sun getting ready to incinerate the earth. Do you know anything about that?"

Lorena gulped.

"Did you spread some crazy rumor?" Peter inquired sternly.

"Have you lost your frigging mind?" Sallye shouted.

"I can explain," Lorena replied, "But I better talk to this guy first. Does the suit have a name?"

"Yes, darling." Sallye answered.

"No, what's his name?"

"Agent Dahling, honey. Agent Tim Dahling."

36

Agent Dahling

The official-looking man stood up when Lorena entered the room. He was a forty-something man of medium height. He was wearing the standard white shirt and dark narrow tie. His haircut was almost military. Lorena knew right away that he had to be a government agent.

At least he stood up when I entered the room, Lorena thought to herself. The dude has some manners.

"I'm Lorena Mae Johnson," she announced.

"I'm Agent Tim Dahling", he returned. "That's with an "h" instead of an "r." It's nice to know you."

They shook hands in a formal, although not too stiff manner.

That's two thumbs up, she thought. He didn't try to crush my hand nor is he a wimp.

The federal man smiled and pulled out a chair for her to sit down.

Three for three, she grinned inwardly. I've missed being around people with manners. Maybe this won't be too bad after all.

"What government agency do you represent?" she ventured.

"I work in a branch of Homeland Security," he replied, "Specifically, it's the N-A-S-T-I Division of DHS."

"Nasty?" Lorena repeated with a snicker, despite herself.

"We get that a lot," he chuckled, "Basically, it stands for "National Agency for Stopping Terrible Information." The people at Homeland have more of a humorous streak than you might expect. In their job, it's a must."

"It is sort of a fun title," Lorena said, "You're the "Nasty Man"."

"We've had so much teasing that they are changing it next month," he advised.

"I hate to ask, but what's the new acronym?"

"You'll probably laugh," the agent told her.

"Try Me", she said with a smile.

"I believe they are calling it "STD"."

"STD?" she whooped.

"It stands for "Stop Talking Damnit"."

Lorena laughed out loud.

Where did they find this guy?

"Well, Agent Tim from STD, why are you here? My bosses are never happy when anyone from the federal government troops into our office."

"DHS received an anonymous telephone tip last week," the agent said. "The caller claimed somebody was spreading a rumor that the world was coming to an end.Somehow your name was mentioned. My bosses asked me to check you out. I did a preliminary online search. You were clean. In fact, you've had a spotless record for your entire life. Pretty dull reading, if I do say so. We also ran a social media scan on your Facebook and Twitter accounts. That's about all you use. I couldn't locate you on Instagram, LinkedIn or any other platform. Anyway, nothing turned up. However, before we closed the file, they asked me to interview you in person. So, with that long explanation, do you know anything about any of this?"

How do I answer him? What I say next could have a profound effect on my life for a long time to come. God, please give me some help here. Do you have anybody on duty today? What should I tell this nice man?

There was a rapping at Lorena's door, surprising both her and the NASTI agent.

"Knock, knock!", a man's voice called out, "Anybody home?"

It was Seth the Angel, dressed in a pinstripe Oxford suit, with Burberry shirt and colorful tie. He was carrying a small black briefcase from Nieman-Marcus.

He extended his hand to the government officer.

"Hello, federal agent Timothy Dahling I presume?" he said in a friendly but authoritative voice.

"Yes," agent Dahling responded. "And you are?"

"I'm Judge William Ormand Douglas, I mean former Judge Douglas from the 13th Circuit Court of Appeals. I'm retired from the bench now but I'm serving pro bono as Ms. Johnson's attorney. I'm a long-time friend of her mother and father. They asked me to check in with their daughter to see if she could use some legal counsel about now. How about it, my dear? Am I intruding or do you need my services? If so, I'm available."

Am I glad to see you, Lorena mused to herself.

"I was telling your client that a tipster called Homeland Security," Agent Dahling explained. "They said someone was spreading rumors that the earth was about to be sucked into the sun. The caller also mentioned Ms. Johnson's name. I was just asking whether she knew anything about it."

"Whoa," Seth said with a palms-up gesture that communicated "Back away, son. Now!"

"By the way, young man," the angel added, "I hate the term "sucked".

Agent Dahling took one step backward as if in a mild retreat.

"Sorry to offend you, Judge," he said.

Then, Seth turned to face Lorena.

"I'm not too sure what this is all about," he told her, "But I think it's past time for this interview to end. However, I do have a couple of quick questions for Agent Dahling? By the way, is that with an "h"?"

"Yes," the agent responded.

"Strange spelling," the "Judge" commented. "Anyway, was the caller a man or a woman?"

"It was a woman," the agent said, "Our voice experts identified her as having a Jamaican accent. The caller mentioned that Lorena was somehow involved, but she wasn't accused directly."

"Then, I don't understand why we're even having this meeting," the angel said. "Here's a card with my private line. If you have any further questions for Ms. Johnson, please direct them to me. Now, I need a word with my client alone. It was nice to meet you, agent."

After Dahling had departed, Seth patted Lorena on the arm.

"I got here as soon as I could," he said.

"You were great," she said. "Now, do you really have something to talk about or were you just trying to just get rid of him?"

"Both," Seth said, "I do have something to discuss. Here's the copy for your Tweet and Facebook post tonight. Don't forget to do it. This is our test, remember?"

Seth handed her two sheets of paper.

The Twitter post read:

Quick! Read Ezekiel 6-7 in the Old Testament. It tells the story of what is about to befall the world if things don't change. This is imminent! Please retweet. God is angry! The end is near! Don't make any long-range plans!"

"Wow," Lorena said. "I'm not sure about this one. It's pretty harsh."

"Remember," Seth responded, "We have two objectives. First, to get some attention about the plight of the world. Secondly, we need to find out if anybody will listen to you. Now, please look at your Facebook post."

The post featured a close-up photograph of Lorena with a note about her "profile picture" changing. It also read:

To my Facebook friends: I have an urgent message for you. Please go get your Bible from the shelf. Brush off the dust. Look in the book of Ezekiel. It's somewhere near the front. Read Chapters 6-7. The world is about to end. Please share this immediately with all of your friends."

"I don't know about this one either," Lorena said, "It doesn't make much sense. People will think I'm nuts. I'll have zero credibility with anybody if I post it. I just don't think I should do it. It doesn't seem cool. Doesn't Heaven have any posters familiar with Twitter and Facebook?"

"I think I understand what you're saying," the angel stated. "But this is where the rubber meets the road. When you become a prophet or follower of God, expect condemnation and disbelief. To have any effect, you must be willing to go against the crowd. It takes considerable courage to challenge the world. I know you have the strength to do it. God and I have faith in you."

"You both have more faith in me than I have in myself," she said.

"Don't forget," Seth reminded her as he stood and walked to the door. "Tweet and post tonight exactly at 6 p.m. Don't worry about my copywriting. I'll admit it isn't very catchy. Just trust me and send them both as is. I'm betting that all hell will break loose once they get out there."

"You're wrong," Lorena cautioned, "The only person catching hell will be me."

37

Social Media

Shortly before 6 p.m., Lorena sat down with her laptop. She pulled out the Twitter and Facebook posts that Seth had composed. Reading them again, something suddenly occurred to her.

If I post these two things on social media, I'll be exposing myself to the government's claim that I'm the one spreading the "Solaster" rumors. That might not be a good thing for me. Agent Dahling said he was monitoring my social media footprint.

Then, having convinced herself, Lorena grabbed a blank piece of paper and began creating her own posts.

I'm sure Seth won't like it, but I'm the one whose head is on the chopping block.

When six o'clock arrived, she began with a Tweet to her "followers":

(Hashtag #spirituality) I believe that life is like a puzzle. I also think God wants to help us solve puzzles like love, work and family. If we can fit these spiritual puzzles together properly, we can find the true meaning of our lives."

That's much better, she told herself. Nothing in that Tweet could come back to haunt me later.

After waiting a couple of minutes, Lorena brought up her Facebook account. She checked her friend-count and found it stood at 154. She posted the exact same message on Facebook that she had placed on Twitter.

Suddenly, her phone beeped. A new text was arriving. It was from Seth

"Lorena," it read. "What's going on? Why did you change my copy?"

She decided to ignore his text for now.

Instead, Lorena checked back to her posts in case anyone might have responded. There was zero activity in her Twitter account and only one "like" generated from the Facebook post

Oh well, give it time, she thought.

Lorena suddenly remembered that she had not responded to Reggie III's invitation to dinner.

That can wait until tomorrow, she thought.

There was a sudden knock at the front door of her condo. She took a quick look outside from the peep hole.

She was shocked to see Franklin standing on her front porch. He had not crossed her mind since the huge "linebacker" angel had ejected him from her condo.

"What are you doing here?" Lorena said in a loud voice through the door, "I'm not having any company right now, especially you."

Franklin did not budge. Instead, he shouted: "Lorena, please, do you remember our terrific night of lovemaking? I'm sure your body remembers. You had orgasm after orgasm. Don't you want to experience that again? I'm sure your body misses me. I know I would like to do it again. I miss you. I want to hold you. Come on, Lorena, please let me in. You won't be sorry. I need to talk with you.Hey, I'll even beg you. What are you wearing?"

The longer Franklin spoke with her, the more Lorena's body tingled.

Sex is such a powerful urge, her mind acknowledged. It can really take control of your brain. Somebody once told me "The mind is the #1 sex organ". It was true.

Despite standing on her porch in public view, Franklin suddenly unzipped his trousers and dropped his pants. He wasn't wearing any underwear. He was on the porch naked from the waist down. Franklin reached down and began waving his enormous penis from side to side.

Oh my God! Lorena thought. He's much bigger than I remember!

"Come on, Lorena," he shouted out, "You know you want it. Let me in now!"

All Lorena could manage was a reflexive action from somewhere deep within herself. She screamed. Her loud shriek traveled through the front door, spilled out onto the porch and ended up on the sidewalk where passers-by were beginning to congregate. A couple of people were already recording the incident on their cell phones.

"Look at the size of that guy's cock!" somebody yelled out.

Lorena opened the door and stepped onto the porch.

Franklin gathered his entire package into both hands and "presented" it to Lorena.

"Here," he instructed her, "Hold it! Kiss it!"

Lorena had the presence of mind to step back inside the hallway. She spied her large real estate briefcase sitting on a table within easy reach. She grabbed the heavy case and stepped back outside. In one quick motion, she landed a roundhouse blow on Franklin's exposed private parts.

"WHOP!" echoed as a direct hit was scored.

"YEOW!" Franklin screamed as the pain cascaded through his body. He fell to his knees.

"Oh my god!" he shouted, "I'm ruined."

The crowd on the sidewalk grew. Several people were shooting the incident on their cellphones from different angles.

One woman yelled out, "Look at the size of that dude's cock. Somebody be sure and get a good shot of it."

Two young women were yelling encouragement to Lorena. "Hit the bastard in the balls again!" one of them screamed.

Franklin tried to hide his private parts from the people filming his obvious distress. His trousers were still gathered at the ankles.

Suddenly, Lorena appeared on the porch again. This time she carried a large broom. She began swatting at Franklin's genitals.

"Ow, ow, ow!" he howled.

"Don't you ever pull out that thing out on me again!" Lorena yelled, while landing two more blows with her broom.

Finally, Franklin was able to roll away from the broom. He managed to get himself into a crouched position.

Lorena got in one more strong whack to the doubled-over man's backside as he began moving away.

"Oh, Oh, Oh!" Franklin cried as he started navigating slowly down the block. He was finally able to sheath his genitals and pull up his pants.

"You'll regret this, you witch!" he called out over his shoulder.

One of the people filming the chaos put her cell directly in Lorena's face.

"What's your name, ma'm?" she asked, "You are one tough lady!"

"Lorena Mae Johnson", she answered without thinking.

Within an hour, the scene had gone viral. Lorena heard later that it reached one million views later that evening.

OMG, Lorena thought. What have I done?

She did have the presence of mind to call 9-1-1 and report the incident to the authorities.

When asked to describe what happened, she heard the female dispatcher suppress a laugh.

"So a man on your front porch came at you with his exposed penis?", the 9-1-1 operator asked. "But you beat him off? Did you happen to see which way the two of them went?"

No, she had not, Lorena replied. She looked out to the porch area where the small crowd had gotten much larger.

"Is this where the cock smasher lives?" one woman cried out. "You rock!"

"I want to see the penis crusher," a teenage girl yelled.

"We have officers on the way," the dispatcher instructed her. "Shelter in place in case it comes back."

Two police officers entered her condo within minutes.

"Ma'm, we have word that the incident was recorded live on a cellphone. We've already received several 9-1-1 calls about it. They all said the man will be easy to identify. Do you know this gentleman, if I may call him that?"

"Yes," she answered, "His name is Franklin. I've got his last name written down here somewhere. I want to file charges."

"Is he related to you? Are you in a relationship with him?"

"No and no," Lorena managed to reply.

"I've already sent out a BOLO to hospitals," one officer told the other. "I told them be on the lookout for a man with damaged large genitalia. I had to tell them a couple of times that I was dead serious."

This whole thing is spinning out of control, Lorena thought to herself.

"You know what, officers, let's just forget the whole thing. I took care of it myself. I don't think he'll be coming around here again. I'm just going to take an aspirin and lie down. Thank you for coming out to check on me."

One of the officers peered outside to the street.

"My God, come and see this," he told his partner.

They both looked out.

"We've got a real traffic jam here. The cars are lined up for a couple of blocks. This lady is going to need somebody to direct traffic. Either that or we'll have to block off the street. By the way, I see a couple of TV trucks coming this way. Ma'm, I believe you're about to become famous."

"Hey lady!" one of the policemen said in his best Jerry Lewis impression, "You've got a problem."

38

Celebrity

Lorena couldn't sleep. She finally went to bed at midnight. The incident with Franklin was spreading into a world-wide phenomenon. Her cell phone began ringing non-stop after the assault video went viral. Her Twitter feed exploded with comments and retweets. She soon began "trending". Unanimous kudos and "you go girl" comments were rolling in from everywhere. Although most of the praise came from regular people, many celebrities and media types also joined in. She found no negative comments, except for one man from Brooklyn who thought Franklin might be his cousin.

Lorena's I-phone mailbox became full immediately. There were calls from friends and family, but also several media inquiries. While none of the evening news "Mainstream Media" had sought her out so far, cable news had gone berserk over the story. Several podcasters were also begging for an interview. A couple of daytime TV talk shows offered standing requests, anytime that Lorena could fit them in. She vaguely wondered how people found her personal contact information so quickly. Her parents left a supportive message, inquiring about the state of her mental and physical health. It was the only call she bothered to return.

Thank God my mom and dad didn't press me too much, Lorena thought. They're the best!

About 2 a.m., there was an insistent knock at her door. At first, Lorena didn't respond.

Damn reporters, she told herself.

Finally, after 10 minutes of steady pounding, Lorena arose from the bed and walked cautiously to the front door. She focused her right eye and stared out of the security hole. To her astonishment, she saw Seth the Angel. He seemed somewhat agitated.

"My Lord, Lorena!" the messenger angel whistled. "We wanted some sort of media response, but this is crazy.""

"Well, I sure didn't plan it this way," she ventured.

"On Facebook", Seth reported, "You have 14,776 likes and 1,350 "shares". I saw only a few snarky comments. Twitter is going crazy. Your "views" are over 1 million. You've generated more than 100,000 likes and 30,000 retweets. That shot of you double-whacking Franklin's genitals is grabbing, pardon the pun, most of the attention. A few of the comments are "killer". I think you'll find some of them downright hilarious. There are so many witty people out there. Meanwhile you might be interested in knowing how your original posts on Facebook and Twitter were received. These are the ones you substituted for what I provided. Your Facebook post drew eight "likes" and three rather bland comments. Your Tweet got three likes and one retweet. Here is what this response says to me: "SEX SELLS". We are off and running. You are #1 trending on Twitter under headings like #"Cocksmasher", #Dickbonker" and #Peniscrusher". You're riding the crest now, PR-wise. This is so much more than we expected. This could not have gone better, Lorena, than if we had planned it."

"What do we do now?" Lorena asked.

"We take our windfall and run with it," the angel said. "This should get you positioned as an avenging angel. We'll get you booked on shows that want to talk about swatting Franklin's "business". However, that only goes so far. The 7 Puzzles, the "Solaster" and God's unhappiness with the world are all stories with "Legs". Add them all up and the overall "awareness" of God's message should skyrocket. We've been blessed, Lorena. You should be proud. I've always said that I would rather be lucky than smart."

There was a knock at the door.

After checking out who was at her door, Lorena told Seth: "It's a reporter with Channel 6. I recognize her. She's got a cameraman tagging along. What should I do? Is it too early for an interview?"

"Let them in," the angel shouted.

As the reporter and cameraman entered the condo, Lorena whispered to Seth: "What do I tell them?"

"This is the good part," Seth said in a low voice, "Just open your mouth. God already has the words prepared. Just get out of the way. Let it flow from you. You'll do fine. I promise."

"So, Lorena, tell me what happened," the reporter began.

For the next 20 minutes, Lorena spun the story. It included how she had been spiritually attacked since God first began channeling the 7 Puzzles of Life idea. Lorena added that she thought the sexual assault was part of Satan's plan to stop her from serving God. After the interview ended, the reporter seemed more than satisfied with the result.

"We've got a good versus evil winner here," Lorena heard the reporter say to her cameraman. "Lorena is a sympathetic heroine who fought back against Satan and won, at least for the time being. And we have the sensational video laced with sex to back everything up. What else could we want?"

God really does work in strange ways, Lorena thought after the news team had departed. Take the classic struggle of Heaven and Hell, a little (or a lot) of sex, a damsel in distress (me) and a good whack on some perp's cock. It all adds up to an unbeatable combination.

Lorena and the messenger angel plopped down in Lorena's small living room. They looked at each other and then both burst out laughing.

"We're on our way!" Seth grinned.

39

The Lost Prophets

Lorena received a text message from Seth about 5:30 a.m.

It read: "Meet me at 7:30 a.m. for breakfast before you go into work. I'll be in the private backroom at the Sunrise Restaurant. I have people that I want you to meet. One of them you know already. Don't be late! —Seth."

At this point, Lorena was beyond questioning the angel. She began her morning routine earlier than usual and departed for the restaurant shortly after 7 a.m.

When she arrived, Seth was already there. This time he was attired in running gear. Lorena recognized a high-end pair of Nikes.

"You look spiffy," she ventured, "Set for a run later, eh?"

"I had hoped to get a few marathons in before my service here is done. You've been a bit more time-consuming than I expected."

"Who's in the backroom?" she asked, "Who am I meeting?"

"We've talked about you about becoming one of God's prophets. Your job will be to go out and warn people about repenting. Do you remember?"

"Yes, I do," Lorena answered, "I told you that I couldn't do it. No way."

"With your new notoriety, it should be easier," Seth said. "But I know you feel inadequate. So today I thought you might enjoy meeting some real "prophets". Every single one of them begged off when God first came calling. But they all eventually said "yes". You've already met Miriam, the first female prophet in the Bible. I also brought along some of the "guys" this morning. I want to warn you. They're all young dudes. They've formed a rock and roll band called "The Lost Prophets". They are cool cats, let me tell you."

"I find that hard to believe," she sighed, "But let's go."

When Seth opened the door, Lorena recognized Miriam. She had on a pair of tight blue shorts with a pink blouse. She looked older than her male companions.

She gave Lorena a wave and called out: "I'm the den mother and also one of the band's back-up singers."

Lorena saw six young surfer dudes strewn about the room. They were wearing green and gold T-Shirts. On each shirt was a picture of planet earth being engulfed by flames. The name of the band was wrapped around the earth: THE LOST PROPHETS.

Lorena turned to Seth.

"These are THE PROPHETS?" she asked.

"Of course," he smiled, "You should read some of their lyrics. They are quite apocalyptic and extremely popular with the kids. Come over here guys, I want you to meet Ms. Lorena Mae Johnson."

The six sauntered over and surrounded her. However, she did not feel threatened. In fact, quite the opposite.

"Boys, this is the cool chick I've been telling you about. Lorena, meet Daniel, Isaiah, Ezekiel, Elijah, Elisha, and Jeremiah."

Here was Lorena's first impression of each prophet:

Daniel was the best looking and radiated intelligence; Isaiah appeared to be the oldest and conveyed an authoritative presence; Ezekiel possessed a mischievous grin of a jokester; Elijah came across as the flirt of the group (he winked at Lorena), Elisha appeared to be the youngest and most shy; while Jeremiah had a palatable darkness about him.

"Jeremiah plays the drums," Seth informed Lorena, "Daniel is the lead singer, Isaiah also sings and plays the keyboards, Ezekiel and Elisha are bass players and Elisha can play anything. He can kill on any instrument. You should hear him wail on trumpet, strum the banjo or play the violin. Together, they've got a sound somewhere between the younger versions of U2 and Led Zeppelin. These boys are supremely talented. No one is older than 22 except Isaiah and he's 25. Their first album drops next month. It's called "World on Fire" and is guaranteed to debut at #1. They are the biggest draw in our culture wars with the other side. Evil has had a few good groups over the years, but these boys are double solid."

"Boys, could each of you say in a few words what being a prophet for God meant to you?" Seth requested.

"I'll go first," Daniel said. "I'm the main songwriter and the dreams and visions guy. I made my chops interpreting King Neb's dreams. I gave him my take on the rise and fall of earthly kingdoms. Do you remember the phrase "the handwriting on the wall"? I coined that phrase. It's still used today. People also remember me from the lion's den and my friends in the fiery furnace. I try and remind people to trust God, no matter how bad things may look. It's a theme in many of my songs."

"I'll go next," Isaiah said. "I prophesied In Judah.I warned the people that Jerusalem and Judah would be judged because of their wickedness. It is sort of like what's happening in the world today. I predicted the Babylonian exile. I specialized in offering comfort to the people. I told them that if they would put God first, he would set up a new and righteous kingdom.

My most famous Bible verse was chapter 40, verse 31: "But those who hope in the LORD will renew their strength. They shall rise up on wings like eagles; they will run and not grow weary; they will walk and not be faint."

"I guess it's my turn," Ezekiel chimed in. "My name literally means "When God is strong." I did most of my work between 593 and 571 BC for my fellow exiles in Babylonian captivity. I was born into a priestly family, so prophesying came easy for me. I grew up around the Temple in Jerusalem, so I was also steeped in religion. After it was destroyed, I proclaimed a new message of hope and restoration. I promised that God would regather the Israelites from everywhere and re-establish them in their own land. And, as you know, everything worked out for the best."

Elijah raised his hand to be recognized. "I don't have a book in the Bible named for me, but you can find my story in First Kings. I told King Ahab about the coming drought and famine. People saw me as a big-time troublemaker, instead of a prophet. You can expect the same treatment. The general public doesn't like bad news. Remember the example of folks wanting to "kill the messenger"? You get that when you start warning people about unpleasant things. I'm also the one who had to confront the false prophets of Baal. That wasn't pleasant either, but necessary. Prophets sometimes must do gutsy things. However, God always gives you the strength to do it."

Elisha waved his hand for recognition. "I didn't get a book in the Bible either," he said, "But my story can also be found in Kings. I was a disciple and protégé of Elijah. I came into my own after he left the earth in a chariot of fire. As he was leaving, he blessed me with a double portion of his power. So, the other prophets back then started deferring to me. Thanks again, "E Number One". However, I don't let him forget that I went on to perform twice as many miracles as he did. You can also find me mentioned in other religious texts, such as the Quran. I did hold the title of "Prophet of Israel" for six decades and spent a lot of time with the soldiers and kings at the time. I was blessed with a great career. I'm sure you'll be blessed as well."

"I guess I bring up the rear, as usual," Jeremiah said. "I was a young guy when God called me as a prophet. Again, like now, public and private wickedness were the main problems. I spent my first 20 years as a prophet under King Josiah. By the way, I thought he was a decent king who tried his best to get folks back in line. Unfortunately, I was always in hot water with political and religious leaders. They hated my negativity. However, God protected me. The LORD wanted me to warn the sinners of what was coming if things didn't change. Of course, nobody paid attention. You must keep on grinding when the criticism comes. I guess my best advice would be to trust in God when the flaming arrows start falling around you. There are many folks in the culture today who don't want to hear the truth. You'll be an annoyance to them. They will try and shut you up. Expect it, but don't let them get under your skin. Keep on keeping on."

"Well done guys," Seth said. "Do you have any questions, Lorena?"

"I'm impressed," she said, "I still don't know enough to ask any questions. Anyway, good luck with your new single. Do you have any last words for me?"

"Trust God and never go anywhere barefoot!" they all shouted.

40

Mr. White

As usual, whenever Lorena was absent for a while, people in the real estate office were trying to find her. The receptionist handed Lorena a stack of messages.

"There's a Charles White for you in the conference room," the receptionist said. "Peter and Sallye have been entertaining him while they've been waiting on you."

When Lorena popped into the room, she saw not only her bosses and Mr. White, but also Reggie Miller III.

"Hi Lorena," Reggie offered casually as though nothing had transpired between them. "I would like to introduce my attorney, Mr. Charles Nelson White. Sir, this is the famous Lorena Mae Johnson that you've heard so much about."

"Please be seated, Lorena," Mr. White said. "It's my great pleasure to finally meet you."

"It's my honor to meet you as well," Lorena returned. "To what do we owe the honor of your visit, if I may ask?"

"Mr. White is here to clear up any confusion about the four listings he gave the firm," Sallye stated in a rather formal tone. "As we all know, the ridiculous charge that Lorena tried to bribe Reggie for the listings has been dropped. Whatever was behind the accusation, we'll mark it down as a business misunderstanding. We'll put it behind us and proceed from here. Secondly, our survey teams have verified that the listings do exist and are available for sale. We have executed new listing agreements for each property, effective today. The agreements were all signed and notarized before you arrived, Lorena. There should be no further misunderstandings. Have I stated everything correctly, Mr. White?"

"Yes, and thank you," Mr. White nodded. "There is one more thing. On behalf of Reggie, I want to apologize for his behavior these past few days."

"I'm sorry for being such a jerk at the restaurant," Reggie addressed Lorena. "I had just been to the doctor that morning. I was diagnosed with Stage IV pancreatic cancer. Still, that isn't any excuse for my acting so crudely and disrespecting you. I'm asking for your forgiveness. It won't happen again. I promise."

He seems genuinely sorry for his behavior, Lorena thought. And I do understand that a diagnosis like Stage IV cancer could throw anybody off.

"Yes, I forgive you," she said. "Let's start over."

To Mr. White, Lorena added "I promise you that our office will do a good job with the listings."

As they all stood to shake hands, Mr. White asked Lorena: "Are you the woman who whacked that terrible man's penis with a broom? I just hope you never get mad at me."

41

A Reminder

After Mr. White and Reggie had departed and Peter and Sallye seemed relieved that the listing chaos was finally over, Lorena went back to her office. Leaning back in her chair, she reflected on her conversation with Seth after meeting the prophets.

As Lorena had prepared to leave the restaurant for work, the angel had taken her aside for a brief word.

"I know you need to go," he said, "But remember that you have an important lunch date."

"I do?" Lorena inquired.

"Yes, it's time for God Herself to speak to you about the 7th Puzzle."

"And that is the Puzzle of God, right?"

"That's correct. Some people have suggested that the God Puzzle should be first, even before Free Will. But I think it works better this way. God is the Alpha and Omega, the first and the last word on everything."

"What should I know before the meeting?" Lorena asked.

"First, you should feel free to ask any question that you think is relevant to your situation. Do not be intimidated or frightened by meeting with God face to face. Remember, Lorena, the Holy Spirit lives within you. You carry God with you everywhere you go. God created you. She knows everything about you, and I do mean everything."

"That's kind of scary," Lorena noted.

"Not really," the angel replied. "That's the wonderful thing about being a child of God. You are loved unconditionally. God knows all your shortcomings and loves you anyway."

"What else should I know before the meeting?"

"When you're with God, don't worry about the time," Seth said. "Many people want to cut things short. They feel like: "I can't take up God's valuable time. He must have better things to do." That's just not so. When you are with God, time stands still. Don't be surprised that when you take leave of God, the time will still be the same as when you first sat down together. You are never charged for any second, minute or hour spent with Spirit. There are no clocks in Heaven. We don't have day or night, morning or afternoon. Eternity is just what the name implies. Earthly time, as such, has no meaning. You cannot imagine how beautiful timelessness can be. Most human beings are always trying to race the clock. This causes untold stress. It can damage your physical body, fog up your brain and scramble your human emotions. When you are with God today, don't expect Her to keep checking the clock. Enjoy every second of your "face time" with the ruler of the Universe. This direct access to God constitutes a remarkable benefit of the spiritual life. When it's over, your heart will overflow with love, contentment and peace. Trust me. You'll sleep well tonight."

"I'm really looking forward to it," Lorena said, "How will I know God when I see Her? Does she still look like my twin sister?"

"Even more so!" the angel laughed.

42

Dream State

Lorena arrived at the restaurant before her "twin sister", otherwise known as God. After she was seated, she sat quietly for a couple of minutes and then closed her eyes. Within a few seconds, she entered a 4th dimensional dream state.

In a realistic dream, Lorena imagined that she was sitting in the orchestra section of a small theatre. She was in Row C, the third row from the stage. The coziness reminded her of an intimate Broadway theatre. She turned to look back at the rest of the theatre goers. To Lorena's shock, she was completely alone.

That's strange, she thought. Where is the rest of the audience?

Soon, a young woman stepped out of the wings, stage left. Lorena did a double take.

That's me, she thought, when I was about 18 or 19. It's either me or a lookalike from when I graduated from high school.

"Good afternoon," the teenage girl said. "I want to welcome you to today's performance of LORENA'S LIFE. I will be playing the role of Lorena. Now, please sit back and enjoy the production."

The Lorena looked around again to glance at the empty theatre. She was still alone.

A very tall man appeared from stage right. He walked confidently to center stage. A pair of spotlights illuminated his face.

It was Franklin, her one-night stand and the man who had tried to physically attack her on two occasions.

Suddenly, the stage lights came up and Franklin stood at the edge of the stage, directly facing her. He was completely nude. Lorena again felt some shock by the size of his manhood. She swallowed hard and felt her Adams Apple move up and down in her throat.

I'm getting accustomed to seeing Franklin without any clothes, Lorena thought. Still, I'm feeling a physical stirring despite my personal animosity toward this guy. Our sexual urges are so powerful that I can't help myself.

 Either Franklin, or the actor playing Franklin, waved at her in a friendly manner.

"Hello out there, Lorena," he called out. "I'm glad you could be here today. I just want to tell you how much I've been thinking about you. I can't wait for us to be together again. How about you? Are you ready to make love all night long? Let's you and I sample the nectar of the gods. I crave your body again, my darling. I know you feel the same way."

Then, "Franklin" vanished. From stage-left and stage-right, respectively, a man and woman walked out. It was her real estate bosses Peter and Sallye. They met at center stage. Suddenly, a roll-down screen came into view from above the stage. Lorena's bosses stood on either side of the screen.

"Just a quick power-point presentation," Peter smiled. Then, one after another, plush luxury items began appearing on the screen. There was a palatial mansion overlooking a vast ocean. In the large home's circular driveway, Lorena saw two new Mercedes automobiles. One was a black 4-door stretch sedan, while the other was a light blue convertible. Sallye beckoned to Lorena, inviting her inside the mansion for a personal tour.

Its furnishings were magnificent. There was priceless artwork throughout. Most of the art was museum-quality. Lorena had never seen any personal residence with such appointments.

"All of this can be yours, sweetie," Sallye called out to the audience of one. "Don't you just love this glitzy stuff! Ka-jing! Ka-jing! Ka-jing!" added Peter. "Money, money, money" they both laughed and shouted.

Then, the screen dissolved to show Lorena boarding a huge private yacht. She was dressed for comfort and fun, wearing an Armani outfit designed by Giorgio himself. Striding a few feet behind her was Franklin, all decked out in Tommy Hilfiger. As the pair was ushered on board, Lorena saw a white bag being handed to Franklin. It contained cocaine, THC-enhanced marijuana and the latest in designer sex toys. "Have a great time!" smiled the ship's captain. It was Charles White, grinning as he clapped both Lorena and Franklin on the back.

Suddenly, an outside presence lightly touched Lorena's arm. "I'm here," a lilting voice called out, disrupting her dream state. "I finally made it," the far-off voice said, "Sorry I'm running late." Lorena turned and beheld her smiling twin. God had arrived on the scene and all was well.

"Did I miss anything?" She said.

43

The 7th Puzzle — God

It was a shock for Lorena to look across a table and see herself. It was like having a large mirror propped up in a facing chair.

I look good today, if I do say so.

"How are you, sweetheart?" God said. "You're looking good. The spiritual life must agree with you.

"Thank you," was all Lorena could muster.

It's not every day that God gives you a direct compliment, Lorena thought. It's a nice feeling.

"You know why we are here today," Spirit said, "I AM planning to share information about the 7th Puzzle of Life with you. That's Me, of course. Now we won't cover one-tenth of 1% of what there is to know about Me. At least it'll be a start. I also want to allow a few minutes at the end of our time together for questions. So, can we start again with a brief prayer?"

"Of course," the real estate woman answered.

"Thank you," Spirit said, bowing her head, "I'll do the honors today."

"Dear Me, please Bless Lorena. Help her be open and receptive to what she hears today. Also, please bless the world. Let it find repentance and salvation. May human beings discover the wonder of Me before their time runs out. Thank you Me, amen."

"Amen," Lorena echoed.

"Would you consider taking one question before we begin?", she asked.

"Of course," God answered. "Please go ahead and ask the one question burning in your brain. Why I would I even consider destroying the earth and every living thing? It's a fair question."

"Well?" Lorena said, awaiting the answer.

"First of all," God began, "You know things have gotten bad if I would even consider such a thing. I've disciplined nations, cultures and civilizations many times. The Old Testament recounts countless situations where I had to apply some punishment. Usually, the sinning involved general debauchery, political malfeasance and blatant idol worship. Of course, your world still has a lot of that still going on today. But things have now escalated in a different way. Your thought leaders regard Me as irrelevant. Technology and science have developed far beyond anything the world has ever experienced before. People are now usurping My divine role in the creation process. You are creating your own "beings". Notice that I didn't say "human beings". The essential part of any human being is his or her "soul". Science doesn't have a clue about how to create a "soul". However, the "soul" forms the essence of life itself. Without a "soul", a "being" can't "be". It can't love, feel, experience happiness and joy or even sadness and despair. The scientific soul has no compassion or empathy for anyone or anything. It's simply a piece of machinery. Do you want to know what a world filled without real souls would feel and look like? It's beyond comprehension. I don't mean that in a positive way. It would also eventually become dangerous for human beings. Artificial Intelligence robots could someday turn on their "masters". If that happens, look out! Real live humans could be at risk. The AI creation could destroy everything in its sight without any remorse or regret. It might become like a "Super Sociopath". I will not allow things to reach that point. We are now engaged in a final battle with the evil forces. What happens next could determine the fate of the planet and every living thing that I created to inhabit it. You are a part of that final reckoning."

"Even if the Solaster incinerates the world," Lorena observed, "You are still planning to take a human remnant to a new star. How will you decide who makes the final cut to go? I'm sure all the billionaires will try and buy a seat."

"Money will never decide who occupies your new home," God explained, "I will search the human heart of everyone residing on the planet before the end comes. I will choose only the purest souls. Anyone I select will possess a humble disposition dedicated to kindness and empathy for others. Of course, seating will be limited. However, I haven't decided on a precise number of spaces yet. I do have three places reserved for you and your parents. That is, if you choose to move forward with serving Me. I'm not trying to pressure or blackmail you, Lorena. You still have Free Will choice. I know the other side hasn't given up on capturing you yet."

"I just can't believe a benevolent God would destroy billions of people," Lorena persisted. "What could change your mind?"

"Well," God responded, "We'll see how the 7 Puzzles of Life are received. Your career in prophesy could impact that outcome. By the way, what did you think of the Lost Prophets group? I think they can play a role in waking people up. At any rate, I'm mildly hopeful that things will get reversed before the Solaster starts. Once the weapons of mass destruction begin igniting, it's too late."

"You say "mildly" hopeful," Lorena observed, "That doesn't sound too positive. I hope you remember there are millions and millions of good people in the world. They'll be cremated along with everybody else."

"I understand that," God said, "But I'm discouraged. I've tried to grab the world's attention with hurricanes, earthquakes and other natural disasters. The public notices them for a few days and then it's back to pornography, gambling, cheating, lying, smoking, snorting and disrespecting Me. That's not to mention the idol worshipping of money, fame, political power, and everything else you can imagine. After a natural disaster fades from the TV, its simply back to business as usual. When the Solaster destroys the entire planet, I AM rid of that negativity forever."

"You are saying that before you would allow evil to win, you would rather see everything destroyed? I have trouble grasping that concept."

"Yes, I AM saying that," Spirit acknowledged, "Evil is already winning. I want to reverse that.I would like for things to change. As you pointed out, there are millions of good human beings ready to take up arms against evil. They just need a sense of urgency."

"Of course, "Lorena argued, "on the new star, you'll still be dealing with human beings. How long do you think it will be before the same problems pop up again? People are still people."

"How well I know that," God replied, "The new star will be humankind's last chance at spiritual redemption. I'm planning to call it Omega. If the people of Omega cannot control themselves, my experiment with humankind is over. But I promise you that I will remain hopeful and positive until the end of human time. Now, this is all interesting, but maybe I should get started on explaining my basic Self to you before we run out of time. I'll begin by telling you something about Myself that you may not know."

"What's that?" Lorena inquired.

"Despite what you or anyone may think, I hear every prayer. I consider and process each prayer request. None of your prayers are ever wasted or ignored. Do you recall that Garth Brooks song: "Thank God for unanswered prayers?" There is a lot of truth in that. There are many more prayers unanswered than answered. However, you must understand that not answering a prayer is also an answer. I give you Free Will, but sometimes I have a vote too. I just don't want you or anyone to think I'm too busy to hear your every concern. Some people think "I don't want to bother God with my insignificant problems." Please hear Me: everyone is important in my eyes. That never changes while you are alive and walking the earth."

"Is there anything else that I should know about You?"

"Yes, there is something I need to share about you. It has to do with your "race". That is a hot button issue for many people. Racial tensions are always around. As an African American woman, you should know some important truths about "race". Not every race is created equal in spiritual potential. You've heard about past lives. Yes, you have lived before as a native American, as both a Caucasian man and woman, as an African native sold into slavery in the 1600s and even as a resident of Judea back in Jesus' time. You entered this incarnation as a black woman. This is My secret: I endowed the black race with an extremely high potential for spirituality. However, that can be both a blessing and a curse. You've always heard about "soul" as being an essential part of the black culture. That's true. But, because of your inherent spirituality, you are a tremendous target for the forces of evil. You have always been subject to prejudice. It's also no accident that violence has been a part of your cultural heritage. Incarceration is also prevalent among families in the African American community. The black family unit is always under attack by the forces of evil. They see your race as an existential threat to their hold on the world. Alcoholism and drug abuse have impacted countless black families. But, on the flip side, there is no greater example of spirituality than the black church. Most every sanctuary of black worship is filled with incredible spiritual power. Go into any African American church and My Presence lifts you off your feet. Yes, evil fears you. Your community will continue to be a target of their schemes. As I said, the principalities see you as an imminent challenge to its control over the material world. In the future, black spirituality will soar to new heights.It could be a bigtime factor in saving the world from destruction.That outcome rests on all races reclaiming their spiritual heritage. In the meantime, the "other side" has increased its attacks on the black community. Expect some ferocious spiritual warfare in the future."

"That's food for thought," Lorena said. "What else should I know about You as the 7th Puzzle of Life?"

"For humankind, the Principles of "Oneness" and "Separation" are key. Oneness means being "At-One" with Me, no matter what. Separation involves what Satan always seeks—a division of the spirit. The devil uses countless ways to split us apart. You name it, the other side has tried it. Worshipping anything material insures separation. Think about it! If you spend all your time working, drinking, drugging, smoking, gambling, sexting, chasing the almighty dollar, watching porn or playing video games 24/7, you are separating yourself from Me and My Kingdom. The material voices around you support you in squandering your spirituality on meaningless distractions. On the other hand, if you commit yourself to Oneness with Me, expect to get razzed and shamed. Family and friends may question your sanity. You'll see the "fun people" start to drop away from you. You'll find yourself alone more, perhaps even most of the time. Some people could tell you: "I liked you more before you went all churchy on us." You'll find that exceptionally true when it comes to your drinking and drugging buddies. Those "friends" drop away from you the quickest. Their implied criticism represents a subtle pressure to win you back to their side. It takes courage to stay on My Path when you begin losing people around you."

"Yes, I can see that," Lorena agreed.

"Most human beings don't understand the concept of placing your trust in something invisible," God told Lorena. "If you have a significant other, drive a fancy car or live in a beautiful home, people can see and comprehend those material things. For them, that's who you are. Telling your family, co-workers and friends that you worship something that you can't see, touch, feel, taste or even smell could make folks question your sanity. It's no joke, Lorena."Finding (and then keeping) Oneness with Me can be a hard thing to achieve."

"I don't know that I've ever experienced true Oneness with God," Lorena mused. "I'm not sure what that would feel like."

"Let Me remind you of the times when we have been aligned," God said. "Whenever you experienced a genuine feeling of love for somebody or something, you were At-One with Me. Anytime you felt inspiration of any kind, such as soul-enhancing music, you were in unison with Me. Oneness can be felt in a House of Worship when a choir sings a hymn or a speaker stirs you. Nature is a magnificent source of Oneness. A beautiful sunset on an ocean, lake or river can bring up feelings of closeness with Me. Standing on the top of a mountain and gazing at the sky above or a peaceful valley below can bring it on. The unconditional love of a beloved pet demonstrates the power of eternal closeness. There are countless opportunities around you to discover unity with Me. However, you must be open to becoming At-One with God. If you've separated yourself from Me for any reason, it could be a struggle. Many souls bounce back and forth between separation and Oneness. But I keep hoping for the day when unity with Me becomes your default choice."

"What else do I need to know about You?" Lorena inquired.

"One of the keys to understanding Me lies in a sacred book that mostly gathers dust on your shelf,"

"Are you talking about the Bible?", the real estate woman guessed.

"Absolutely," God replied, "The Bible is My Holy Word. It offers priceless wisdom, interesting stories, timeless inspiration, needed comfort and examples of courage, strength, wisdom and fortitude by both men and women. The Bible also includes explicit warnings that must be heeded. That's the part that most people want to skip. The cautionary tales about disobeying Me are something that human beings do not want to hear. Denial is a common human character flaw. We've talked about the Old Testament retribution that consumed the idol-worshippers. It's all true. But the real key in saving the world lies in the words and teachings of the New Testament. There is one specific book in the New Testament that demands constant study and understanding. No, it's not the book of Revelations. Nor is it located in the letters of Paul, as important as they are. The most crucial writings in the New Testament can be found in the Gospel of John, the disciple that Jesus loved."

"Why is that?" Lorena questioned.

"First of all, John is different from the other three Gospels. I referred to John as "the Disciple that Jesus loved". There was a special bond between John and The Master. John informs us about five specific miracles not mentioned in Matthew, Mark or Luke. He also reveals mystical information about Jesus' relationship with Me. The key observation can be found in John 10:30. Jesus says: "I and the Father are one." Several times, Jesus emphasizes that God is in every person. In John 14:40, the Christ repeats: "I AM in the Father and the Father is in Me." Most humans picture Me sitting up in Heaven on a throne. Nothing could be further from the truth. Yes, I AM both a Transcendent and Immanent God. I AM both above and within. I reside at the core of every human being that walks the earth. Since I live inside you, I can dispense My Grace through you by way of the Holy Spirit. I give you the ability to heal, encourage and uplift others. I can make you a spreader of hope and peace. I do miracles in and through you. The Book of John explains it all. I want you to use this book in your work as a Prophet for Me."

"So, you do see Me as a Prophet?" Lorena observed. "I'm just not sure I see myself in the same way."

"I have full confidence in your ability to prophesize," Spirit said. "You have visionary capabilities far beyond what you imagine. Please remember that you do not do the work. The Holy Spirit within you does the work. I speak and act through you to accomplish My goals for the world. Now, I just have only a couple more things that I need to share before we wrap up today. It only requires a couple more minutes."

"Certainly," Lorena said, "I'm listening."

"Here is the first thing you should know about Me: I will never leave or forsake you. Once you are mine, I AM yours as well. Then, you can move onward and upward, unafraid of anybody or anything in the material world. I provide every resource you require to accomplish My Work."

"And?" Lorena asked.

"I always love and accept you, no matter what."

Lorena closed her eyes, bowed her head and murmured softly "Thank you, God."

When she looked up, her twin had disappeared. Lorena glanced at her watch. As Seth predicted, time had stood still.

44

Media

Seth the Angel requested a meeting for the following day.

"We need to talk about your media interviews," he texted her. "Plus," he added, "I would like to set up a new Twitter account for you under a different name than your own. We need something more up to date, like "#dongdonker" or "#peniswhomper". I think a more descriptive handle will increase your number of followers."

While Lorena felt somewhat offended, she could see Seth's reasoning.

Social media is one strange place, she thought to herself. It's a different world and I'm not sure I understand it.

The angel was waiting when she arrived, decked out from head to foot in Ralph Lauren.

"What happened to you?" she asked, "Did you have a session with your "Polo" rep? You look spiffy."

"I must be cool when I'm out there representing you to the media," he stated, "Oprah's producers won't talk to anyone that doesn't look awesome".

"Were you able to book me on her Sunday spiritual show yet?" Lorena asked. "I hope my beating up of Franklin's manhood isn't the only angle."

"You have to understand," Seth explained, "That whacking is your claim to fame. You'll need a big-time platform to get your other points across. If I tried to get you on as a "prophet", I wouldn't get to second base."

"What else do you have for me?" Lorena asked, "Anything on "The Today Show", "CBS This Morning", "Fox and Friends" or "Good Morning America?"

"No, not yet," the angel responded, "But we do have our choice of podcasts. There is also a porn site that wants to interview you."

"Absolutely not," Lorena huffed, "I don't want to do anything raunchy that my folks might see."

"You may want to reconsider," Seth cautioned her, "The porn show has higher ratings than most of the cable and even some network shows. They're also offering to pay you 5K for a solo interview or 10K if you can convince Franklin to go on with you."

"Franklin!" Lorena exclaimed, "I never want to see him again."

"You might want to reconsider that stance," Seth said, "But let's not get into it right now. Now, can we quickly go over the talking points for any show that books you?"

"Sure," she said.

"God and I want you to focus more on "The 7 Puzzles of Life" and less about the "Solaster". Nobody wants to hear about the earth getting pulled into the sun. Getting yourself tagged for cremation for buying an extra lottery ticket or smoking a little weed seems a bit harsh. If you get defined as a nutcase, that destroys your overall credibility. People will tune you out. We need to go a bit lighter on the heavy stuff for now. Please hear me, Lorena: God wants you to stir people up. Just do it slowly. Let them get used to the idea of a disaster on the horizon."

"Am I getting any criticism on social media so far?" Lorena inquired.

"Of course," Seth informed her, "I've already counted 39 death threats. All, except one, are from men. Not many guys enjoy seeing what you did to Franklin. Some people view him as an innocent victim. On the other hand, you've received thousands of "Attagirls". You've also been nominated for various women's groups awards. I even received one serious query about a possible "Made-for-Streaming" movie. The working title is "I Clobbered His Junk". Don't laugh. They have a couple of real-live female movie stars who want to play you. I'm going to hold out for "The Lorena Mae Johnson Story" as the title. That would give you some identification and credibility. If the streaming project jells, we should be able to book you anywhere. Speaking of "book", several agents want you to consider writing a book. They say it would be an easy sell to publishers."

"I guess it all sounds good," Lorena said. "Just know that I still might back out of everything. I don't think my real estate bosses would be OK with this idea. By the way, what about saying that God asked me to become a prophet? That really seems far out."

"I would downplay that for now," Seth advised. "Maybe you could say that defending yourself against Franklin somehow made you feel more spiritual. I don't know. Again, we just don't want anybody writing you off as a fruitcake. At least, not yet."

"Am I going to be targeted for any more spiritual attacks in the near future?" Lorena inquired. "I would appreciate a heads-up."

"I wasn't going to bring this up, but since you asked," Seth said, "Don't you have an annual physical with your gynecologist later today?"

"Dr. Williams?" Lorena asked in a surprised tone. "How did you know about that?"

"We received the top-secret alert yesterday," the angel said. "You had some lab work done last week. We got the results the same time as Dr. Williams."

"So?" Lorena asked.

"Are you sure that you want to hear it from me and not your doc?"

"Now you're scaring me," Lorena observed, "What is it?"

"You're pregnant," the messenger angel announced.

"Oh, My God," Lorena shrieked.

"That's not all," the angel said.

"What else?"

"You're having twins."

45

Doctor Williams

For the second time ever, the real estate saleswoman learned the meaning of the cliched phrase: "time stood still". Lorena's heart leaped straight into her throat. She was shocked, speechless and barely able to function.

After leaving the angel, Lorena placed an immediate call to the office of Dr. Margaret Williams.

"I can't wait until this afternoon for my appointment," she told the receptionist. "I'm coming in now. Please work me in."

The drive to the doctor's office was blurred. She could barely breathe.

This must be a mistake, she thought. A double-sized one. Franklin was my only sexual partner in the last two years. Please God, don't let this be happening.

She was ushered in to see Dr. Williams within five minutes of her arrival.

"How did you hear about the results of your test?" the doctor asked. "We just got everything back yesterday. Do you have a contact in the lab or what?"

"With all due respect, you don't need to know," Lorena said. "Are you sure? Could there be a mistake? I've only had sex one time in the past two years."

"For what it's worth, I'm surprised too," Dr. Williams said. "I didn't remember you being involved with anyone. Do I know the father?"

"I barely know him," Lorena answered.

"Was he the dude that you wailed with the broom?" Dr. Williams asked.

"Yes," Lorena confirmed, "I forgot that you might have seen that. I'm so embarrassed."

"I did see it, along with a couple million other people. I must say your boyfriend gave a whole new meaning to the phrase "big one"."

"I don't what to say," Lorena offered, "Could your lab be wrong?"

"It sometimes happens," Dr. Williams said. "Right now, all I can tell you is that the lab results confirm that you're pregnant. Unless someone provided the wrong sample, I don't know what else to say. Would anybody want you to think you're having twins? Even if they did, I don't know how they could have faked the sample?

"How far along am I?" Lorena inquired.

"A little more than six weeks," the doctor replied. "I'm sure it's too soon for you to think about your options. You just found out. But there is something else you need to know. Now, Lorena, I want you to take a deep breath before you hear what I'm going to tell you. Ordinarily, I would recommend you wait until nine weeks before doing an ultrasound. However, I think we should do one right away. I'm talking about this week."

"Why is that?

"It might even be triplets."

Maybe I should act surprised, Lorena thought.

"Jeez, Lorena," Dr. Williams said, "You don't seem surprised. You must really have some good contacts that gave you a heads up."

Lorena did not recall much more of the visit, except the scheduling of the ultrasound for the following day.

OMG, she thought while staggering out of the doctor's office. How much more of this crap can I take?

46

Lorena's Lament

Lorena couldn't sleep. She laid on top of her bed and stared straight up at the ceiling. Then, she uttered the common cry sent heavenward from millions of people over the years:

"Why me, LORD?" she called out, "Why have you forsaken me?"

Her cell phone rang. She saw that Seth was calling.

For a second, Lorena thought about not answering.

Oh well, she thought, maybe he could offer me some spiritual insight.

"God heard your prayer and asked me to call you," he said. "Bummer, huh?"

"Big-time bummer," she replied. "Why did God allow this to happen?"

"Some things are just mysteries," the angel responded. "It's above my pay grade. I feel for you. I want you to know that."

"What does this do to my work as a 'prophet'? I don't see doing much prophesying while I'm nursing twins or triplets. I just don't understand it, Seth. What should I do now?"

"How did your lunch with God go?" Seth asked, changing the subject.

"O. K. I guess," Lorena responded, "Why didn't God mention this to me? I'm sure She must have known about it."

"You would think," Seth agreed, "However, some things are just mysterious. I do know that Spirit never leaves or forsakes us under any circumstance. You can always find comfort in embracing that Truth, no matter what happens to you."

"I don't feel like embracing anything right now," she said."I guess abortion is a possibility. It might even be a probability. I have never considered it as an option before because this is a new situation for me. Ordinarily, I would be against it. Now, I don't know what to think."

"It's a hard decision for many people," the angel observed, "Others not so much. Having the "right to choose" dovetails nicely with Free Will choice, which is a gift from God. I know that God places the soul component into the fetus at conception. So, an aborted soul returns to Heaven basically unused. A lot of work goes into creating the life journey for any soul. I think God cries when the process gets short-circuited. So much can be lost. Maybe one of those aborted souls could have cured cancer. Perhaps another might save the planet from destruction. Still, I must be honest, I understand the other side. There is nothing sadder than an unwanted child."

"I'll just have to think about it," Lorena said. "This news only happened a few hours ago. It takes some getting used to the idea. And, as for the father being Franklin, that just adds a whole new negative aspect. Of all people, he would be the last person I would choose as the father of my baby or babies in this case."

"I don't disagree with you," Seth said. "Now, you asked earlier about whether this changes your spiritual call. Absolutely not. It just poses another challenge to surmount."

"I'm about surmounted out," Lorena lamented.

"May I make a suggestion?" the angel asked.

"Of course. What do you have in mind?"

"I'm sending you all of the "Puzzles" tomorrow. Why don't you go to work on the "Family" Puzzle? Maybe that will give you some extra insight into everything. I don't see that it could hurt."

"Right now, I'm open to anything. Oh Seth, I'm so discouraged."

"Let me share an insight with you," the angel said, "You are experiencing almost non-stop spiritual attacks, culminating in the one today."

"Yes, and I want it stopped!" Lorena interrupted.

"That's one way to see it," Seth acknowledged. "But let me offer another perspective. God wants you to develop complete faith and trust in Her. If you never had any challenges, you would lose the chance to practice faith and trust. "Trouble" eventually finds every human being. Getting through the "bad" times takes a strong belief in God's Grace. You could look at any problem as God's way of making you into the finest steel. Spirit is basically preparing you to handle anything the devil may throw at you. Your pregnancy might be part of your "basic training" for the spiritual life."

"If that's true, it's pretty tough training," Lorena nodded. "I think I'm ready to wash out. I can't handle much more. I hope you or God won't judge me too harshly if I beg off this whole thing. There must be somebody else out there who can do a better job than me."

"Don't give up just yet," Seth advised, "Pray about it. Have faith. Trust God to help you over the hump. You've come this far."

"I hear you," Lorena said.

"Besides," the angel concluded, "I just got you booked on Oprah's Sunday show".

47

The Puzzles Arrive

The Fed Ex truck had just pulled away when Lorena arrived back at home the following day. As Seth had promised, there was a large package containing the Puzzle boxes that she did not yet have.

This is exciting, she thought to herself. This also gives me something to think about other than the news I got from Dr. Williams yesterday.

As she tore open the main package, Lorena could see that Seth had sent the complete set. Each of the seven Puzzle boxes had a bright and colorful cover. As promised, they were labeled "Free Will," "Family", "Love, "Work", "Spiritual Service", "Death" and "God". There was also a note on each box that said "365 pieces". Lorena plopped the main box next to her dining room table. She figured the table would probably accommodate one puzzle. She noticed that the size of the puzzle itself was about 24 by 30 inches, a bit larger than most. The pieces themselves also seemed bigger.

I'm going to do the "Family" puzzle first, as Seth suggested. Maybe I can unravel more about what will happen with my pregnancy.

Lorena surveyed the "Family" box cover. The first thing she noticed were the sharp and dazzling colors. She examined the cover more closely. There were several recognizable scenes. Some were photographs, others were done in a stylized or artist's rendering. "Panorama" was the word that flashed across Lorena's brain.

As she began sorting out the pieces, Lorena could discern some of the images. A few were familiar, while others seemed obscure and even confusing. On the box cover, she could make out a line drawing that resembled federal agent's Tim Dahling's face. Another, more photographic look, featured Lorena's mother and father. It showed them on their wedding day. One image intrigued Lorena immediately. It was a happy teenage girl, smiling at the camera.

I've met her before, Lorena concluded.

The real estate woman searched the box cover for any sign of "twins" or even triplets, but none was evident. She did spy a small photo of her bosses, Peter and Sallye. In a way, they were her "work" family. Lorena also found several scenes from her childhood. One triggered a memory of a family outing at a beach amusement park. Lorena had ridden the roller coaster that day with her parents. Everyone looked happy, which was how she remembered the event. There was an artist's rendering of a birthday party depicting her blowing out 13 candles. There were also two smaller photographs of each of her two husbands. Neither of those reminders triggered much emotion for Lorena. The dominant image on the cover was a bright red heart. To Lorena, the heart image signified 'LOVE". It looked large, healthy, and harmonious. It radiated the love she felt for her family.

If I had to use one word to describe my "family" experience, she thought, it would be "love". I feel so blessed to have been a part of it. I know many people struggle with their family of origin. That wasn't true in my case. I still love and appreciate my family. I would be more than devastated to lose either my mom or dad. I know that will happen someday, but I'm not ready for it yet.

She noticed an artist rendering that depicted a panel of street addresses. Lorena recognized them as places she had once lived, either with her parents, husbands or alone. There were also a couple of addresses on the panel that she did not recognize.

Could these be places where I might be living sometime in the future, she wondered. One looks especially intriguing: "4484 Cheyenne Mountain Road." I wonder if that could have anything to do with Colorado Springs or Pike's Peak?

One thing that startled Lorena was the timeliness of the "FAMILY" cover design. Some things in the puzzle were quite recent, such as meeting agent Tim Dahling. For such an elaborate print job, she would have thought more time would have been required. Yet, it all seemed so current.

Lorena turned the box upside down and emptied the 365 pieces onto a plain white covering atop the dining room table. She purposely searched the unattached pieces to locate anything resembling "twins". She found nothing.

She also searched for anything about Franklin in the puzzle pieces. There was no trace of him.

That's a good sign, she thought to herself.

Lorena was about to plunge ahead with the "FAMILY" puzzle, when she noticed an instruction sheet. It had fluttered out of the box and onto the floor when she dumped the pieces on the table. It read:

BEFORE BEGINNING THIS PUZZLE

YOU ARE ENCOURAGED TO SPEND

A MINIMUM OF FIFTEEN MINUTES

IN SILENT MEDITATION. PLEASE

ASK FOR THE GUIDANCE OF YOUR

HIGHER POWER IN PUTTING THIS

PUZZLE TOGETHER. THANK YOU.

That absolutely makes sense, Lorena thought.

She bowed her head and said this prayer:

My LORD, I seek your divine guidance in

exploring this puzzle about Family. Please

fill my mind and heart with your wisdom

and insight. Thank you, God. Amen.

As Lorena lapsed into meditation, the still, small voice of God filled her consciousness:

I AM here, closer than your hands and feet

I AM in you, as you are in Me

I AM the Holy Spirit living in your midst

I AM the Light that illuminates your Path

I will guide you

Trust Me

I want only the best for you.

When Lorena opened her eyes, she glanced at her watch. She had been in meditation for 35 minutes.

I should be more than ready to tackle anything, she thought.

Lorena worked on the puzzle for more than an hour without a break. She found a few pieces that showed her pushing a pink baby stroller. It only accommodated one baby. Lorena and the baby were both dressed for warmth.

I wonder if we are living somewhere up in the mountains, she mused.

Then, a strange thought came out of nowhere.

Could I be living on another, colder planet or star? Hmmm

Lorena kept working on the Family puzzle. There was one drawing of a large and fierce looking Native American woman. She looked like a warrior, with piercing black eyes.

Does this woman look strong! I wouldn't want to be on her bad side.

There was another unfamiliar image of a woman in Biblical times, standing by a well. There was also the face of a bearded man. The face was positioned in an elevated fashion, overlooking the woman as if he might be advising or protecting her. The woman appeared thoughtful and appreciative.

Could one of my ancestors have been "the woman at the well"? Lorena questioned. That's an intriguing possibility.

Spurred on by what she was seeing, Lorena continued working on the "FAMILY" puzzle. Again, she checked her watch. Another two hours had passed.

It's time for me to hit the sack, she thought. I have a feeling that tomorrow could be an interesting day.

48

A Busy Day

Lorena began her day by meeting with Seth on their bench. She had expected a brief session before heading into the office. However, Seth looked much too comfortable in his walking shorts for a quick get-together.

Uh-oh, she thought, he must have something on his mind.

"I've got something on my mind." The angel confirmed. "First of all, both God and I think it's great that you started the "Family" puzzle. How did you find it?"

"I liked it," she responded, "I can see how that puzzle could be helpful to someone trying to figure out how "family" fits into his or her life."

"That's good," Seth said. "Now, the main reason I'm here today is that Spirit felt some things were left unsaid at your meeting with Her yesterday."

"Like what?"

"She asked me to go over four things with you," the angel said. "This is important because any of them could come up in your interview with Oprah or someone else in the media. Some things you may have heard before, but they bear repeating again."

"Go ahead," Lorena nodded, "I'm listening."

"First of all, God is always God. That means whoever you are, wherever you may live or what religion you might practice, God is God. You may call your Higher Power names like Jesus Christ, Allah, Confucius, the Buddha, Dharma or whatever. God still functions as the Supreme Being. Spirit reigns as the One Power and One Presence in the universe and in your life. The essence of God, known as the Holy Spirit, is strategically positioned at your core. This is the "soul". Everything spiritual dwells in either your mind, soul or both. The second thing is this: Absolutely nothing happens without God's direct or indirect involvement. There are no accidents in the spiritual universe. However, that doesn't mean God causes bad things to happen. Remember Free Will Choice? Spirit wants you to understand Its pivotal role in everybody's life, whether they acknowledge Him or not. Thirdly, God doesn't punish people for being human and making mistakes. She, or He, loves and accepts everybody. You can never say, do or be anything that will cause God to reject you. You bring punishment on yourself by negative choices and behavior. Some people call it "karma", others say you "reap what you sew." God understands that people are just people. He created human beings. He understands and forgives them for the sins of "error" and "missing the mark". Everyone possesses the capability of acting out of a sinful nature. The last thing is this: God does not persecute any one person or any one race. In fact, Spirit detests spiritual or religious persecution of any kind. God does not tolerate or condone bigotry, racism or anti-Semitism in any form. God detests anyone or any nation using "religion" as an excuse for their evil deeds. Right now, the material world has lost favor with Spirit for many reasons. God feels disrespected by idol worship and a sudden desire to usurp His divine function of creating human life. In terms that perhaps human beings can understand better, the world has gotten "too big for its britches". Thus, discipline must be applied. The people of the earth are living on borrowed time. It's their choice as to how things play out from here on. However, God doesn't see His justice as being "persecution" per se. It's just karmic and spiritual law in action."

"Wow," Lorena said, "That's a lot of information."

"You and the other prophets have a big job ahead of you. Addictions are rampant and getting worse. Distractions are everywhere. Pornography, video gaming, gambling, pot smoking, misuse of pain killers and recreational drugs are making things much harder for those who want to reverse their spiritual decline. Countless obsessions also slow people down. For example, many people are obsessed about sports of any kind. That wouldn't ordinarily be a bad thing, if other things were equal. But they are not. Politics has become another obsession. Trust me, it constitutes one of the most amoral endeavors imaginable. Political temptation can corrupt anyone. Are things hopeless? Personally, I believe human beings are capable of change. They possess a great ability to overcome adversity. People are generally smart, tough and resilient. They can come back from the depths of anything if they choose to do so. However, the material world is struggling right now. Just maybe, with the help of you and the other prophets, you make it through. In your media appearances, God wants you to emphasize the positive. God wants you to talk about "Hope". Spirit isn't advocating that people give up on surviving this crisis. If there is life, there is hope."

"Is that all?" Lorena asked. "That all sounds daunting."

"Yes," the angel said, "That's all for now. I believe in you, Lorena Mae. So does God. That counts for a lot. I hope you choose the right path. The world is counting on you to do the right thing. Somewhere in the world tonight, a fellow human being is praying for a savior. That could be you."

49

Real Estate Showdown

Lorena did not even ask the receptionist if Sallye wanted to see her. She just headed straight back to her boss's office. A perturbed Charles White was seated across from Sallye. This time he did not look happy.

"What's wrong?" Lorena asked.

"We just don't know what to make of you," Sallye stated with a frown. "You've gone back and forth on these major real estate listings. One minute you're in. Then you're out. Now we are hearing that you've gone and gotten yourself pregnant!Can you tell us what the hell is going on, Lorena? We don't know you anymore. Mr. White is a patient man. He showed you that in our last meeting. We thought everything was back on track. Now he just doesn't know what to think."

"I'm confused, Lorena," Mr. White agreed.

"How did you know I was pregnant?" Lorena inquired.

"Reggie dropped by yesterday and laid the information on us," Sallye frowned again. "Evidently he and your baby's father Franklin are friends. So, yes, we found out about it. When were you planning to tell us?"

"I just learned I was pregnant myself," Lorena stated, "I didn't think that Franklin even knew about it. I guess there aren't any secrets."

"It's not any of my business," Sallye observed, "But do you plan to keep the baby?"

"You mean the twins?"

"What!", Sallye and Mr. White exclaimed in unison.

"Yes, it appears that I'm having twins. Maybe even triplets. Franklin must be one potent dude. That's good for him, not so much for me."

"Well, I never," Sallye sputtered.

"And, no, I haven't decided yet what I'll do about keeping them. It's a big decision. Since they are twins, I wouldn't want to split them up."

"Well, Lorena," Mr. White chipped in, "If you decide to keep the babies, you'll need to support them. Need I remind you that those big commissions would go a long way toward doing just that."

"I'm sure that's true," Lorena acknowledged.

"Besides all of that," Sallye piped up, "What the hell is going on with these TV appearances about the 17 Puzzles of Life or whatever it is? I hear you're scheduled on Oprah's show Sunday after next. With you, I don't know whether I'm coming or going."

"Neither do I", Lorena agreed.

"Let me ask you straight," Sallye continued, "Do you really believe that business about the sun swallowing up the earth? If so, I guess that's the end of the real estate business."

"And everything else too," Mr. White added.

"I'm just the messenger," Lorena said defensively. "I'm hoping that it won't happen. I'm trying to help turn things around."

"Will that be a full-time job?" Sallye asked sarcastically, "Or do you plan on doing a little real estate now and then?"

"Saving the world sounds like a pretty big job," Mr. White observed, "Maybe I should take my real estate listings somewhere else."

Just then the receptionist burst into the office. She looked startled.

"We've got to get out right now!" she shouted.

"What's the matter," Sallye said, jumping to her feet. "You're acting as though the place is on fire!"

"It is!" the receptionist yelled.

50

Spiritual Attacks

Two large firetrucks with about a dozen firemen, local police and Sheriff's Department officers, EMT crews and other first responders flooded the street outside of the real estate office. Investigators were to later determine that the fire originated from some ancient aluminum wiring that had melted down and ignited. The old wiring had been overlooked when new copper wiring had been installed four decades ago. The building itself was more than 50 years old.

Hours after the fire had been extinguished, parts of the damaged area still smoldered. Peter and Sallye busied themselves consulting with insurance reps and comforting other agents and employees. Even a small fire can be extremely disruptive, the assistant fire chief told them.

Lorena wandered around discussing the unexpected blaze with her co-workers. Mr. White had departed, with no final resolution of the four listings. He promised to contact them soon.

As White had headed to his car, he turned to Sallye and admonished her for Lorena's indecision. "That young lady needs to get with the program," he said gruffly, "I've lost my patience with her. The clock is ticking. Is she in or out?"

Sallye took Peter aside as they consoled each other about the fire.

"Maybe we should just go ahead and let Lorena go," Sallye told her husband, "She seems unhinged. Her nuttiness could damage our reputation. I had a call this week from a client who heard Lorena being interviewed on the radio. He said that she sounded like a first-class nutcase."

"I hear you," Peter agreed, "I've been waiting for her to get past this Bible-thumping phase, but things keep getting worse. Ever since she got some notoriety from slamming that guy's business, things haven't been the same. I agree with you. If this keeps up, our reputation might take a hit. Maybe we should give her an official warning to cover our asses. You know how every personnel decision, especially involving a minority, must be documented. I don't want her suing us on top of everything else."

"Giving her a warning sounds like a good plan," Sallye agreed. "As soon as things calm down, let's move on it. I'm sorry things haven't worked out. Lorena had big-time potential before becoming a religious wingnut."

Although Lorena was standing some distance from her bosses, she saw they were engaged in an animated discussion. She could tell they were talking about her.

I'm sure it's about me, she thought to herself. They're probably disgusted with my flakiness. I've got to get things straight with myself as well. Do I have what it takes to serve God on a big stage? More importantly, do I want to do it? I'm really mixed up. All I really wanted to do was sell houses and make money. How did I ever get caught up in this mess?

Her cell rang. She saw the ID as "Mom".

"Oh, Lorena, I'm glad I caught you," her mother said.

"You won't believe what just happened at the office," Lorena said, "We had an electrical fire. No one got hurt, thank God. Everybody made it out. We have some smoke and water damage on the inside, but I'm OK. Where are you?"

"That's why I'm calling. Now don't get excited, honey, but your father experienced some chest pains this morning. I called the doctor and he said to call 9-1-1. So, I did. They took him straight to the ER. That's where I am now. They did some tests as soon as he arrived. I haven't gotten any results yet. Please don't worry, honey. He's strong. I'm sure he'll be fine."

OMG, Lorena thought. What else can happen?

"I'm on my way," she told her mother.

51

Doctor John

When Lorena arrived at the hospital, she went first to the General Information desk to inquire about her father. He was still listed at the ER, but that was in the process of changing. In fact, his room number in the Cardiac Care Unit was now becoming available.

"Has my father been moved yet to CCU?" she asked the registration clerk.

"They're getting him ready to go now," the clerk said, "You might catch him in the ER first, if you head straight over there now. Or, you can meet him in his room in Cardiac Care. It's up to you."

Lorena didn't want to wait. She walked briskly toward the ER. As she rounded a corner, she came face to face with Franklin. Garbed in an auxiliary-type uniform, he was transporting a patient to another location.

They spied each other about the same time and the shock was mutual.

"Lorena!" he exclaimed, grazing the wall with the patient's gurney.

"Hey, buddy, watch out," the surprised patient called out in an irritated voice.

"I'm sorry, sir," Franklin apologized.

Then, over his shoulder, he called back to Lorena, "I'll see you later!"

The encounter only lasted a few seconds and Lorena had not said a word to the expectant father of her babies.

I can't believe it, Lorena thought to herself, I thought things were weird before. What the hell is he doing here?

When Lorena arrived at the ER, she was directed to her dad's location. Clad in a white gown, he was sitting on the side of the bed. Lorena's mother greeted her daughter with a hug.

"Well, this is a big surprise," her dad said with a smile.

"And not a good one," Lorena said, "How are you feeling?"

Her mother answered for him.

"He's doing fine," she said, "The tests are inconclusive, but they think it could have been a TIA or mini-stroke.We'll know more in a couple of hours. Right now, he needs to get over to CCU where he can rest."

"Good luck with that," Lorena observed, "The hospital is the last place for getting any rest. Does he have a heart doc assigned yet? If so, could we speak with him?"

"I'm not sure about a specific doctor," her mother said, "I think you must be in your room first."

Just then, the curtain in her dad's ER space parted. Lorena saw a tall African American man clad in a doctor's smock. Her heart took an instantaneous and unexpected leap upward.

Now that's what I call a good-looking guy, she thought.

"I'm Dr. John Wilson," he announced, "I'll be handling Mr. Johnson's care after he gets to CCU. But I wanted to come by and say hello now."

He extended his hand directly toward Lorena and flashed a warm and friendly smile.

"I'm John," he said.

"Yes, that's what you said," she responded, "I'm Lorena."

"I already knew that," he said teasingly.

"How is that?" she asked with surprise.

"Well, for one thing, you and I have a mutual friend. He speaks quite highly of you. I can see why after meeting you."

"A mutual friend?" Lorena inquired, "Who would that be?"

"Seth", the doc answered, "He's the neatest guy. What a character! He's a real stitch. Don't you think so?"

52

John And Lorena

Before asking the doctor how he knew Seth, Lorena wanted to inquire about her dad's medical condition.

"How is he doing?" she asked.

"Your father should be out of the hospital this weekend," Doctor John said. "He probably experienced a TIA. I expect a complete recovery. He'll need some anti-clotting medications. I believe blood thinners will handle the problem. I think this episode was probably a blessing. Anyway, I'll put together a plan for what he needs to do. I'm not sure yet what it all may involve. However, as I said, your dad may have avoided something much worse. God was looking out for him."

"Speaking of God," Lorena said, "What's the story? How do you know Seth?"

"Let me finish up about your father," the doc said, "I won't be following him going forward. I'm wrapping up my residency here. I've accepted a position at a new hospital in Colorado Springs. I'll be the #2 cardio guy, which is a nice little gig. I'm looking forward to being in the mountains. I'm a Connecticut guy and went to Yale pre-med and medical school. I've spent most of my life on the East Coast. I love the outdoors, so Colorado should be like heaven on earth for me."

OMG, Lorena thought, there's Colorado Springs coming up again. Is there something going on here? This is spooky.

"How close will you be to Pike's Peak?" she asked.

"The hospital is about seven miles from the Peak's entrance, so not far," John replied. "I'm going to be staying at a nearby hotel my first few weeks, until my condo is finished. The hotel is right next door to Cheyenne Mountain. I'm a little bit excited about it all. Do you know the Rockies?"

Only in my dreams, Lorena felt like saying.

"Well, I'm sure my father will miss not having you as his lead doc," Lorena said.

"Oh, I think your dad will be perfectly fine," Doctor John replied, "There are some terrific "heart" people here. I think he still has some mileage left on him. However, this was a warning shot across his bow. He needs to take care of himself."

Lorena was still thinking about seeing Pike's Peak in her "Family" puzzle, when the doc lightly touched her arm.

"Say," he said, "I'm wrapping up my rounds in about 20 minutes. Can I buy you a cup of coffee? There's something I want to ask you about."

"What's that?" Lorena inquired. "If it's about our mutual friend Seth, I'm still interested in how you know him."

Lorena and John decided to fetch their coffee from a nearby vending machine. They then found a private lounge area.

"I can finish my rounds in a few minutes," he said, "I have a feeling this could be an important conversation."

"Me too," she said, "What did you want to ask me about?"

"I'm not sure you've begun working on any of the 7 Puzzles of Life yet," he said, "But I've already started on "The Family". I found some interesting things. And they might involve you. There is somebody on my box cover that looks just like you. And then I meet you today. It's kind of strange!"

Lorena's heart jumped into her throat again. No kidding, she thought.

"I worked on "The Family" last night too," she said, "And I saw someone who resembles you. I'm assuming you were introduced to the Puzzles by our mutual friend Seth?"

"Yes, that's right," the doctor said. "I really haven't gotten many pieces put together yet. But I can see your face already forming. That tells me we might be seeing each other again in the future. What do you think?"

"It could be," she acknowledged, "I don't know. How did you meet Seth?"

"He came to the hospital asking for me about a month ago. I thought he was strange at first. But I've been dabbling in spiritual things for a while now, so I was receptive. I agree that the outside world has gone crazy. It's affecting many people physically, mentally, and emotionally. I see it here at the clinic every day. People are lost spiritually. I'm also a Bible reader, so I know about the Old Testament judgments. I'm especially interested in the book of Revelations. I think I've seen the Four Horsemen of the Apocalypse circling around the earth for some time now. So, I guess you might say that I was open to what Seth was saying. How about you?"

"I honestly didn't know what to think," she said. "Unlike you, I haven't been on any kind of spiritual "Path". I rarely ever go to church. My folks aren't especially religious.This all came out of the blue for me. Seth stopped me one day as I was coming into work. He offered to pay off my car. I owed about $8,500, so I listened to his pitch. Then, I started having some bad things happen to me. Attacks of one kind or another began occurring. Some of them haven't been pleasant. To tell you the truth, I'm a little freaked out."

"I saw the beat down you gave that dude's private parts when he attacked you," the doc commented, "Good for you."

"By the way," she said, "He works at your hospital. I just ran into him about half an hour ago."

"My God," Doctor John exclaimed, "What does he do here?"

"He transports patients," she returned, "You might watch out for him. He's bad news."

"Maybe I should alert security or HR," he said. "Do you think he's part of your spiritual attacks?"

"Absolutely!" Lorena exclaimed, "However, I can't prove anything. What else did Seth tell you?"

"Well, if God follows through on the Solaster threat, I guess I'll be taking a road trip to the new star or planet. Are you on the manifest too?"

"As far as I know, I am. In the meantime, I've been tapped for some "prophecy" work. I'll be a guest on Oprah in a couple of weeks. If I start talking about the world coming to an end, I'll be labeled as a mental case. I don't look forward to that. I'll try to be honest though. Sometimes I waver back and forth. I just don't feel adequate for what God and Seth want me to do. What about you?"

"They haven't really assigned me any particular job," he noted. "If I'm in the new place, I'll probably be a doctor taking care of people. That's all I know."

"How do you feel about that?" she asked.

"For now, I'm trusting that God knows what He or She is doing. I'm not surprised that His patience finally ran out with this crazy world. I do think it's sad that all the beautiful things and innocent people would die. I suppose a Solaster won't be sparing anybody or anything."

"I want to try and convince God to spare the world," Lorena said. "I don't know if I can pull it off, but I'm going to give it a shot."

"I can't believe God would go to such extremes," Doctor John said. "If you want, please count me in on your idea of stopping the Solaster. There are so many great and loving people in the world. I see them every day at the hospital. I would hate to think about losing anyone, especially the children. That would be a real tragedy."

"Are we sitting here plotting against God?" Lorena asked. "Remember, Seth and God already know everything. We're both probably toast already."

"By the way," the doctor noted, "in my family Puzzle, I see one nice thing."

"What's that?"

"I think you and I could someday be the proud parents of a lovely daughter," he smiled, "And she looks just like you."

53

Problems

As she was preparing for work the next day, Lorena's cell phone went off. A text was coming in. She quickly checked and saw that it was from her angel friend.

"Meet me before work, but not at the bench," Seth texted. There's too much activity around your office because of the fire. I'll see you at Starbucks. Order me a Blonde Americana if you get there before me."

Sure enough, Lorena arrived early so she was able to place Seth's order along with her own. A regular tall dark roast sounded perfect to her today.

"What's so important?" she asked the angel in a somewhat irritated voice.

Seth seemed almost annoyed by her impatience.

"What's going on with you?" he asked. "I thought you had a good visit with your folks at the hospital yesterday. Isn't your dad OK?"

He didn't mention a thing about my meeting Doctor John, Lorena noticed.

"Plus, I'm glad you and the handsome doc finally had a chance to meet," Seth added, "What did you think of John?"

Oh-kay, she thought to herself. I wonder if he knows anything about the two of us plotting against God to foil the Solaster?

"I liked him," she stated simply.

"Don't worry about God being angry that you and John want to change Her mind about the Solaster", Seth offered. "Spirit almost expects resistance about Its plans, even from folks inside the tent. She won't hold anything against you."

"Do you think John and I together might actually change God's mind?"

"I don't know. It's still too early to tell. Anyway, that's not why I texted you."

"What is it now? Did the Oprah interview fall though? I almost hope it did,"

"Oh no, it's still on. You'll be taping a week from Tuesday in the backyard of her mansion. Her people will be calling you to confirm travel arrangements. I hear she's looking forward to meeting you. I'm here because God wanted me to share some other information with you."

"Like what?" she inquired.

"She wanted me to counsel you about quote-problems-un-quote. You've started to experience quite a few of them lately. I know you feel bummed out. God wanted me to give you some "inside baseball" ideas about handling "problems" when they pop up."

"I could use some help like that," Lorena said, "I'm feel overwhelmed. Should I take notes?"

"No," Seth answered, "Just listen. I'll e-mail you a summary later. Are you ready?"

"Shoot", she said.

"Number one: everybody has problems. That's just "Life" being "Life". Be sure there really is a bona fide problem before you get yourself all worked up. If left alone for a while, most problems work themselves out. Most of the time, people worry and stew about things that never happen. If you can back off from situations or people, most everything will solve itself. Secondly, when a serious problem does crop up, don't react too fast and do something impulsive. Let things simmer for a few days before making any move. Don't jump in and make a rash decision that you might regret later. This is especially true where social media is concerned. Monitor your comments, posts and Tweets. Watch your clicks. Hesitate before you "send" anything. Never Tweet out or post a hateful comment when you are angry. Practice restraint. The third thing about problems concerns meditation. Go into the silence and ask for divine help when a problem crops up. Remember Lorena: Spirit wants you to seek divine guidance about any concern, big or small. Don't worry about bothering God. Let Her untangle your skein of yarn. Life is full of confusion and contradictions. Knock on God's door when things get balled up. She will help you get back on track."

"Those are all good thoughts," Lorena said, "Anything else?"

"Yes," Seth replied, "Number four, don't try to control or manage the problem yourself. That's a sure path to failure. Many people want to exercise total control over their problems. They believe in their own managerial expertise. They don't want God's help. Believe me, that is not the smart way to go. Trust me. Spirit has seen and resolved every problem under the sun. Remember that TV commercial for an insurance company: "We can handle everything because we've seen everything." That's God. Get into Oneness with the divine. Use His universal experience and knowledge to solve your problems. You won't be sorry."

"This is all good information," Lorena said. "I hope I can remember to practice it when I'm in the middle of something."

"OK," Seth said, "I'm almost done, but there are a few more quick things. Fifth, you must be cold blooded and practical when trouble comes. Take off the rose-colored glasses. Get out a piece of paper. Write down the facts. Writing something in the starkest of terms makes it more real. Sixth, you must engage any problem without becoming emotional. It's almost impossible to solve anything when you let emotions take over. If you are a journal keeper, go back and read about similar situations and how you dealt with them. What did you learn? What did you do right? What could you have done better? Seventh and lastly, don't be afraid to ask for help. Of course, going to God for divine assistance remains the best idea. Just be wary of seeking advice from the wrong people. Who are the wrong people? Anybody who wants you to "sell your soul" doesn't have your best interest at heart. Avoid the "soul sharks". You can't afford to pay their kind of interest. Some price tags are just too high. Never do anything because of money alone. That's the worst bargain possible. Staying in the pain is better than a short-term fix that bankrupts you spiritually in the end. There, I guess that's all."

"Wow, that's a lot," Lorena said. "Thank you. Please don't forget to send me the hard copy version."

"Let me add a P. S. about problems," Seth said, "Ask yourself why a specific problem has cropped up. Is there a lesson for you to learn? If so, what might it be?"

"Tell God thanks for this information," Lorena said. "I appreciate it. Now I have a question. What's the deal with your Doctor John?"

54

Free Will Again

"Did Doctor John tell you who he was?" Seth inquired.

"Of course," Lorena replied. "Secrets are impossible to keep in your spiritual world. There is too much honesty floating around. The question I'm asking you is what does he mean for me?"

"What do you think he means?" the angel returned.

"What do I believe it means? For one thing, this guy is already showing up in my "Family" Puzzle. I'm seeing "Pikes Peak" pieces everywhere. John is moving to Colorado for his new job. He said that strange things are showing up in his Family Puzzle too. John thinks that he and I might have a child together sometime in the future. So, Seth, I'm asking for your informed opinion. Do you think John and I will get married and be parents together?"

"Here's the thing, Lorena," Seth explained, "I could give you an opinion, based on today's outlook. However, there is a reason why "Free Will" is Puzzle #1. Things can change, based on somebody's free will choices. There are still lots of twists and turns before you decide which person to marry. You remember federal agent Tim Dahling, right? You'll also find him turning up in both your "Family" and "Free Will" puzzles. I seem to recall that he's being transferred to Colorado Springs too. That makes for an interesting coincidence, don't you think? Of course, we know there are no accidents."

"I accept that," she said.

"The young girl you saw in the puzzles might be your and Tim's daughter," Seth noted. "I think you could have a couple of possible choices for a new mate. That's what makes life interesting, my dear girl."

"What do you know that I don't?" Lorena asked.

"My lips are sealed," the angel teased.

"Doctor John says God has a seat reserved for him on the spacecraft to the new star if the Solaster happens," Lorena observed, "How about agent Tim? Is he on the manifest too? I'm sure he must have some skills."

"You're a bit ahead of me," Seth revealed, "I'm planning to talk with him next week. The "remnants" will need "security" in its new home. Agent Dahling would be the perfect candidate for a job in that area. Just because we're starting over in a new place doesn't mean there won't be security problems. Human beings are who they are. All are capable of both good behavior and bad behavior. Now wouldn't it be something if you, Tim and John were all traveling together?"

"In the meantime, do you have any advice for me?" she ventured.

"Just keep working your puzzles," Seth advised, "Try to keep an open mind about everything. It's possible that God may change Her mind and there won't be a space voyage ahead for anybody."

"If I have my way, there won't be a Solaster," Lorena said, "It's just too drastic. That must be another way to satisfy God."

Seth's pager went off. He read the incoming text with a frown.

"I have some bad news for you," he said to Lorena.

"What? Tell me, please."

"Your dear father just took an unexpected turn for the worse," he said. "His blessed soul just entered Heaven. He is being welcomed as we speak. I'm truly sorry for your loss, sweet Lorena. The Kingdom of Heaven has received its newest angel. It was a shock to everybody, including him."

55

Saying Goodbye

The next few days were an extended nightmare for Lorena. She had raced immediately to the hospital. Doctor John met her at front door and confirmed her father's unexpected passing. Lorena found her mother in a complete state of shock at his sudden death. Doctor John also seemed blindsided by his patient's demise. He explained, as best he could, that the fatal event had not involved heart failure. A blot clot in her father's leg had dislodged and traveled to his lung.

"It was fast," the doctor told Lorena and her mother, "He didn't suffer."

That offered little comfort for the grieving widow and daughter.

It's just one damn thing after the other, Lorena thought. I don't blame God for my father's passing, but everything seems so weird these days. My life was peaceful before Seth stopped me that day.

Her father's memorial service was held exactly 10 days after his death. He had chosen cremation, so the local cremation society handled the details and furnished the chapel for the memorial service. Lorena was pleasantly surprised that nearly 250 people attended. Many were former students and fellow faculty members at schools where both he and his wife had taught.

Lorena's mother asked her to handle the main eulogy. She later received many compliments for the remarks. Seth had texted her some ideas, which included a stylized version of the 23rd Psalm. Lorena had not expected any angelic assistance, but she used the Psalms idea. Seth also came and sat directly behind the family. Lorena was overwhelmed by the kind and generous remarks from numerous people who were touched by her father's life.

"Your dad was the gentlest and kindest man I ever knew," was the most common thing she heard.

Peter and Sallye also showed up, as did several real estate agents and other company employees. The spray of flowers from the firm dwarfed the others. Lorena also was a bit surprised, but pleased, that both Doctor John and Agent Dahling attended the service. She had brief but pleasant conversations with both. The two did not cross paths, which was fine with Lorena.

She saw Charles White sitting about half-way back in the chapel. He had also visited with her, offering his heartfelt condolences. There was no sign of Reggie III or Franklin, for which Lorena was eternally grateful. However, she did spot a subdued looking Shanice on the back row. She was dabbing at a tear.

Several days after her father's memorial service, Lorena went in for work at the temporary offices leased by Peter and Sallye. They had decided to fully renovate the damaged section of the old office. The smoke smell was still prevalent throughout the structure and there had been water damage.

Upon leaving the office after her first day back, Lorena decided to stop for dinner at a nearby fine dining restaurant. As she entered, she noticed a long line of patrons waiting for a table. She overheard a hostess telling a couple in line that the wait might be 45 minutes.

I'm not about to stand here for that long, she thought. I'll stop at 7-Eleven and get a Hot-to-Go sandwich and a Slurpee.

As she turned to leave, Lorena noticed a middle-aged black woman being advised that her table was ready. The woman suddenly looked back at Lorena and then whispered something to the waiter. He then approached Lorena and said: "Mrs. Smith would like you to join her for dinner." Lorena shook her head no, but the smiling woman beckoned for her to come ahead. "Please," the lady called out, "Don't make me dine alone."

The real estate woman gave in and followed the waiter to where the woman was standing.

"This is very nice of you," Lorena said as she extended her hand. "I'm Lorena Mae Johnson," she added.

The attractive woman looked straight into Lorena's eyes.

My name is Helen Smith," the woman said. "I'm Franklin's mother. I'm the Nana for your grandbabies. This is the least I could do for my future daughter-in-law. I believe we have a few things to discuss."

56

The Confrontation

On one hand, Lorena was surprised by this strange woman coming out of nowhere. However, for some unknown reason, Lorena also felt powerful and prepared for anything. Although she hadn't sought a relationship with God, the spiritual connection made her feel strong and enhanced. As the young real estate woman took her seat at the table, she was almost eager for what might be coming.

Bring it on lady, she thought. I'm ready for you.

The older woman led with a smile. The whiteness of her teeth was startling.

I'll say this for her, Lorena thought. Somebody furnished this woman with some nice choppers. There must be lots of dentists in hell for some reason, The thought almost made her giggle.

"I call myself Helen now," the woman grinned, "But my real name is Jezebel. However, that moniker carries too much baggage for today's world. I'm quite famous in the Bible, you know. I was with King Ahab, the old scoundrel. I heard you met Elijah and Elisha recently, I had quite a tiff with both of those boys back in the day. They even prophesied about how I would die. Getting tossed out of that window wasn't pleasant, I can tell you that. Anyway, I've been involved in lots of battles with God. Another bigtime fight doesn't bother me a bit. Since this your first real skirmish, I'll try to be gentle with you — not!"

Then, the woman let out a loud cackle that caused some of the other restaurant patrons to turn around and stare.

"Oops, I'm sorry," she apologized, "My public manners are a bit rusty."

"What should I call you?" Lorena inquired, "Helen or Jezebel?"

"Call me Jezzie," the woman answered. "May I call you 'Little Bit'? I think we both know what that means. It fits what you did to my son Franklin. The poor boy still hasn't recovered from that beat down you gave his privates. You're a mean one, Missy. Using that broom? I better be watching out for you."

"You don't sound too pleasant yourself," Lorena replied. "By the way, can I ask you a personal question?"

"Certainly, Little Bit, shoot?"

"How old are you? I have to say that you're an attractive woman for someone who was around in the Old Testament."

"That's hard to say," Jezzie answered, "I've been coming back in so many forms over the years. There is always a demand for a crafty and unscrupulous woman, so I've been back lots of times. I've had a few interesting gigs. My favorite was as a courtesan in Charles II's palace in England in 1660. Charlie was such a fun guy. They called him "The Merry Monarch". Too bad about the Great Plague and that Bakehouse Fire. They were both bad timing for him. He was a real stud. The guy sired an even dozen kids out of wedlock. However, he missed me for some reason. Anyway, I had a good time. People knew who I was back then. I could drink any of those boys under the table."

"You are really full of it," Lorena opined, "Are you drunk now?"

"Never ever touch the stuff these days", Jezzie confided. "However, I do love watching what alcohol does to other people. As for me, I probably should stay sober so I can watch for opportunities to make mischief. That's where I get my real kicks. I dig disharmony and conflict of any kind. How about you? Would you like a drink? It wouldn't bother me."

"No thank you," Lorena responded, "I'll probably need to stay sober for our discussion about Franklin and the grandkids."

"Where would you like to begin?" the woman said, pulling her chair up closer to the table.

Jezebel stared intently at Lorena and then placed her own wrinkled hand on top of hers. Unusually large and colorful rings adorned all four of her fingers.

I wonder if she's about to make a pass at me, Lorena wondered.

"I'm not going to make a pass at you, "Jezebel said. "This is a business dinner for me. I do want to make a direct appeal to you. I prefer persuasion over persecution."

"What are you talking about?" Lorena asked.

"What is it you want, Little Bit?", the she-devil inquired, again leaning close. "We've tried everything on you. Sex, money, and vanity don't seem to have any effect on you. Why are you holding out? What is it that you want? I'm sure we can reach some sort of agreement. Everyone has a price. I guess we just haven't found yours yet."

"Maybe I don't have one," Lorena responded.

"Then just back off and don't choose either one of us. Believe me, you don't want any part of those do-gooders. If you go with them, expect nothing but trouble. They'll make you feel guilty about ever having any fun. These straight arrows don't know how to party. All you'll get from them is loneliness, pain and suffering. Do you hear me, girl? Even if you don't go with us, at least tell them to get lost. Look, I'm on your side. Some folk in our principalities want to kill you off right now. I tell them "Give our girl a break". I say to them that "she'll see the light" before it's too late. Don't Make me a liar, kid. Listen, we've been easy on you so far. You wouldn't like it if we got really rough with you."

"Easy?" Lorena said with sarcasm, "I'm pregnant with your worthless son's twins, I just lost my dad and I've been in a bad car wreck.I'm about to lose my real estate job, the cops have been chasing me, and my office just burned down. Besides killing me, what else could you do to me? Or is that the next part of your plan? I wouldn't be surprised."

"We had nothing to with the car crash or your dad dying," Jezebel argued, "You know, a lot of people blame God whenever bad things happen. Maybe you should look in His sorry-ass direction for a while. Right now, nobody on our side wants you dead. Or course, that could change. We don't usually work that way because God overprotects his fools. But we've already had a few serious battles over you. However, our group doesn't relish physical conflict. We prefer to make you wish that you were dead."

"I didn't realize this spiritual warfare business was so fierce," Lorena said, "I don't understand it. Why do you all fight so hard over one little soul?"

"It may seem like one soul to you, but never underestimate the strength and power contained in just one human soul," Jezebel said, "There is no gain so crucial nor any loss so devastating as losing your soul. He who controls the world's souls rules the earth. For many years, we've had a clear majority. Our numbers are growing daily. This is the reason why God has become so desperate. Negative influences are rampant. Evil is everywhere these days. You may think it's just human nature at work. To some extent, I agree with that. But look at the past century. Two World Wars in in a period of just over 30 years? Over 50 million dead? Now, that's real negativity. The Holocaust? That was the epitome of evil. And now, dear Lorena, so many nations and terror groups have collected many weapons of mass destruction. The world is less than one minute from a nuclear calamity. Will it happen? I wouldn't bet against it. World history is rife with miscalculations of one kind or another."

"I'll do my best to prevent any destruction from happening," Lorena said.

"You should be on the winning side," Jazzie said, shaking her finger at Lorena. "We control the negative influences that bedevil most human beings. Sorry about the pun. We corrupt world governments and then destroy them. We encourage the use of alcohol and drugs. We utilize greed, money and power to tear families apart. We create and promote abusive relationships between people. We even get human beings to injure or murder one another. Our side promotes intolerance, bigotry and prejudice. We feed the fires of racism. We make human beings hate each other over skin color and religious differences. We laugh at how gullible people can be. They do not realize or comprehend that every soul has lived many lifetimes with different backgrounds and skin colors. You've been black, white, yellow, brown and red more times than I can count. You've been rich, poor and in-between. If humans understood the principles of reincarnation, there would be so much less hatred in the world. But, what the hey, we hope people never wake up to the truth. Racial hatred and intolerance are the best tools in our trouble-making arsenal."

"You really are a she-devil," Lorena said.

"Thank you," Jazzie sneered. "That's the nicest thing anyone has said to me all day. Now, I must ask you again: Where do you stand? We want you with us. I am ready to increase our compensation package to snare your soul. Is it more money? Drugs? Fame? Power? Eternal youth? It's all there on the table for you. How could you possibly say no?"

"I say that I need to find the little girl's room," Lorena interjected, "Could you order me a vodka gimlet while I'm gone? I'll be right back."

"Now that's my girl," Jezebel cackled.

57

Angel Wisdom

Lorena raced straight out the front door of the restaurant. She looked both ways, while trying to decide her next move.

The parking valet had just pulled up a baby blue Porsche 911 coupe. The real estate woman was admiring the sporty vehicle when its owner stepped out from the shadows behind her.

It was Seth.

"Need a ride, honey?" he said with a smile. "If you do, get in."

The parking valet swung the passenger door open and Lorena was drawn in naturally.

She saw the angel give the parking attendant a twenty-dollar tip. "Thank you, Mr. Angell", the attendant said.

Seth looked back to check for oncoming traffic and then roared off.

"I thought you could use a get-away car right about now," he told her.

"You weren't wrong," Lorena replied, "How did you know?"

"I saw Jezzie as she was loitering in front of the restaurant before you showed up. I figured she was trying to connect with you. She's a piece of work, right?"

"Yes, she is," Lorena sighed. "Did you know that she is Franklin's mother and the grandmother of my twins?"

"Well, about that," Seth said, "Try to act surprised when Dr. Williams calls you tomorrow. The lab had the tests mixed up. The twins belong to someone else. However, you are still pregnant with the one baby."

Lorena almost fainted with relief.

"Thank you, God," she shouted out loud.

"God is good," the angel agreed.

"Where do I go from here?" she asked.

"Now that you are centered again, you can refocus on your interview with Oprah and the rest of your media commitments. It's time for you to do some prophesying."

"I was really scared back at the restaurant," Lorena reflected. "I felt that I was in the presence of pure evil."

"You were," the angel agreed. "Jezebel is a seriously bad spirit. She even makes me nervous. With her, I try to remember the Boy Scout motto: Be prepared."

"Amen to that," Lorena agreed.

"She must have thought you were wavering in your commitment to God," he said, "Is that true?"

"Honestly, yes and no," Lorena answered, "I still don't know what God sees in me. I'm spooked by these spiritual attacks. However, something strange happened tonight. When I was sitting in the restaurant with Jezebel, I could feel my dad's presence. I sensed his spirit sitting right there at the table with us. He lifted me up and helped me see everything with more clarity. I could never choose evil over good. I know that I have free will choices. I could choose the Dark Side and be rewarded materially. I understand that. Evil really knows how to frame temptations to make them seem attractive. I'm grateful that my parents taught me right from wrong. I felt my father's spirit reminding me of those teachings tonight. I feel so grateful for my upbringing."

"Human beings need all of the help they can get," Seth noted, "Even after you make a solid commitment to God, evil still researches your weaknesses.If they find something, look out! You must always keep your guard up. They can strike when you least expect it. Put your spiritual resources on speed dial. Somebody will be there to respond. I'll let you off at the next corner. I think I'll just ride around in my toy here a bit longer. Angels love to fly, especially in a Porsche."

58

More About The "Family" Puzzle

When Lorena arrived home for the evening, she decided to look through the "FAMILY" Puzzle box again. Although the "FREE WILL" puzzle contained important "family" elements, she wanted more insight about the issues related to her own family situation.

Lorena noticed that the pieces in her puzzle contained many images of Africa. The beautiful scenery, the wild animals and the colorfully dressed people were everywhere. However, she found some of the images disturbing. In one section of the puzzle, a lion was mauling someone.

Could that have been one of my relatives, or even me? What a painful way to go, she mused.

Then, the puzzle seemed to shift scenes and continents. She saw a picture forming of colonial America, probably in the late 1700s. Lorena remembered a similar setting in the "FREE WILL" puzzle. It was apparent that many of her ancestors had lived during the Revolutionary War as slaves. She also discerned an artist rendering of the "Stars and Bars" flag of the Confederacy during the Civil War. It was flying in the vast front yard of a large plantation.

That makes sense as well, Lorena thought. Her ancestors were probably still trapped in the bonds of slavery decades later.

Then she noticed the cover of the "FAMILY" puzzle box. There was a beautiful photograph of the current American flag. Lorena counted the "stars" depicted on the flag. There were exactly 50, so the photograph was obviously current. She took it to mean that, whatever her family's past, they were now full partners in the great American mosaic of one nation, with liberty and justice for all.

That gives me hope for the future, she told herself. If my people could overcome their past, maybe all of us working together can surmount the possibility of losing everything.

After spending a little more time with the "FAMILY" puzzle, Lorena searched for and found the "LOVE' puzzle. Again, she saw immediate similarities with "FREE WILL". However, in one unfolding scene, Lorena saw a gigantic waterfall.

Wow, she exclaimed to herself, that is one huge waterfall. I wonder where it might be located.

As if to answer her question, there was a puzzle piece with the words "NIAGRA FALLS" clearly visible. Lorena could also see the image of a man and woman standing next to the sign.

I know that many people go there on their honeymoon, she thought. Maybe that's me with my future husband.

She had started searching for faces in the "LOVE" puzzle when her cell phone beeped. A text was arriving. It was from Seth, the messenger angel. It read:

"Coffee tomorrow at 9 a.m. Special Guest joining us. Don't be late."

Lorena immediately texted back: "Who Special Guest?"

A text returned in less than 10 seconds: "God who! B there or B square."

59

God Speaks

Lorena was right on time for the God meeting. Both Seth and her mirror image were already sipping their lattes when she arrived. Spirit stood and greeted Lorena with a warm hug.

It's like embracing my twin sister, Lorena thought.

"We were a little early," Seth explained, "Grab something and then we'll get started."

After Lorena was seated, God spoke.

"I wonder if we might begin our time together with a word of prayer?"

I would never say no to praying with the Deity, Lorena nodded.

"I send this prayer forth to the universe," Spirit began, "Bless the world and its wonderful people. Let our efforts here today bring healing and peace to one and all. Help us remain open and receptive to becoming a Light in the darkness. For that possibility, we say thank you, thank you, thank you Me."

Lorena stifled a small chuckle at God's personal reference to herself again. She noticed that Seth also was suppressing a grin.

"I'm pleased that you are getting closer to choosing the spiritual Path", God said. "You won't be sorry. There could be a few times when things get dicey. In the long run, however, you'll be happy with your decision. I realize that My Path can sometimes be lonely, hard and even dangerous. Just think about your final reward whenever the hard times keep coming."

"Thank you," Lorena responded, "I'll keep that in mind."

"Now, there are several things I want to cover today," Spirit said, "I know you still have your day job at the real estate office, so I'll keep that in mind. Are you OK with that?"

I'm not about to decline spending time with God, Lorena nodded again

"I understand you'll be doing media interviews in the next few days," God continued, "You've got your big interview coming up with the "Talk Show Queen". Expect to receive lots of spiritual vibrations from her. Don't let that throw you. She comes by it naturally. Her soul has a long history with My Kingdom. She walked the earth in Biblical times as the famous Queen Esther. Yes, she's the one who saved the Jewish people from being murdered. Unknown to everybody, Esther was a Jew herself. But she prevailed on her husband King Xerxes to spare her people. Esther has a strong and savior-type personality. However, remember that "The Queen" is a master interviewer. "O" is a real pro. Be prepared and concise. Don't ramble."

"Any other tips about the media?" Lorena inquired.

"Up to this point, you've been a media curiosity because of the viral event with Franklin," God answered, "Now it's time for the focus to shift. You need re-introducing to the public. It's time to put on your prophet mantle."

"How do I do that?" Lorena asked.

"First, you must shift your mindset. Put aside everything except acting as a prophet for Me. Yes, it will shock some people and put off others. Expect blowback on social media. Some people will call you deranged. Don't be surprised when you become a controversial figure. Develop a thick skin.

Speaking out on My behalf requires extra courage. The evil doers are savage fighters. Be prepared to feel the sting of their wrath. You will become an existential threat to them. They've been trying to topple you already with temptation and intimidation. None of it worked so far. Get ready for bigger threats. Many of my staunchest supporters have perished in some epic spiritual battles. I don't mean to frighten you, but this won't be a walk in the park. Ramp up your faith. Put on My whole armor. Avoid the flaming arrows that fall around you. Strangers will spit at you and call you the worst names possible. They'll say you're a loser, a fraud, a lunatic and a deadender. Some will want you physically committed. Even moderates may dismiss you as an alarmist and prone to conspiracy theories. Those who sing your praises won't get by unscathed.They also can expect attacks from the media and other critics. Even some of your supporters will urge you to dilute My warnings. "You're scaring the old people and the children" could be something you hear. I AM not overstating the negative reactions about to take place. You must stay strong in Me. Do not be shaken or deterred. You've got Heaven on your side, Lorena. You'll never be abandoned or forsaken."

"You paint a pretty scary picture," Lorena said haltingly.

"That's because it is scary," Spirit agreed, "But besides being My prophet about the coming dangers, there are several other specific areas that need addressing."

"What are those?" the real estate woman asked.

"They fall into one general area: addiction. I want you to take on gambling, pornography, alcohol and drug addiction. First, on gambling, I want you to warn people about the negative results of "betting". You would be surprised at what compulsive gamblers find to bet on. Many people see gambling as a harmless, benign and fun activity. The results say otherwise. Once gambling becomes a full-fledged addiction, your very soul is at risk. Many "types" are susceptible to the disease of gambling: alcoholics and drug abusers, risk takers in general, and adrenalin junkies. The adrenalin addicts crave the "rush" that comes with winning or losing a bet.It's an instant payoff. The rise of gambling demonstrates how low the world's culture has sunk. Many problems are linked with this addiction: poverty, family break-ups, depression, a sense of hopelessness and even suicide are normal outcomes for compulsive gamblers. Yet, it doesn't seem to deter anybody. The legalization of certain types of gambling adds to the problem. Sports betting has become the fastest growing aspect of this addiction. Wagering on sports was always a serious mental health issue before it was legalized. Now some people regard it as unpatriotic if they don't place a bet on their favorite team. Speaking of how the world sometimes legitimizes bad behavior, that brings me to another area of concern."

"What's that?" Lorena inquired.

"The recent trend to legalize marijuana is an extremely bad decision with many negative outcomes for humanity," Spirit explained, "Believe me, I know all of the arguments for it, especially in the area of taxation and medical use. Some of them even make sense.Here's the problem: the THC content of weed today is three or four times greater than just a decade ago. This is not your grandpa's or grandma's pot. It's simply not cool to have 10% of the population stoned at any given time, especially if they are out driving around in cars and trucks. Marijuana is becoming the replacement for the terrible opiate problem. You know how devastating that addiction was and is. Yes, in many ways, opiates are more deadly than pot. Marijuana won't kill you per se. But you can expect DUI's, ER visits and mental health issues to spike in states where marijuana is already legal. But, my dear Lorena, let me warn you about this one. Speaking out against pot will bring a swift, loud and negative reaction. You will be roundly condemned. Anytime you stand up against the current culture, expect the brickbats to start flying your way. The idea of making weed legal has countless supporters."

I can identify what God is saying about both gambling and pot, Lorena mused. I still spend a few dollars every now and then on the lottery. I do get a small rush when I check my numbers. Also, when I went to Vegas last year, I spent hours playing the slots. You get a shot of adrenilin every time you spin the wheel. I've never won much money gambling. I just mark it down as "entertainment" dollars, like going to the movies or out to dinner. Regarding marijuana, I've smoked a few joints along the way. It's never done much for me. The same is true with booze. Neither of my parents were big drinkers, maybe once or twice a year. I guess I've been lucky. I do know both gambling and pot can create problems. If I start weighing in big-time about them, I'm going to get unpopular fast.

"What are you smiling about, Lorena," Seth asked.

"If I start speaking out against either gambling or smoking grass," Lorena noted, "I'm going to become persona non grata with a lot of folks. I won't be the first one invited to the parties, that's for sure."

"Yes," God said. "It can get lonely. Now, let me add a bit more about alcohol. Booze has been around big-time both before and after "Prohibition".Almost every family has one, two, 20 or more alcoholics somewhere in their family history. Colleges and universities help enable the alcoholic tendencies among their students. Excessive drinking is part of the college experience for many college students. Fraternities and sororities encourage the use of alcohol. You probably can't affect or change that much, even if you tried. Part of the rite of passage for kids in their teen-age years is to have their first drink. Or, it could be to smoke that first cigarette or first joint. Human beings love to create trouble for themselves. That will probably never change. Don't get discouraged by human nature. And that brings me to the last addiction that I want you to take on: pornography. Porn is a secret addiction that is being ramped up by the internet. There are many hidden aspects of being a smut addict. It's almost always done privately, and away from others. Some people you would never expect are hooked. When you go after pornography, expect many heads to nod in agreement. Yet, some of these folks could be the worst addicts. It's a tough one."

Addictions must be a much bigger problem that I ever thought, Lorena told herself silently. Practically everybody I know smokes, drinks, takes pills, uses pot or watches porn

"Addictions are why it's so hard to stay on the spiritual Path" God explained. "However, let me share why it's important to stand up against them. The #1 problem with being addicted to anything is "separation". They separate you from Me spiritually. When you and I are not united, things go "South" in a hurry. Separation from your spiritual self (which is Me) causes money problems, confusion, bad decisions, physical sickness, unhappiness, depression and even suicide. That's just for starters. Addictions can play havoc with any love or family relationship. You must avoid separating yourself from Me. Always stay bonded in Oneness with Me, no matter what."

Just then an elderly woman approached their table.

"I had to ask," she said, "Are you two girls twins?"

"Without a doubt," God answered.

"I just knew it," the woman smiled, "Which one of you is the oldest?"

"I AM," God replied as she stood to depart, "by a few billion years."

60

Pushback

Seth's media interview schedule for Lorena kept her busy the next few days. Her real estate bosses Peter and Sallye granted her the week off, which helped. She was forced to lie about the commitment, saying it would only last for a week or two and then she would be done with it.

The experience itself proved rewarding, problematic and a bit unnerving for someone not accustomed to being in the public eye. Lorena's most important and rewarding interview came with the "Talk Show Queen." They met in the backyard of her palatial home. As God promised, the iconic woman was gracious, professional and possessed a genuine spiritual aura. The interview predictably began with the viral incident involving Franklin. It evolved into a discussion about women defending themselves from sexual harassment. Only the last few minutes covered Lorena's spiritual work. God's concerns about the evils of gambling, pornography, alcohol, drugs and marijuana did not come up at all.

When Lorena confided to Seth that she felt the interview was a failure, he reassured her. "You're learning," the angel said, "You did fine and you'll get better."

Sure enough, after the interview aired on the Talk Show Queen's channel, a producer called with positive news. "We had a great reaction to your interview," she told Lorena, "especially on the part about women defending themselves.

Oh yes, people also liked how you were committing yourself to spiritual work. We'll have you on again in a year or so to see how that's going for you."

 However, another interview went in a not-so-great direction. The male host was a long-time "comedian" on a popular TV subscription channel. His anti-religious views were well documented. He usually spent most of his on-air time spewing left-wing political rants. The man was smart, articulate and funny. He specialized in skewering anyone who dared mention spirituality, religion or God. He quickly put Lorena on the defensive by asking if God had told her to whack Franklin in his privates. She stuttered around a bit and never fully responded to his question. When Lorena tried to bring up her new spiritual calling, the host cut her short with a sarcastic comment: "So you talk to God, eh? See if you can get me a couple of good tickets to the Super Bowl next year." He basically dismissed Lorena as not being credible. After the interview ended, he was more friendly and kidded around for a while. He even told her: "I'm actually kind of spiritual."

After the show aired, Lorena was dismayed how fast social media began attacking her with mean-spirited comments. For a day or two, she was "trending" on Twitter. She drew several thousand negative and snarky tweets, mostly from men who identified with Franklin. Lorena's comments about spirituality also drew widespread condemnation. She did manage to bring up gambling and pot just briefly. She was booed and hissed by some in the live studio audience. Later, her comments were almost unanimously panned in Twitterland.

Once she finished the two interviews, Lorena reached out to Seth to express bewilderment with the negative reactions. His response was not comforting: "Toughen up, Lorena. Grow a thicker skin. This is only the beginning."

She did not realize how right Seth had been in his observation. Two late- night TV talk show hosts began routinely mocking her. Their observations were uniformly crude, tasteless and unfunny. One host was a man on a major network, the other a foul-mouthed woman on a large cable network. The network host was relatively mild with Lorena. However, the woman comic was merciless. She equated Lorena's beatdown of Franklin with having an orgasmic experience. She also applauded God's role in bringing His wrath down on the hapless young man. The female host accused Lorena of being a witch and leaving the scene on a broom. Neither mimicking made the real-estate woman feel positive about herself. She felt like withdrawing from the spiritual battlefield.

"It's not easy," Seth had counseled her in a more understanding and soothing manner. "You've ruffled some feathers," he added.

Lorena was also now being recognized in public. It didn't happen every day, but often enough to make her feel uncomfortable. She was interrupted by so-called "fans", curiosity seekers, some detractors and a few outright mental cases. Thankfully, most people were nice and even supportive. She signed a few autographs and always granted requests for selfies. But not every encounter was pleasant. The people with negative religious experiences were the worst. She received several direct and online threats of physical violence. A couple of obvious mental cases leveled specific death threats. The most deranged she passed on to local authorities, who added the information to their "celebrity" file. So far, it appeared that nobody was openly stalking her.

Lorena conferred with Seth about the harassment. "I don't like being a public figure," she told the angel.

"I'm sorry," the angel said, "I understand, and losing your privacy can be a demeaning experience. You're lucky that the federal or state government agencies haven't noticed you yet. Agent Dahling did question you about the Solaster rumor, but that's about it so far. Do you remember what Jesus Christ had to endure? Jewish religious leaders were worried about His influence. They openly plotted against Him. Even the authorities in Rome were concerned. Jesus got so much attention that eventually it led to his crucifixion.So far, you haven't been on the government's radar. However, that could change. When and if it does, getting noticed at the supermarket could be the least of your worries."

"Where are all these threats coming from?" Lorena asked. "Do they all originate from Satan?"

"Probably not every last one," Seth advised, "But some are, for sure. Personally, I think the online stuff is the worst. One twisted individual could be responsible for hundreds of negative posts on social media. It's kind of a faceless manifestation of evil. I've always regarded those people as cowards."

"The negative attention has affected what little real estate career I still have," Lorena noted. "My income has dried up. I'm getting paid a few bucks for some of my interviews, but I'll be tapped out soon. Who do I see about a short-term loan in your high-level organization?"

"Have you prayed about your financial situation?" Seth asked, "It might be something to think about. In the meantime, don't worry about it. God has promised to cover you. He keeps His promises."

Lorena's cell phone beeped to indicate an incoming text.

"Let's get together for lunch tomorrow," it read, "I really want to see you."

It was signed "Agent Tim Dahling".

I don't know whether to be happy or concerned, Lorena thought. He might honestly want to see me. Or, he could be coming to arrest me. On the spiritual path, one never knows. At least it's never dull.

61

Agent Tim

Although they had not spoken for a while, Lorena always felt comfortable with Agent Tim. From the first moment they exchanged a semi-hug, she felt at ease in his presence. They agreed to meet for lunch at an unpretentious neighborhood eatery near her old real estate office. There seemed less chance that Lorena might be noticed and/or bothered.

However, within a couple of minutes of pulling up their chairs and before their server could appear, an elderly gentleman walked up to their table.

The man looked at Lorena and began shaking his finger in her face.

"No, no, no, no," he kept repeating, "You're wrong, you're dead wrong! God wouldn't do that to us. Why are you lying? Liar, liar, pants on fire!"

A waiter approached and gently tried to take the man's arm and steer him away. However, he jerked loose from the waiter and kept berating Lorena.

"I hope you rot in hell," he shouted. "You she-devil!"

That was enough for Agent Tim. He stood up and stepped to within two inches of the man's face.

"Sir," he said in a commanding voice, while pulling his official badge from an inside coat pocket, "That's enough. You can back off now. I'm a federal agent. Step away from our table. If you don't leave right now, I will arrest you. Now go!"

The man looked at the agent, inspected his badge, and retreated. Meanwhile, the restaurant manager arrived and escorted the intruder outside.

The scene attracted some notice among other patrons. Most of them just stared down at their food. However, as the man departed, one couple applauded.

"Give 'em hell, Lorena!" the woman called out. "We're with you, honey," her companion said in support.

"Do you get that much?" Agent Dahling asked.

"Every once in a while," Lorena responded, "I try to ignore it. I'm always concerned that somebody might get physical."

"Maybe you should consider hiring a bodyguard," Dahling ventured, "Talk of religion stirs up the crazies big-time. If you need somebody, I'm available nights and weekends. My rates are low."

Lorena laughed.

"Thanks, but I'll take my chances for now," she said. "However, I appreciate the offer. I might even take you up on it at some point. Being recognized in public is a new thing for me. I understand now why some celebrities never go out."

"Remember, Lorena, it just takes one nut case with a weapon. Please be careful."

"I will," she said, touched by his concern for her safety.

For a while, both stared at their menus. Lorena put hers down first. She took some time to size up her companion.

"Why are you staring at me?" Tim asked as he also placed his menu on the table.

I'm not too cool, she thought. I had forgotten how clean-cut Tim looks. I would absolutely pick him out as a government agent of some kind. Maybe the IRS. However, I'm not sure that's a compliment.

"I'm not surprised that man turned tail when you flashed your badge," she smiled. "You look official."

"I am official, and I get that a lot," he smiled.

"I apologize for being so obvious with my staring," she said, "We haven't seen each other for a while. It's really good to see you, Agent Dahling."

"I've been taught how to hide my own staring," he said, "But I'm kind of obvious when it comes to you. Honestly, Lorena, you take my breath away. It may not be cool to say this, but you get prettier every time I see you. I hope you take that as a compliment."

Are you kidding me? Lorena thought to herself. More, more.

"I feel some real chemistry between us," the agent stated with a shy grin, "I hope I'm not wrong. You may not know this, but I've never been married. I was engaged once, but my girlfriend broke it off. She said I was too "earnest". I'm pretty sure that wasn't a compliment."

Lorena nodded in agreement.

"She may have been right, but I like earnest," she said with a smile.

"Maybe we should order," he stammered.

"Yes," Lorena agreed, "We should do that."

"How are you taking all of this attention?" Tim asked, "And especially the criticism? I would have a real hard time with it."

"I was warned about it," she admitted, "I sort of knew what to expect. But it's still much worse than I imagined."

"Let me be honest, Lorena," Tim explained, "People don't like bad news. Nobody wants to hear about the world ending anytime soon. That doesn't scan on their radar. If it's going to interfere with their bowling league or keep them from watching the ball game on Sunday, then they might pay attention. No one in their right mind craves a major dose of horrible news. You've heard the cliché about "killing the messenger." Well, you're the messenger. You're in a no-win situation. Now, if you want to prophesy about who will win the lottery? I promise you'll get plenty of positive attention. I might tune you in myself."

"I understand," Lorena agreed, "Maybe I just don't have a tough enough skin."

"I know you've got a good and sensitive heart," Tim smiled, "You could have easily blasted that old guy who waved his finger in your face. You didn't do that. You have a gentle and non-confrontive mindset. I can see why someone would choose you to do spiritual work. You're a good soul."

"At heart, I'm a wimp," she said. "I'll bet that man has a long-suffering wife at home. She would probably be mortified at him approaching us."

"I'm sure you're right," he agreed, "I guess my law enforcement background makes me cynical. I'm skeptical about people's motives. Just about anybody is capable of big-time mischief and deceit. You need to keep your eyes open."

"Well, I think most folks are good," Lorena said, "But there are a few who won't hesitate to take advantage of another person."

"Let me give you an example as a cynical lawman," the agent said. "If people really believed the world was ending, con men (and con women) would be selling insurance protection and seats on the space ark. And there are tons of folks who would be ponying up big money for the best seats. Trust me. I've seen it first-hand. This is the world you're up against."

Changing the subject, Lorena asked: "How are you doing?"

"That's one thing I wanted to share with you," he said, "I'm being transferred."

Let me guess where, Lorena thought. Colorado Springs!

"I guess somebody at headquarters knows I love the mountains," Tim told her. "I'm being moved to the Colorado Springs office."

Why am I not surprised? Lorena smiled inwardly.

"Have you ever been there?" Tim asked, "It's beautiful."

Only in my dreams and the 7 Puzzles, she thought to herself.

"There's something else I want to tell you," the agent said with some shyness.

"What's that?"

"You've been in my dreams lately. In fact, I've had the exact same dream now three nights in a row. In it, you and I are happily married and living out in Colorado. I can see the big blue mountains on the horizon. We also have a daughter. She's a lovely young girl in her mid-teens. We're a happy family. Then, something sad happens. I'm not sure exactly what takes place, but everyone is in big-time mourning. It's as if somebody died. I think it pertains to an event that took place when we were out hiking up in the mountains. Anyway, I've had the same dream now for three consecutive nights. What about you? Do you ever dream about us?"

I think I'll keep quiet about "The Puzzle of Love", Lorena thought.

62

Seth Has News

As Lorena and Agent Tim were leaving the restaurant, a text from Seth arrived.

"I have important news. Meet me in an hour at our old bench. Don't worry about the construction."

Seth and I haven't met on the bench since the fire, it occurred to Lorena.

She arrived within 45 minutes. The angel was already waiting.

After the barest of greetings, Seth got straight to the point.

"This is the last time I'll be seeing you," he said with a frown.

"Why?" she asked, a bit startled by the news.

"I'm being reassigned," he answered.

"Where?"

"I'm headed to Paris, France," he announced, "It's a dirty job, but I guess somebody has to do it."

"Why Paris? What's happening there?"

"It has to do with the rebuilding of Norte Dame Cathedral after the fire," Seth explained. "It seems the other side is determined to slow things down or prevent it altogether. Lots of spiritual warfare is happening over there right now. So, I'm being summoned. I could be involved for several years. The Cathedral is a top priority in the Higher — and lower — realms, so I'm not surprised. Angels are being pulled in from everywhere. I wanted to tell you the news in person. I'll miss you, my sweet real estate girl. However, I'll be keeping tabs on you. But I'm sure you will do just fine here without me."

I feel a little blindsided, Lorena thought. Just when I'm getting started, my best angel resource is leaving me. I wonder who'll replace him.

"Change happens, even in the spiritual realm. To answer your question, they are replacing me with Celestina. I believe you've met her already. She has been a warrior angel in training, but now it's time for a promotion. You'll like her. She's winding up her last few days of orientation as we speak. I'm leaving for Paris in the morning, so I won't be around when she arrives. You shouldn't have any big problems before then."

"I hope not," Lorena sighed.

"As we wind down our time together," the angel said, "I want to talk with you about something else."

"What's that?"

"Life and death".

"That's a weighty subject to end things with," Lorena observed.

"With a Solaster in the mix, I agree. Personally, I'm still hoping it doesn't happen. I'm counting on human beings to make the changes that God wants. The stakes are high. I would like to see a spiritual revival throughout the world. Of course, even then, not every human problem will disappear. Evil won't ever go away. However, even a small turnaround could cause God to change His mind. I'm expecting some success with "The 7 Puzzles". I also think the emergence of prophets like yourself will make a difference. Call me an angel-eyed optimist, but I'm hopeful that the world gets spared."

"I hope you're right." Lorena said, "I'm just not as optimistic as you."

"Now," Seth began, "I want to explain something about life and death. Here's the bottom line: don't ever be afraid of human death. Making your physical transition may be painful for a short time, but then it's over. Never fear transitioning onward and upward to Heaven. It is like being here on earth one minute and in Glory the next. When your body dies, your soul exits and rises. You shed the outer skin and soar straight up to Paradise. Very few departed souls ever want to go back. In some near-death experiences where the soul does return, God and the individual have made that decision jointly. What comes right after dying physically? You see and feel a thousand rainbows enveloping you. Yes, you can feel a rainbow! Your spirit literally soars upward in complete freedom and release. If you've been sick, all pain vanishes. It's like being on the most exciting Ferris Wheel in the universe. Leaving earth for Heaven produces a rushing sensation. In sexual terms, think of it as a hundred nearly simultaneous orgasms coming one right after the other. I'm not exaggerating. Then, when that aspect of transition ends, a stunning peacefulness and serenity hits you. You also see a series of blinding and exploding lights bombarding you from everywhere. As I said, all physical, emotional and spiritual pain disappears. After a brief time of transition, your spirit awakens amid the beauty of Heaven. You are dazzled and engulfed by the absolute purity of God's divine Love. New souls always comment about the stunning beauty and peacefulness that radiates all around them. You are not fearful. Spiritual clarity infuses you with acceptance and understanding. Every negative thought about anything or anyone disappears. Eternal life has begun for your soul in eternity and all is well."

"You make it sound like quite a trip," she said.

"Oh, but here is the best part," Seth continued. "When you die physically, your loved ones are there to welcome your soul back into Heaven. These dear souls have waited patiently for this moment. They are happy that you have finally arrived. They are eager to share God's Kingdom with you. It's always a beautiful reunion. Think about the happiest moment you ever experienced on earth. This joy exceeds it a thousand times over."

"Heaven sounds fabulous," Lorena said.

"However good I've made human death sound," the angel stated, "I also need to make a point about the beauty and importance of human life. No matter how bad you think your life may have turned out, God always has a plan for everyone. No one should ever consider ending his or her life prematurely. That would short-circuit Spirit's Will for you. If you're still walking the earth in human form, God has something important in mind for you. You are needed somewhere on earth. Vow to keep going until the end arrives naturally. If you are in pain, God knows about it. She hates suffering as much as anyone. Just allow your moment of transition to arrive at its appointed hour. Don't try to hurry things along. That upsets the natural order of the universe."

"Can you tell me anything else about Heaven?" Lorena asked

"Yes," Seth said, "First of all, Heaven was your original home. God creates each soul from scratch. However, your various incarnations either have raised or lowered your spiritual consciousness. You are a somewhat different soul than when you departed Heaven for this parenthesis in eternity. You carry any growth or lack of it forward. Understand that you are made in the image and likeness of Spirit. However, as I've mentioned before, every soul possesses its own uniqueness. When you depart God's Kingdom for earth, you forget every memory of Heaven until the day you return. Then, in an instant, you realize again its wonder and beauty. Everything comes back to you."

"I'm sure Heaven must be beautiful," Lorena said.

"There are many wonders of the world," the angel stated, "However, nothing compares with the magnificence of God's Kingdom. The surroundings are stunning, but that isn't what sets it apart. The uniqueness comes from the incredible souls that reside in Paradise. People who can barely move on Earth fly unencumbered through the halls of Heaven. Illness and pain have vanished forever. There are no cloudy or stormy days. We don't allow them. It's always blue skies and green lights. Negativity is banned. Everybody loves and accepts one another. An aura of love permeates everything. Your soul soars just by being in such positive surroundings. There is zero prejudice. Bigotry and racism are long-gone. People aren't judged by their skin color, because there isn't any skin. As I said, when you return home to Heaven, you suddenly remember your past lives. Of course, you've lived in other genders and as a part of other races. That fact alone binds souls together into a glorious tapestry. You'll love the camaraderie of Heaven. Everyone is appreciated because of their soul's beauty and uniqueness. No one ever gets lost or abandoned. You are always honored and loved by all. Unconditional acceptance begins with the Creator, who cherishes each soul. It's like knowing your Father/Mother will always love you, no matter what you said or did on earth. There is no judging, only acceptance. No criticism, just ongoing adoration and appreciation."

"All of that sounds wonderful to me," Lorena said.

"Oh, but there is yet another fabulous aspect to Heaven," Seth smiled. "You cannot conceive of the learning experiences available to all. You'll be thrilled by the famous souls you get to meet. I adore fine art. I especially like the French Impressionists. I've attended many exhibits by Manet, Monet,

Cezanne and Renoir. I know all of them. I especially enjoy Auguste Renoir. I like his quote "The pain passes, but the beauty remains." I know you enjoy classical music. Expect to attend intimate recitals by the masters. I've been blessed to hear Mozart play his Piano Concerto No. 21 in C major. I've attended a performance of Beethoven's Ninth Symphony on more than one occasion and heard Chopin do his nocturnes and etudes. Ludwig hears perfectly now. That's the healing power of Heaven at work. By the way, the great souls in every area are always thrilled to meet new fans, so expect a warm welcome."

"You certainly make it sound like a terrific place," Lorena said, "But it's hard to believe that no friction exists. I'm thinking about the bad feelings sometimes between family members or ex-husbands and ex-wives."

"There are lots of glorious reunions in Heaven," the angel said. "However, there are many souls who never meet up with certain people they knew back on earth. Here is the arrangement once you enter Heaven. For any meetup to take place, BOTH parties must agree to it. Nobody needs to explain or justify their position. If someone desires to meet with you, they must schedule things through the Main Exchange. You then receive the request, punch a button "yes" or "no" and the scheduling goes from there. If you decline somebody's request, they are not allowed to ask why or stalk you. Remember, Lorena, negativity has no place in God's Kingdom. You might think this policy is hard to enforce. It isn't. Nobody wants to test the rules. Life outside of Heaven's Gates represents something that no one wants to think about.

"What if someone says "NO" in the beginning, but later changes their mind?"

"That's allowed," Seth said, "But we have a three-strike rule in Heaven. Once someone says "NO" three times, that's it. No more invitations and no more turndowns. We never make souls meet against their will."

"That sounds fair," Lorena observed.

"Believe me," Seth stated, "For every turndown, there are 10,000 Happy reunions. We have lots of singing, dancing and downright joy up there. Expect tons of joyous music. It's non-stop. Some of the most touching reunions take place between pets and their masters. After you get situated, please take a trip down to the Rainbow Bridge. There are thousands of pets and their masters meeting up every day. Those joy-filled reunions are always something to behold. I go down to the Bridge sometimes just to watch the joyful interactions. It beats the human-to-human emotion hands down."

"Is there some sadness or anger if and when meetings are turned down?" Lorena inquired.

"It might be hard to understand, but most people make their peace about it early on. We don't allow grudges or hurt feelings to enter or remain active in Heaven. They must stay earth-bound. Therefore, there is no latent anger or hidden resentments lurking in the halls of Paradise. God's Kingdom reeks of non-judgement, clarity and honesty. It's a wonderful way to exist throughout eternity. For many human beings steeped in backstabbing and double dealing, it's a real eye-opener. But most adjust quickly."

"Doesn't anybody ever get mad or get their feelings hurt about anything?"

"No," Seth allowed, "I've certainly never seen it and I've been around for a while. If anything did happen, we have a "Council of Higher Angels" who serve as God's administrators. They keep Heaven flowing smoothly."

"You make it sound like a fantastic place," she said.

"I'm not overstating it," Seth confirmed, "It's the best. I want you to anticipate the experience, not dread it. Everyone will depart the physical earth at some point. What people discover is an afterlife filled with wonder, joy, peace, beauty, love, and freedom. You'll love the "freedom from worry" part of eternity. No more illness, sickness, pain, money worries or family concerns hold your soul back from enjoying eternity."

"Thank you for that perspective," Lorena smiled.

"I have just one more bit of information to share before we say goodbye on this side of the veil," the angel concluded. "I know your love life conflicts you. Please do more work on your "LOVE" puzzle. It might clear up things for you. No matter what happens to the Earth, your human life should keep going for a while. The "LOVE" puzzle could give you a few clues about who could be sharing the journey with you. Let me caution you about one thing. Be careful about taking any mountain hikes. Make a free will choice to avoid any bigtime climbing above the tree line. Something could happen in the mountains that might affect your human happiness. Now, my dear, I must say goodbye until we meet again in Paradise. I look forward to that glorious day, my sweet earth angel."

Before Lorena could respond, the messenger angel vanished into the ethers. She was suddenly alone on their beloved bench.

63

More About Death

Although Seth had urged Lorena to focus on the "LOVE PUZZLE", his description of Heaven intrigued her.

She decided to forego "LOVE" for now and focus on "DEATH".

I'm wondering about how much time I have remaining, she thought. When I do die, will it be quick or long and painful? Who will greet me in Heaven when I pass over to the other side?

Lorena rummaged through the seven boxes and found the one marked "DEATH". The first thing she noticed about the box cover was an absence of dark and mournful colors. The individual puzzle pieces were all bright. The "blackness" usually associated with "death" was completely missing. Instead, there was a colorful and radiant theme that almost suggested joy and happiness.

This "DEATH" puzzle feels uplifting, she thought. If I were creating titles, I would label it "SPRINGTIME". I see much more "joy" in these particular pieces than "sadness". This is the most colorful and brightest puzzle that I've found so far. It's not what I expected at all.

She could see many beautiful cloud formations among the puzzle pieces. Bright shades of blue and green permeated everything. There was an unmistakable serenity and peacefulness floating up from the box. Lorena thought about the many clichés about death: "Rest in Peace" and "May the Peace of the LORD watch over you". Suddenly she could understand better their deeper meaning. She did not sense any hint of pain and regret. In fact, the word "RELEASE" was plainly forming in the puzzle.

This is such a surprise, Lorena decided. I've always thought of death as a downer. I'm starting to see that might not be true. There seems to be little pain or regret after human transition. I'm sure death relieves great suffering for some. Still, most folks want to live out their years and beyond. I understand that. Life can be beautiful. But this puzzle certainly seems upbeat about the cycle of life and death. It's so different than the sadness and regret you might expect.

In several pieces, Lorena could make out her own face. She was looking back over her left shoulder. Perhaps it was akin to reviewing one's entire life at the moment of death. In another sequence, she was seated at table with a pad and pencil.

Could I be taking an inventory of my life, she wondered. That could make sense, totaling up the plusses and minuses. I'm sure there must be some sort of "accounting" or review process when your life ends. What gains did I make? What losses did I experience? What lessons did I learn? What was my greatest regret? I could almost begin doing that now. I wonder what grade God would give me for how I handled my life. At this point, I probably deserve an "incomplete." I still have lots of unresolved things going on.

In the silence of the moment, Lorena heard a discernible voice.

"Every soul comes back home to Heaven. Period. End of story."

"What?", she said.

The voice seemed to originate from her Siri digital personal assistant.

"Someday, I recall every soul home to its point of creation," the voice said.

It's absolutely coming from Siri, Lorena marveled. I wonder how long that has been going on?

"There are no exceptions," Siri continued, "I harvest every soul. No matter how much damage a soul inflicts on others and the environment, it becomes blameless when it reenters Heaven. I wipe the slate clean."

I wonder if my working on the "Death Puzzle" activated Siri, Lorena thought.

"The bright colors of death intrigue you.," Siri observed. "With death comes absolute clarity. What you are beholding now can be called "revelations of the unknown".The moment you pass over brings extreme understanding. Prepare to be shocked at the revealing of "Truth" with a capital "T"."

"What kind of Truth?" Lorena inquired,

"One of the first revelations concerns the futility of human worry. Virtually, 99.9% of the things you worried about in your lifetime have zero meaning after death. Your preoccupation with worry and fear was a waste of time. Human beings invest far too much emotional and physical energy worrying about things that either didn't happen or just faded away. Occasional worry may be rational and necessary. Living your life in fear of the present or future is useless and counterproductive."

"I don't think life would be life without some form of worry," Lorena injected.

Siri answered without pause.

"Then you're accepting "worry" as legitimate," Siri argued, "Being a constant worrier is not a normal state of being. Too much fearfulness causes stress overload. Stress then becomes a killer itself. It shortens your life. Too much fretting about anything can produce a "self-fulfilling prophecy.""

"What are some of the other revelations when I pass," Lorena asked.

"Spending your time obsessed with "work" is not a good thing," Siri opined. "When you put your job or career ahead of family, relationships and life experiences, you're not choosing wisely or well. You'll see that clearly during your first minute in Heaven. Nobody ever says they did not "work" enough."

"It sounds as though the purpose of death is to teach us how we should have lived."

"Bingo! That's it, my dear girl," Siri said, "Over and out!"

64

An Invitation

The gold engraved invitation arrived at Lorena's condo by special courier. It read:

 Your Presence is Requested

At a Special Screening of

GOD'S DECISION

Next Sunday Evening

7 P. M.

4th Dimension Theater

4040 Main Street

As a real estate professional, Lorena knew her city. There was no movie theatre located at 4040 Main Street. It was a vacant lot where an old warehouse once stood. The building had been torn down over a decade ago. The property wasn't even being advertised for commercial sale, at least as far as she knew.

That's odd, Lorena thought to herself. I wonder what's going on.

On Sunday afternoon, she dressed up in her "Sunday Best" and drove to the designated location. As the real estate agent drew closer to the address, Lorena was surprised to see that a small but modernistic structure had sprung up. The sign on the building read: "4th Dimension Theater". It had magically unfolded from the ethers. From the number of vehicles parked around the building, Lorena surmised that perhaps 100-150 people might be inside attending the "Special Screening".

Lorena drove around the theater until finding one of the last remaining parking spaces. She quickly claimed it and then headed for the front door. She was stopped at the building entrance by a tall African American gentleman in a tuxedo. He requested Lorena's invitation, matched it to a master list of invitees and then waved her inside. She walked into a nicely appointed lobby with lush carpeting. It was empty, except for an attractive young black woman in a stylish white dress.

"Good evening, Lorena," the woman greeted her. "I'm Celeste. I believe you know my mother Celestina. She'll be replacing Seth as your angel contact here on earth. I'll be escorting you to your seat tonight."

Celeste was carrying a large flashlight, which was needed. The theater was extremely dark, and the young woman cautioned Lorena to watch her step.

The seating consisted of enclosed individual cubicles. Lorena saw that each individual space was small but comfortable, about 5 by 7 feet. It featured elegantly furnished details that included a slender desk, a padded chair with arms and a modernistic lamp. A sleek new laptop was open on the desk. The logo on the empty computer screen simply read "GOD" in a Quadron style font. Beside the laptop was a Namaki Nippon fountain pen and an embossed writing tablet with her initials on the cover.

First class all the way, she thought. But hey, we're talking about "God".

Lorena had yet to see anyone else in the theater. The separate cubicles guaranteed privacy. Except for the cars parked outside, there was no indication that anyone else was in attendance.

This is all a bit spooky, she thought. Could I be dreaming?

At precisely 7 p.m., the laptop on her desk flickered. The screen was filled by the face of a famous actor who had passed about 40 years ago. Then the camera dissolved to show him standing behind a gold-plated podium. The handsome man was dressed in a classic Kilton black tuxedo from head to toe.

The actor spoke:

"On behalf of God, the Supreme Being and Ruler of the Universe, I want to welcome you here tonight. You are about to see a special screening of "GOD'S DECISION". The message this evening concerns the fate of the world. Each of you has been pre-selected to hear this historic pronouncement. God wants to personally inform you of Her decision. There is a writing tablet in each cubicle. After seeing the revelation, God would appreciate your comments. Please leave the pad on the desk when you depart. You will also find a waiver stating that you will not share this information with anyone. It must be kept confidential. Leaking this material is not permitted, under the severest penalty imaginable. If you cannot keep what you hear private, please vacate your cubicle now. If you under-stand and accept these conditions, please push the red button directly underneath the table. Do it now." The actor then stepped back from the podium.

Lorena quickly found her button and pushed it, signaling her compliance.

After a minute or so, the actor returned.

"Can I have the attention of cubicles 46, 78 and 92," he said, "If you don't respond in the next 60 seconds, I must ask that you either leave the theatre or be escorted out. Please respond immediately."

After a brief time, the actor made the following announcement:

"Thank you for your patience and cooperation. The next voice you hear will be that of God, the Good, omnipotent."

There was a brief interlude of Pachebel's Canon in D lasting approximately three minutes. The screen saver on Lorena's laptop depicted peaceful scenes from nature, such as a snow-capped mountain, a deep forest and a tranquil lake.

This is just too weird but also exquisitely beautiful, Lorena thought. I'm getting chills just waiting to see what comes next.

65

The Announcement

Lorena's laptop went dark. There was a momentary pause before an image appeared on the screen. Lorena watched a form spin up. As it came into view, her heart jumped. Then she audibly gasped.

That's ME, she realized. There I am, getting to play the role of God announcing the world's fate. OMG! I can't believe it!

Then, another thought cascaded through her mind.

I wonder if other people are seeing my image or their own.

She heard a deep and commanding voice, not her own, begin to speak.

It looks like me. However, the voice doesn't sound like me. It's a masculine voice. Maybe everyone sees themselves as God, but then Spirit speaks with Its own voice. That's way cool, she thought.

The voice sounded almost recognizable. After scouring every corner of her memory, she finally placed it.

It's that famous actor who played Moses in the TEN COMMAND-MENTS movie, she realized. Perfect casting!

God spoke:

"For the purpose of My Announcement today, I AM assuming your individual image. Please don't be startled or concerned. I AM still God, but in your human guise. I AM also choosing to use a familiar voice from an old movie about Me. For the non-English speakers, this message is being translated into your own language. There won't be an official transcript of My remarks. You are free to take notes, but everything must stay behind in your cubicle after you depart. I AM asking that you pay close attention to what I will be saying today. I promise this will not be a long presentation. You'll get follow-up information later. First, let me thank you for your commitment to spiritual service. I realize that My Path can be hard, complicated and dangerous. I promise that, at the end, you will find it glorious and fulfilling beyond your grandest dreams. I compliment you on your dedication and courage. Many of you have already experienced persecution, temptation and ridicule. In future days, some may of you could also be subjected to imprisonment, injury or human death. Any soul that surrenders his or her physical life on My behalf will be celebrated and honored in My Kingdom. Now, before I announce my decision about the world's fate, I want to remind you again of a spiritual principle. You still possess "Free Will" choice. You may rescind your commitment to Me, if you so choose. You can walk away from this moment. Just turn off your electronic device and leave the building. You are free to re-enter the material world. I will think nothing less of you. I allow you to pursue whatever road you choose. You can become the best—or worst—human being. That choice is up to you. Now, for those who choose to remain, here is My decision about the future of your planet and every living thing that inhabits it. I will now speak to you in boldface:

I have come to judge the world. Rendering My decision is painful, but necessary. I have found myself in this situation before. During Biblical times, many people worshipped golden idols and engaged in sinful behavior. They chose to turn away from Me, just like today. I was cast out into the wilderness. I was disrespected, ignored, shunned and cursed. During similar times, I assigned many talented prophets to warn people about my anger and dismay. You have read about many of them—Isaiah, Ezekiel, Jeremiah,

Daniel, Elijah, Hosea, Elisha, Micah, Jonah, Nahum and Zechariah were among the most famous. I dispatched them as My Holy Messengers to warn the world of My unhappiness and impending judgment. I wanted to give the world a chance to repent of their behavior. Again, just like now, I also resorted to natural events such as famine, earthquakes, floods, hurricanes, wildfires, volcanic eruptions, tornadoes, cyclones and tsunamis to get the world's attention. Sometimes these disasters worked, at least for a while. But human beings can be willful, oblivious and self-involved. As all of you remember, I once drowned the earth with a 40-day flood. That calamity was against who I AM. I still regret the loss of human and animal life. I AM a benevolent and loving God. I created every living thing that walks, creeps, swims and even slithers across the earth's face. I made a beautiful world full of oceans, lakes, rivers, mountains, forests, jungles and deserts. I approved when humankind added magnificent cities and other human-made wonders. I even blessed the exploration of outer space and countless other scientific discoveries. I also provided human beings with incredible material wealth far beyond anything imaginable. Today's largesse would have been unthinkable in Biblical times. However, as the world has become materially richer, things have gotten much worse for Me. My relationship with human beings has deteriorated to the lowest point in recorded history. There are many reasons for this freefall. People worship themselves now. They are their own golden idols. Science and technology are drunk with materially inspired power. They are even usurping My sacred role in creating human beings, albeit without an anchoring soul. Many regard Me as outdated, irrelevant and unnecessary. Add addictions of every stripe to this negative concoction and you can understand my upset. Humans are acting as if they are beyond My jurisdiction. I have news for everyone with ears to hear. I AM always relevant and still very much in charge. It is past time for Me to reassert myself. Remember, I have been forced to discipline human beings before. However, the cloning of human beings and the rise of Artificial Intelligence have caused me to act now. What are My options? I could purify the world again with a flood, but I made a sacred covenant not to repeat that event. As a few of you know already, I AM considering a cataclysmic event that would consume your planet. Some call it a "Solaster". The sun would pull the earth into its flames, destroying everything and everyone. What a tragedy! Believe Me, I do not wish for that terrible outcome. I personally created our beautiful world as a sacred laboratory for spiritual growth. I regret that things have not worked out as planned. Is destroying the earth My wish for humankind? Absolutely not! Yet here we are. I have some final details about what's next. I will share everything with you after we take a 20-minute break. I ask that you remain in your individual cubicle during the intermission. Please use this respite as a sacred time of meditation and contemplation. After I return, I will provide you with the specifics of My decision. Thank you, My children. I love you."

66

Lorena's Fantasy

Lorena closed her eyes and tried to meditate. However, she soon fell asleep. Within seconds, she lapsed over into a dream state.

She felt herself being transported back in time to First century Judaea. She recognized several Biblical landmarks. She identified the Temple in Jerusalem, bustling with political activity and religious fervor. The Sanhedrin was in session and listening intently to an address from Pontius Pilate, its Roman governor. The prefect was cautioning against giving rogue religious figures any credibility. His message kept referring to a fur-clad preacher called "John the Baptist". He had been roguishly baptizing followers in the Jordan River. Then, she saw the River itself in her dream. It was smaller than she had visualized it. After that, the larger Sea of Galilee came into view. Lorena spotted several fishing boats dotting the water. She could clearly discern some of Jesus' future disciples manning the boats. There was Peter, short and stocky but rugged looking. He was engaged in a deep conversation with John, the disciple whom Jesus loved. To Lorena, John was strikingly handsome. Then her dream shifted to a group of shady looking men. They were obviously plotting something. However, she was too far away to hear their conversation. Then, Lorena watched as thirty pieces of silver exchanged hands. Finally, the dream whisked her away to the Judaean countryside. She could make out three separate crosses at the top of a small hill. She recognized the young man on the middle cross. It was Jesus the Christ. He appeared weak and near death. Suddenly, Lorena sensed the presence of a man standing next to her.

"Hello, my dear Lorena," the man said. "I'm Joseph of Arimathea. I'm here to claim the body of Jesus after he passes."

They both looked up to see the young man on the cross beckoning to them.

"He wants us to come closer", Joseph told her. "Follow me," he added.

The Roman soldiers barely noticed them as they walked toward the three crosses. A crowd of gawkers also had also begun congregating. The soldiers seemed more interested in controlling the unruly crowd than monitoring their movements. Finally, Lorena and Joseph stood at the foot of Jesus' cross. They stared at him without embarrassment or pity. Jesus' remarkably blue eyes found them. There was a pained expression on His face. His countenance was only partly visible because the crown of thorns had slipped down on his face. The young man had a benevolent look about him, despite the circumstances. It projected an aura of love, peace, understanding and grudging acceptance.

Jesus' lips were moving. He was trying to speak. Lorena and Joseph strained to hear His words.

"Hello Lorena and Joseph," He said. "Do not cry or be sad for Me. I predicted this day would come. It was inevitable. Yes, I feel the physical pain. I am fully human and fully divine, so I do feel the nails. Yet I know my wounds are only temporary. I will be with My Father soon. Then, the pain disappears forever. Someday, I'll see you both in Heaven. Everything that happened today will seem so small compared to being in God's heavenly Kingdom. Now, Lorena, I have a special message for you. Record these words in your heart. God plans to ask much of you, just as He did from Me. When he summons you to help save the world from destruction, remember my sacrifice. I hope you will say "yes" when that time comes."

Then, Jesus closed his eyes. His head fell forward. He was silent.

A group of Roman soldiers walked up and began ushering Lorena and Joseph away from the three crosses. As they backed off, she watched as one of the soldiers used his spear to pierce Jesus' side. The Master's human scream was the last thing Lorena remembered until she woke up. The lights were flickering in her cubicle and a soft chime had begun to ring.

The intermission was over.

67

God's Decision

Lorena stared at her electronic device and awaited God's reappearance. Strangely, she felt no apprehension or fear. It was more a resignation of what might be coming.

Then God, again in her own likeness, appeared and began speaking:

"I hope you enjoyed your time in quiet contemplation. I AM now ready to share My decision about the world's fate. I have tried to balance My judgement with fairness and compassion. However, a punishment must be rendered. When I created the world, I warned humankind to have no other gods before me. The people of the earth have once again ignored My basic law. Yes, in the past, I have mostly forgiven them. I always hope for the best. However, My breaking point has been reached. Here is what I plan to do. First, I have decided there will be no immediate destruction of the planet. For now, the "Solaster" is off the table. I AM granting the world a 5-year reprieve. I AM hoping that human beings will use this Grace period to repent and shift the focus back to Me. The earth has approximately 1,800 days to turn things around. I have created THE 7 PUZZLES OF LIFE program to engage people about their spiritual lives. During the first two years, I AM sending out designated prophets to warn the world of its impending doom. You are one of those prophets. Then, at the beginning of the third year, a "Savior" will appear. She will come to instruct and inspire people of all nations. My designated Messiah will teach though miracles, stories, parables, precepts and other means of mass communication. The new Master will use social media, films, television, radio, the internet and other communication avenues to bring My warnings of a final judgement. The world will either pay attention, continue to ignore Me or react by crucifying My messengers. Unfortunately, this has all happened before. In other times, those who spoke for Me were routinely stoned, imprisoned, tortured, murdered or (even worse) ignored. I hope for a different response this time. Perhaps humankind will have learned its lesson, although I doubt it. We'll see. As I said, I always hope for the best. As for the world, it should prepare for the worst. There is a penance that must be extracted during this 5-year period of Grace. I plan to deal with the worship of money, fame, ego, and materialism in the near future. The largest and most vibrant economy in the world will experience a second Great Depression. Its national government will go bankrupt because of reckless overspending. The stock market will lose 90% of its value. Huge corporations will falter, fail and disappear. I will cause the digital economy to stall. The internet, as you know it, will cease to exist. The world will face major economic disruption. The only nations holding their own will be those with not much to lose. Taking away economic arrogance is necessary for the beginning of humility and cultural change. After the 5-year Grace period ends, I will reassess the situation. If nothing has changed, I AM prepared to act with swiftness. The earth can expect to be pulled into and consumed by the sun in a matter of weeks. This is not the outcome I want. During the final days, a remnant of earth's living things will be transported to a new star. I will start the process of human experimentation one more time. Yes, I realize and accept the definition of insanity: doing the same thing over again, while expecting different results. Yet, I AM forever an optimist.

Now, I want to tell you briefly about the new Messiah. I AM designating a woman to act as the Savior this time. In two years, the female Messiah will appear. Our new "savior" is currently living as a real estate salesperson named Lorena Mae Johnson. She will come in the guise of an African American female, one of the most spiritual of all races and genders.

Oh my God, Lorena thought to herself. Did God just say what I thought She said? No, no, no, no. I can't do that. I'm not a Messiah! Is this why God and the Devil have been fighting over me so much?

I AM speaking to you now in the guise of Lorena. She will spend the next two years preparing for this sacred assignment. It won't be easy. Although the world teeters on extinction, it seems blissfully unaware. I hope things change. I do believe in miracles. I know there are many heroes, healers and human angels among you. I AM asking that you support Lorena Christ Johnson in her message of hope. Maybe it's not too late. I love you all. Thank you and good night.

In her small cubicle, Lorena wept with joy, gratitude and fear.

68

Busy Times

The next few days were a busy blur for Lorena. She dropped by the real estate office to offer Peter and Sallye her official letter of resignation. They both expressed sadness about the imminent departure, but Lorena could also sense some relief. Since the incident with Franklin had gone viral, things had changed. There were still unresolved issues with Charles White and Reggie III. All in all, the real estate owners yearned for more normal times again. With drama always swirling around Lorena, that seemed impossible. They wished her well on all future endeavors.

Lorena met Doctor John for a late lunch on a Saturday afternoon. It was pleasant, but the chemistry had vanished. They parted as acquaintances but without any plans to meet again.

Government agent Tim Dahling was a different matter. They each now possessed a shared secret. He had seen God's presentation at the theater and knew about her future role. Tim was also a potential fellow voyager to a new star in five years. They met on Sunday after church at a downtown restaurant to discuss their respective futures.

Agent Tim got to the point.

"How are things going with your pregnancy?" he asked.

"Wow, you're subtle," Lorena laughed.

"Well, you have a new situation to consider," he noted, "A baby could complicate things for you."

"I'll manage," she replied. "I'm planning to deliver in four months. At least, there are no twins involved. I don't want to know the sex of the child, only that it appears healthy. So far, so good on that score. I've even chosen the names. If it's a boy, I'll name it Paul. If I have a girl, I'll call her Ruth. You can't go wrong with a couple of Biblical famous names."

"Well then, I'm happy for you," Agent Tim said, "What about the father?"

"Franklin is no longer a part of my life," she said, "I don't even know how to contact him. It looks as though I'll operating as a single mom."

Agent Tim stared at Lorena for a few seconds.

"I wanted to talk to you about that," he said, "Would you be open to exploring a relationship with me? Subtlety isn't my strong suit. I want to act super cool about the way I feel, but I am who I am."

"I honestly don't know," Lorena answered, "I'm going through some unbelievable changes right now. I have no idea what this "Messiah Training" entails. It sounds almost like a joke to even talk about it. I would never share about that with anyone on the outside. They would think I'm ready for the funny farm. I don't see how I can get involved with anyone until I know more."

"Well, Jesus shared a lot with Mary Magdalene, or so they say," Dahling responded.

"We all know how that turned out," Lorena said ruefully.

"You just seem almost detached about everything," Tim responded, "I hear what your head is saying. What about your heart?"

"I'm not sure I can afford to have a heart right now. First, I need to deliver my baby. Then, someone needs to explain my spiritual assignment in terms that I can understand. I don't think I have the emotional strength to take on much else."

"I need to ask you a direct question," Tim said, "And, I want you to give me an honest answer. Can you do that?"

"I'll try," Lorena answered.

"Does race have anything to do with it? Does the fact that you're black and I'm white cause you to hesitate?"

"Absolutely not!" she responded, "Love is love, whatever color anyone may be. I'm surprised you would ask me that. I'm one of those fools that believes love is colorblind."

"By the way," Tim smiled, "FYI, I really am colorblind. I thought you should know."

He reached over and gently touched Lorena's hand. This time her heart responded.

"May I ask you one more question?" he asked.

Lorena nodded her head and said: "Sure. What's on your mind?"

"Is there any chance our friend Satan might ever get off your back?"

"I don't see that happening," she replied.

Lorena couldn't possibly know how right she was. A meeting about her spiritual future was being convened in Hell at that exact moment by the Devil himself.

69

The Devil You Say

Satan was in a foul mood. That meant he was having a good day. From his ancient castle adjacent to the Lake of Fire, he surveyed the human carnage on planet earth. Everywhere his evil eyes took him, things and lives were falling apart. All was well.

"Ah, progress," he smiled. "Things are good. Lots of wars and threats of war, terrorism, murders, multiple addictions and souls being consumed by their human problems. What more could I ask? I'm happy! I still rule the world."

The devil looked around his conference room. Ministers from every principality in Hell had been called together for a special meeting. They needed to consider God's most recent moves. There was much to talk about.

"That damn fool is throwing us another curve ball with His bizarre 5-year plan," the Devil snarled, "That could get some attention. I'm not too sure about the 7 Puzzles gimmick. I don't think it has legs. Human beings are too damn lazy. I'm not sure how many people will even work on those crazy puzzles. If they do, we must do our best to distract, deter, and disillusion them. I love taking a wrecking ball to God's plans. Corrupting His religious frauds makes my heart sing. What do you all think?"

"Think about what, Boss?" The Minister of Mind-Altering Drugs inquired.

"Pay attention, dopey," the Devil teased, "Are you high? Shooting up your own stuff again, eh?"

"Listen your excellency, I've got my group under strict control," the Gambling Czar responded, "We opened 25 more casinos worldwide last month. That should be a bonanza in bankruptcies, broken homes and general unhappiness. Our business is booming! Legalized online sports betting is just now getting cranked up. We're talking hundreds of billions these fools will be wagering on their precious teams! We'll grab the market before people understand what's happening.I can barely wait for college and pro football seasons to begin. We'll be raking it in. Times are booming for me! Gambling is king. We'll have people betting on today's weather before it's over. Hallelujah!"

"Watch your language!" the Devil cautioned.

"Things are also rolling for Me," the Prince of Pornography added, "I've just scratched the surface with my addiction. We've got fabulous growth potential. I'm planning to branch out to elementary schools at one end of the spectrum and assisted living communities on the other. The Baby Boomers are already going nuts about soft porn. Wait until we introduce the hard stuff! There are lots of sex-starved people out there—and I'm not just talking about the men. The new sex bots are really taking off with the gals."

"I love going after spiritual hypocrites!" the Minister of Religious Chaos called out. "I think we can easily start a couple of big intra-church feuds before they know what's happening. I love to see these Bible-thumpers fighting among themselves. The congregations are so easy to stir up. They've got more in-fighting than we do in Hell. The church choirs are still the hot beds of unrest, pardon the pun. I get such great pleasure from pitting God's people against each other. I especially enjoy ruining ordained ministers, priests and lay leaders. Religion is a happy hunting ground for me. It's Hypocrite Central! There is never a dull moment!"

"Throw all of these two-faced bastards into the Lake of Fire!" the VP of Resentments yelled out. "Anything else is too good for them."

"Hear, hear," the VPs of Anger, Deceit, Political Corruption, Organized Crime, Dangerous Drugs, Anti-Semitism, Racism, and Gossip all shouted out in unison.

"I like these old-fashioned pep rallies," Satan commented, "it makes my blood boil. As we all know, that's a good thing."

"When are we going to deal with that real estate tramp?" the Director of Dirty Tricks asked, "Ms. Lorena Mae Johnson? Hah! She's a stone-cold loser!! I can't believe God would choose her for anything, much less a Messiah. They must be scraping the bottom of the barrel with that tramp. She should be easy for us to pick off. Right, boss?"

"Hold your horses, Tricks," Satan said, "We'll get to Missy Lorena in a minute. I've got some special plans for that witch. When we're done with her, she'll long for the days of staging open houses in real estate."

"I don't know, Chief," Dirty Tricks said, "We've already hit that bitch with everything — big money, sexual temptation and eternal good looks. Nothing worked. She showed some grit, damn her. She might not be easy to corrupt."

"Don't worry," Satan assured the gathering. "I've got a few more surprises up my crooked sleeve. Have some faith in my cunning and baffling ways, people. I'm an old hand at destroying the best of do-gooders. She won't be any different."

'Why don't we "off" her and be done with it?" The Director of Final Solutions ventured, "Why don't we just kill her?"

"You know how God reacts when we begin talking about murdering one of his precious prophets," Satan interjected.

"Sometimes we get away with it, but most of the time we get our butts kicked. I'm got some past bruises to prove it. That old bastard and his army of angels can fight like hell, excuse the reference. Those angel dudes never fight fair. They've chewed us all up at one time or another. I prefer to use some guile. First, I plan to confuse Missy Lorena as much as possible. She likes being in control and what human being doesn't? We'll strip all control away from her. I think we can accomplish our goals without murdering her, at least for right now. But I won't rule anything out. Now, who wants to serve on the "GET LORENA" Committee?"

"Me!" Final Solutions yelled.

"Count me in too," Dirty Tricks called out.

"I'm on board," the Evil Plots Co-Ordinator boomed.

"That sounds like something I could go for," Emotional Pain said.

"Of course, I'll head up the group," the Devil concluded. "Let's all think about the worst possible things we could do to this wench. Don't rule anything out.We're EVIL! Let's prove it. Ye-hah!"

The raucous cheering caused waves to erupt on the Lake of Fire.

70

God And Friends

God and a few of Its closest friends met often in "HALLOWED HALL OF HEAVEN #1" to discuss universal issues. Major spiritual decisions sprang from these important gatherings.

For this meeting, The Supreme Being of the Universe had assembled a special group to consider the fate of the world. The sacred souls present included Jesus the Christ, Confucius, the Prophet Muhammad, Lord Krishna, Saint Francis of Assisi, Maimonides (author of the Torah), Gautama the Buddha, Moses, King Solomon, the Apostle Paul, Mother Teresa and Mary Baker Eddy (founder of Christian Science).

"I've asked the twelve of you (plus Abraham when he can make it) to meet with Me for an important reason: to consider the fate of the world. I want you to act as an informal jury to help me decide this crucial question. Is there anyone here who does not feel adequate for this task?"

Every soul indicated that it did not feel qualified.

"I expected that response," God smiled, "However, I can assure you of your qualifications. Now, I have provided you with the details of My 5-year Plan to avoid the "Solaster." I realize that none of you would vote for the complete eradication of the planet earth. I understand that. I agree that such a terrible outcome would appear harsh. I know that even considering such a drastic move causes you discomfort. All of you have descendants who still walk the earth."

"LORD, may I ask a question?" King Solomon asked.

"Of course, Sol," God said. "I want your thoughts and opinions."

"Have you considered all of the good people who would be affected?" the King inquired. "Yes, there are individuals who are guilty of bad things. However, they are a tiny minority compared to so many wonderful human beings. I'm sure you agree with that. You created every one of them."

"I agree that most human beings are decent and good people." God said, "But I reached this decision because of many factors. Scientific and cultural trends leave me no choice. I cannot have the scientists ripping away my prerogative of creating human souls. I AM the Creator, with a capital "C". I cannot leave the creation of human beings to humankind itself. I AM also fed up with being disobeyed and ignored. Can you all understand and appreciate that?"

Every soul nodded in agreement.

One special soul indicated that she sought to ask a question.

"Mother Teresa?" God acknowledged the newly created saint.

"Many of those individuals who have brought you unhappiness dwell in the wealthier countries of the world. Do you understand that the least wealthy will bear the ultimate sacrifice in much greater numbers? It is the poor in countries like India and continents like Africa who will suffer the most from a "Solaster." Is there not a better way to somehow discipline the people causing the problem?"

"That's obviously true," God responded. "However, I also understand that the poor always carries water for the rich. The least among us are always the most affected by any upheaval. However, I must come back to the blatant misuse of science. I believe it is only be a matter of time before the cloning of human beings becomes prevalent everywhere. That practice devalues human life in every form. In addition, some selfish people now want to live forever. I did not intend for mortal life to exist in perpetuity. Whether you are rich or poor, I want each soul to return home. That allows us to inventory everyone's spiritual progress."

"LORD, I have a question," said Moses, "I know you are an environmentalist. You created the world's natural beauty. Thousands of lovely lakes and forests, the tall mountains and the deep vast oceans would all be lost forever. Are you willing to give up all of that wonder just to discipline some human negativity?"

"The loss of nature would be hard for Me to take," God said, "I think about that a lot. I could always re-create natural beauty in a different location. However, considerable work, effort and love have gone into shaping the earth's wonders. It was my desire to provide human beings with a grand setting for their lives. Did they appreciate it? I'm not sure they have been good stewards of the environment. I don't think most people appreciate what they've been given."

"Could we please come back to the real problem here?" said Mary Baker Eddy. "We're witnessing some wrong-headed thinking. If we can change the world's thought processes, maybe we can alter this terrible outcome. I know the world has many spiritual seekers. These people might help lead the world to a shift in consciousness. We need a mental revolution in which human beings raise their level of spiritual awareness."

"I actually agree with you, Mrs. Eddy," God replied, "That's what the 7 PUZZLES OF LIFE project is all about. I want the human mind to grow spiritually. That's happens when people move their thinking away from materiality. If people thought more about their inner life, maybe that could change things. It would certainly be a significant step forward."

"Pardon me," said Gautama the Buddha, "But I think the world needs greater humility. The earth teems with arrogance.

The "selfie" culture proves my point. Everyone lives for "me and mine". Humankind has lost touch with acts of kindness and consideration. I agree that discipline must be applied. I'm just not sure that the "tough love" of destroying the planet offers the best way to proceed."

Mohammad's soul listened to the comments and then added: "No matter what anybody thinks about Islam right now, we have always been about promoting discipline, peace and reconciliation. These subjects are emphasized throughout the Qur'an. I think the biggest threat to the world comes from nations developing Weapons of Mass Destruction. The world has no way to measure how devastating these weapons might be to their planet. Unless we can slow this insanity down, the world will destroy itself. I also believe that drugs, alcohol and immoral behavior are destroying the social fabric. I know it is testing the Islamic culture as never before. From that standpoint, a lesson of some kind should be applied. However, I too would hate to see the entire world erased."

"I agree with Gautama the Buddha," Maimonides offered, "Humility must be restored. There is too much disobedience in general. The Torah warns about what can happen when people get rowdy and forget to worship the Creator. Big trouble! Human beings are short-term thinkers. They live in the "now". If it feels good, do it. That's the real problem here!"

Confucius was always thoughtful and slow to comment on important matters. Finally, he said: "I agree with the Buddha and Maimonides. Human beings enjoy playing God. Evidently, they don't think that souls matter anymore. I also worry about these AI robots. They seem to be more advanced than their human masters. Reflective thinking is no longer deemed important. Everything has been relegated to a device. Who are Siri and Alexa? Strange birds, these human beings. I'm not sure I understand them. To quote one of my sayings:

"Real knowledge is to know the extent of one's ignorance." I'm not sure today's people understand that."

Moses stood up to speak. He spread his arms out and said, "I remember when you gave me those stone tablets with the 10 Commandments. What wisdom! But when I brought them down from the mountain, quite a few folks were not thrilled. I heard some murmuring right away. Some urged me to cut the Commandments back to six or seven. "Coveting" in those days was quite popular. Self-discipline has never been a popular human trait."

Everybody in the Hallowed Hall looked over at Jesus the Christ for his input.

He glanced up and told the group: "Let's pray about it."

Every soul complied, each praying silently in its own way.

After the prayers were completed, the soul of St. Francis spoke softly: "I prayed that You, Father, would grant forgiveness to the world for its sins. Having the blazing sun cremate the entire planet just seems too final. Surely there must be another way to set the world back on course."

God turned to Jesus and asked: "And what did you pray for, My Son?"

The soul of Jesus replied: "I don't believe human beings have ever appreciated the spiritual power they possess at their core. Yet now they act like material gods, without remorse or concern for the consequences. So, I prayed today they might better understand their spiritual relationship with You. They think real power exists in themselves, politics, money, power and fame. Each one of us here knows how wrong they are. However, here's the thing: except for a few exceptions, the so-called enlightened thinkers of today don't know much. The materiality and sexuality of the earth has mesmerized them into false beliefs. I'm not sure it can be corrected. Human beings are locked into their current thinking. We need the miracle of all miracles to affect any kind of shift in consciousness. I believe in forgiveness and redemption, but I just don't see it happening in today's world. I wish I could be more optimistic."

Paul's soul asked for recognition: "I agree with the Master. I saw lots of discord in the churches back in the day. After more than 2000 years, it has only gotten worse. The credibility of many established faiths is almost gone, especially after the various scandals. If you don't have religion leading the moral turn-around, it's a steep climb. In some ways, organized religion today is more of a drag than a help. I'm not optimistic either."

"Who haven't we heard from?" God asked. "Sri Krishna, what do you think?" Lord Krishna, the central figure of the Bhagavad Gita, spoke so softly that the other souls strained to hear his thoughts.

"Righteousness declines while unrighteousness prevails," he said, "The earth needs unity with God, yet it pushes God away. Realized souls are few and far between. I fear the battle between spirituality and materialism has already been lost. The bad guys won. Now we must deal with it. I'm not hopeful either."

"What do you all think about my choice for a "Savior"? God asked. "Please speak candidly."

"A Savior or Messiah is needed," the Apostle Paul said, "But whoever you send will automatically be compared to the soul of the Master who sits among us today. I'm not sure anybody could ever measure up to the Christ. Jesus is a tough act to follow."

"I'm in favor of a Messiah-type figure," Maimonides offered, "You know how we Jews are always looking for the designated One. However, I come from a male-dominated culture. It would take some adjusting, in my opinion."

Just then, another soul entered the Hallowed Hall.

"Sorry I'm late," Abraham said, "Did I miss anything?"

"I think you already know that we're discussing the fate of the world," God said, "Now we're talking about My choice of a female "Messiah". As a founder of three great religions— Christianity, Islam and Judaism-- what do you think?"

"With all of the hatred I see between religions, I wouldn't be too confident that anybody could pull it off again," Abraham said. "The world has had 2000 years to get things right between different faiths. Instead, it has gone the other way. Quite frankly, things are in a mess. I am not bullish about any kind of reconciliation."

Jesus sought recognition to say, "Let Me say that I am in favor of a woman as the Messiah. Women are the mothers and natural peacemakers. I know that my dear Mother Mary would agree with that. I believe that women of the world could lead the way. Lorena Mae Johnson might be the right person at the right time."

"I want us to take a vote now on three items," God said. "Of course, I will still act as The Decider. However, I AM interested in your opinion. We will cast our votes by secret ballot. First, how many are in favor of Lorena Mae Johnson as the new Messiah who will carry our spiritual message to the world?"

The vote was 7-6 in Lorena's favor. God abstained.

"Well, that's not exactly a ringing endorsement," Spirit noted. "However, although I didn't vote, I believe in her. I have no current plans to deselect Lorena, at least for now. I'm sure that those who voted against her have their reasons. Now, vote #2, How many of you think the 7 PUZZLES OF LIFE could have a positive effect on changing the world's consciousness?"

This time, the vote was a resounding "No" 11-3. On this question, God did vote in the affirmative.

"That's disappointing," Spirit reflected. "Heaven has spent considerable time and effort developing the 7 PUZZLES. Would anyone like to share why they voted as they did?

"I'm sorry," Lord Krishna said, "I don't think a "puzzle" can attract more followers than say online sports betting, Happy Hour at the pub, pornography, or weed. It's just not likely. A few "thinkers" may go for it, but not many. You're just not understanding human beings at this stage of their mental development. I could be wrong, but I doubt it."

"All right now," God stated, here is vote #3: If the change in the world's spiritual behavior does not occur in five years, would you be in favor of the earth's total destruction?"

The vote 12-1 "No", with God abstaining, and Maimonides voting "yes".

"You're a tough old soul," the Buddha jibed.

"Hard core," Paul the Apostle added.

"I'm not a Pollyanna", Maimonides responded.

"Thank you all," God said. "At least I know how you feel. I want to thank every blessed soul for its input. As I said earlier, I'm giving human beings five years to change. If they remain the same or fall further into the abyss, I must act. Let us all hope for the best and prepare for the worst. I, the LORD of all, have spoken. And, so it is. Let it be written. Let it be done. Amen."

The End Of The Beginning

About The Author

Rev. Allen C. Liles is a graduate of Baylor University in Waco, TX and the Unity School of Religious Studies at Unity Village, MO. Before being ordained as a non-denominational minister, he served as vice-president of public relations for the 7-Eleven Stores and communications manager for the McLane Company. He was also Senior Director of Outreach for the Unity School of Christianity and served as senior minister at Unity churches in Sun City, AZ, Minneapolis, MN, Bloomington, MN and Oakdale, MN.

PRINT BOOKS by Allen C. Liles

OH THANK HEAVEN! THE STORY OF THE SOUTHLAND CORPORATION

SITTING WITH GOD/MEDITATING FOR GOD'S DIVINE GUIDANCE

THE FOREVER PENNY/HOW OUR LOVED ONES STAY CONNECTED AFTER DEATH

E-BOOKS by Allen C Liles

Friends Of Jesus
https://www.smashwords.com/books/view/455617

R-Spiritual Rehab
https://www.smashwords.com/books/view/481978

The 12 Promises If Heaven
https://www.smashwords.com/books/view/444920

The Book Of Celeste
https://www.smashwords.com/books/view/593856

The Book Of Floyd
https://smashwords.com/books/view/615914

The Book Of Ethan
https://www.smashwords.com/647665

AUDIO TITLES by Allen C. Liles

https://www.audible.com/pd/The-Peaceful-Driver-Steering-Clear-of-Road-Rage-Audiobook/B002V59SMS

THE 7 PUZZLES OF LIFE: God's Plan To Save The World by Allen C. Liles is a fictional prophecy about God's final attempt to save the world from a planetary catastrophe. It features commentary on "The 7 Puzzles of Life" that include Free Will, Family, Love, Work, Spiritual Service, Death, and God. It also serves as a cautionary tale about the fierce struggle between good and evil for the soul of every human being.